THE MAN WITH THE SILVER SAAB

Detective Ulf Varg is a man of refined tastes, and quite familiar with the art scene in Malmö. So when art historian Anders Kindgren visits the Department of Sensitive Crimes to report a series of bizarre acts that have been committed against him, Ulf and his team swing into action. Fish stuffed into the air vents of Kindgren's car and a manipulated footnote in a publication would be cause enough for an investigation — but when a painting Kindgren had confidently appraised as genuine is later declared to be a fake, it's clear that someone is out to tarnish his reputation. Meanwhile, Ulf is also weathering personal issues, which quickly spiral out of control, and lead to him being investigated himself . . .

ALEXANDER MCCALL SMITH

◆

THE MAN WITH THE SILVER SAAB

Complete and Unabridged

ISIS
LARGE
PRINT

ISIS
Leicester

First published in Great Britain in 2021 by
Little, Brown
an imprint of Little, Brown Book Group
London

First Isis Edition
published 2022
by arrangement with
Little, Brown Book Group
London

A catalogue record for this book is available
from the British Library.

ISBN 978–1–78541–998–0

Published by
Ulverscroft Limited
Anstey, Leicestershire

Printed and bound in Great Britain by
TJ Books Ltd., Padstow, Cornwall

This book is printed on acid-free paper

This book is for Harold Short and Vanessa Davies

1

An Attack with Impunity

It happened very quickly. One moment, Ulf Varg's hearing-impaired dog, Martin, was enjoying his outing to the park, sniffing about in the bushes, pursuing ancient and tantalising smells, the next he was bleeding copiously from a number of severe head wounds. Above him in the trees, the unrepentant perpetrator of this outrage, a large male squirrel, bloodstained himself but clearly the victor, looked down on his victim with all the mocking impunity that the arboreal have for the land-bound.

Of course, these things often take place against a background of entirely ordinary events. A big thing happens while small things are going on all about it. Take suffering: Auden's poem 'Musée des Beaux Arts', a reflection on Brueghel's *Landscape with the Fall of Icarus*, reminds us of just that — of how the Old Masters understood only too well the human context of suffering, about how it occurs when people in its vicinity are going about their ordinary business, their innocent routines. The tragedy of the boy falling into the sea unfolds while a ship sails blithely on, while a man ploughs a field unaware of what is happening in the bay. Ordinary human business. So it was that when misfortune struck Martin on that Saturday morning, Ulf himself was chatting in the park to a fellow dog owner; a small boy was trying — unsuccessfully — to launch an un-cooperative kite, the boy

1

being still too young to understand that kites require wind; and a young couple, newly in love, were having their first disagreement, on a park bench, about what to do that evening.

At first, Ulf barely noticed what was happening. His conversation with the other dog owner was about a puzzling series of incidents that had taken place in the park a few weeks earlier and that, in the opinion of the other man, had been scandalously under-investigated by the police. The incidents in question had occurred at night, and had all involved young women being approached by a man who, without warning, danced up and down in front of them shouting, 'Cucumber! Cucumber!' before rushing off into the trees.

'It's utterly bizarre,' said Stig, Ulf's friend in the park, about whom he knew very little other than that he was a doctor, and often overworked. 'Seemingly, it was not all that serious, but the victims have all been young women in their late teens or early twenties and they've been pretty shocked by the experience. I know one of them — she works in the hospital pharmacy. A very open, friendly girl — and robust, too, I would have thought. But she was pretty shaken.'

Ulf tried not to grin. As a member of the Department of Sensitive Crimes in Malmö, he had seen just about every sort of bizarre behaviour that people were capable of, and he had long assumed nothing would surprise or shock him. Human perversity, he realised, was endlessly inventive. No sexual fixation or aberration, however ridiculous, struck Ulf as being unlikely or impossible: no private fantasy was too odd not to have its secret practitioners; nothing was out of bounds or unlikely as a vehicle for concupiscence. Eyebrows may have been raised in the past over these

2

things, but not now, when all judgement as to personal erotic preference had been more or less abandoned in the name of . . . in the name of what? wondered Ulf. Freedom? Personal fulfilment? That must be it: our ability to disapprove had been blunted. And as disapproval waned, so too did morality itself change. It was no longer about goodness; it was about freedom to do what you wanted to do. In a world in which the concept of sin was so outdated as to seem like a medieval survival, the real offence seemed to be disrespect for the tastes and ambitions of others.

Ulf managed a serious face. 'That's not good,' he said at last. 'People should not frighten other people with . . . with cucumbers. That's bad.'

There was a note of accusation in Stig's tone. 'Then why did your colleagues in the uniformed police not do anything? Why did they say: probably just a harmless crazy person? Why did they not lift a finger to investigate?'

Ulf felt he had to explain about operational discretion. 'The police can't do everything,' he pointed out. 'We have to pick and choose — according to what's most urgent, or most serious. If somebody threatens to kill somebody, for instance, we drop everything to investigate.'

Stig nodded. 'So you should.'

'But if it's something minor — a small theft, for example, or a row between neighbours — we might decide we just don't have the time to look into it.'

'All right — triage.'

Ulf thought the analogy apposite. 'Yes, it's what you people do in the emergency department, isn't it? People come in and you decide who's bleeding the most or who's in most pain. It's the same sort of decision.'

3

'Yes,' said Stig. 'But . . . ' He paused. 'It's just that people think the police have become soft. They think the police will let people get away with anything. And that's particularly the case here in Malmö, where the police are anxious to not be seen to be picking on people.' He paused, looking hesitantly at Ulf: one had to be careful what one said, and many people said nothing. 'Is it because the police are party to our great Swedish pretence that crime doesn't exist here? That people are imagining it? Or that it's all socio-economic?'

Well, it is, thought Ulf. Or, at least, to an appreciable extent: crime was committed by those on the outside. But he looked away; he knew what the other man meant, but he knew, too, that he could quite quickly be drawn into the sort of conversation that he wanted to avoid. He reached for the anodynes. 'We do our best,' he said. 'Sometimes, if you come down too hard on a particular group, it makes matters worse. They think you're picking on them. And you might be — even subconsciously. You have to keep everybody onside — as far as possible.'

The doctor sighed. 'I know, Ulf. I know. You're right about that. We wouldn't want Sweden to become an oppressive society.'

'No, we wouldn't.' His agreement was real, and heartfelt; he would not have wanted to be a member of the Criminal Investigation Department of a heavy-handed government. Policemen could sometimes find themselves becoming oppressors because of the very nature of what they did, but Ulf had always seen the police as public guardians — the protectors, rather than the destroyers of people's freedoms. That was his vision of police work in general, and in particular

4

it was the philosophy that guided his approach to the unusual complaints with which his own department, the Department of Sensitive Crimes, was concerned.

'And yet,' Stig continued, 'a light touch should not allow people to go around frightening people by shouting 'Cucumber' at them.' He fixed Ulf with a challenging stare. 'In the dark. In a park. Whether or not a cucumber is threatening is surely contextual, wouldn't you say?'

It would be easy to laugh now, thought Ulf. Of course, cucumbers were capable of being threatening in a way in which peaches and nectarines, for instance, were not. But this man, this *cucumberist*, was really a minor irritant, in the way of those day-release patients from the psychiatric hospital who go about the town carrying on one-sided conversations with their individual demons . . . or talking on their mobile phones — it was sometimes difficult to tell the difference between those who were talking to themselves and those who were merely having a telephone conversation through microphone headsets.

'I'm sure they'll do something,' he said. 'When they have the time, they'll have a word with him.'

This was greeted with incredulity. 'Have a word with him? Is that what policing has become? Having a word with people?'

'It's sometimes the most effective response,' said Ulf.

'But this is clearly sexual assault,' Stig protested. 'You don't have a word with people who do that sort of thing.'

'Does he have a cucumber with him when he jumps out in front of people?' asked Ulf.

Stig shook his head. 'I don't know.'

'Well then . . .'

Stig was not sure whether Ulf understood. Sometimes policemen were a bit literal, he reminded himself. Did he have to spell it out? Surely not, and yet not everybody was sensitive to these things. 'But the whole point, Ulf, is that the cucumber is phallic. It's the most phallic of vegetables.'

Ulf felt a momentary irritation. He had read Freud, and felt that Stig's remark verged on condescension. But his friend was probably right about the phallic nature of the cucumber: there was no other vegetable that matched it in that respect. And yet he reminded himself that people looked at things in their particular ways; cucumbers might mean different things to different people. That was not to say that they had no significance here: of course, symbolism was important in the investigation of crime, as the psychological profilers were at pains to point out. Those people found, in the criminal *modus operandi*, all sorts of clues as to motivation, and these clues often led directly to the perpetrator. There had been that man who had kidnapped domestic cats, always picking on Siamese, sometimes leaving them injured in their owners' gardens or in the streets. The public had been revolted, as gratuitous cruelty to animals always met with disgust. The case caught the eye of the press, and this in turn brought in the Commissioner of Police, who said that every effort had to be made to find the culprit. A profiler was approached, and he suggested that enquiries should focus on finding somebody who had been raised by a stepmother, and particularly by a stepmother who kept Siamese cats. 'He'll be transferring his dislike of his stepmother — a very common problem — to the cats,' he advised.

The police had paid heed to this diagnosis and had interviewed the entire membership of the local Exotic Cat Appreciation Club — fruitlessly, as it transpired. And then, quite by chance, Ulf had seen a magazine feature on a local pair of conjoined, or Siamese, twins. The author of the article had been sympathetic, but conveyed the impression that the twins were unhappy with their lot. Unhappiness, thought Ulf, does not always keep its head down: it may mould our response to the world. And at that point it occurred to him that the profiler had ignored the most obvious of all possibilities: attacks on Siamese cats might be (a) carried out by persons of a Thai background, or (b) by conjoined twins.

The twins, under investigation, proved blameless, and before Ulf had time to interrogate members of the local Thai community, the perpetrator of the attacks was filmed on CCTV chasing a Siamese cat down a street. He was apprehended and interviewed by the duty police psychiatrist, who reported that far from being motivated by animus against Siamese cats, he was, in fact, trying to steal them. This was to sell them across the border in Copenhagen, where unscrupulous dealers were prepared to take expensive pets without too many questions as to provenance. It was when the cats resisted that they were damaged, and that was entirely through ineptitude on the thief's part.

It had become an open-and-shut case, but it gave rise to debate in Ulf's department about how one might go about arresting a conjoined twin. Erik, his colleague in charge of filing and general support, had pointed out that if you took one such twin into custody, you would have to detain the other. And yet, the law would not countenance arresting somebody whom you knew, or even suspected, to be innocent. The courts would become involved and once that happened there would be only one outcome. In Erik's opinion, the law was resolutely on the side of anybody who came to be detained by the police. 'Once you're arrested,' he said, 'you're in a very strong position. A presumption arises that you're being wrongfully held. It always happens like that.'

Anna, Ulf's closest colleague, and one with whom he had for some time been secretly in love, was dubious. Erik was given to exaggeration, she thought, and was, by any standards, remarkably ill-informed on all subjects except fishing, on which his knowledge was extensive. What did Erik know about the doings of the Swedish criminal courts, bearing in mind that his only reading matter — as far as she could tell — was angling magazines such as *Fish Today* or *Big Trout* — copies of which were to be regularly spotted on his desk.

'I don't think you can say that, Erik,' she said mildly. 'Or not in so many words. The courts try to balance interests.'

'That's probably true,' Ulf contributed. He was not entirely sure that this was the case, as he had seen many instances in which lawyers had managed to snatch manifestly guilty people from the jaws of justice. These people knew they were guilty as charged; their lawyers knew it too, as did the judges themselves, but the words of the penal code and the code of criminal procedure had somehow been interpreted in such a way as to allow wrongdoers to walk free. He had sometimes wondered how these notorious defence lawyers managed to sleep in their beds at

8

night, knowing that their efforts had allowed anti-social elements of every stripe to be returned to society. Or did they not see it that way? Did they feel that it was better for the system to be weighted that way than to punish the occasional innocent defendant, the occasional victim of a police misjudgement? Nobody was perfect, and Ulf understood that this applied to police officers every bit as much as to others. At least his department, the Department of Sensitive Crimes, had, under his leadership, a reputation for being scrupulously fair to those whom they investigated. If he ever felt that they were investigating the wrong person, they would abandon the inquiry. That did not happen in some departments, where a far more cavalier approach was adopted and what seemed to count was that *someone* was apprehended, in order to keep the clear-up rate looking impressive.

Ulf thought there was a grain of truth in what Erik said, but he could not express this view in front of Anna, lest she think he agreed with Erik's general opinions. It would not do at all if Anna suspected him of having anything in common with the world view of *Fish Today*, which occasionally published articles on subjects of a political or social nature. That, thought Ulf, was inexplicable: why should the editor of *Fish Today* stray outside his area of undoubted competence — fish — to opine on other matters? Was it journalistic frustration at being the editor of *Fish Today* when he might have wished to be the leader-writer on one of the national newspapers, or the editor of a respected political review? Plenty of people were in the wrong job altogether, or on a lowly rung of their chosen ladder; plenty of people were not where they wanted to be and might from time to time try to show what they saw as their true mettle.

Now, on the subject of conjoined twins, Ulf was unequivocal. 'It's quite right that the courts would order the release of the innocent twin. It would be completely wrong to imprison a person who had nothing to do with the offence in question.'

Erik thought about this for a few moments before replying, 'Except for one thing, Ulf: how would you know that he — the other twin, that is — had nothing to do with the crime? How would you know that?'

Ulf shrugged. 'We're talking about a hypothetical case here, aren't we? Let's imagine that one of the twins has been seen doing something illegal. Let's assume there are witnesses who say: *That twin did it, the one on the left* — or the right, as the case may be. Let's assume we know beyond any shadow of doubt which one did it.'

Erik pointed out that this was not what he meant. What he meant was that the other twin — the one who had done nothing — might be guilty of abetting the offence because he'd failed to do anything to stop his twin from acting. 'He becomes an accessory,' he said. 'By doing nothing to stop his twin brother, he becomes party to the offence. Simple.'

Anna thought ahead. 'All right,' she said, 'but let's think this out. Let's say that we've gone beyond the issue of whether a suspect might be detained. Let's say that we're at the trial stage and the guilty twin has been duly convicted. The issue of accessory guilt has not arisen and there's just one convicted person. What then? How do you punish the guilty twin without punishing the innocent sibling?'

'You can't,' said Ulf. 'You have to let him go free. He gets a warning, or something similar.'

This was too much for Erik. 'But what if the crime is really serious? What if it's homicide? What if the court thinks the offender is a danger to the public?'

This question was greeted with silence. At last, Ulf said, 'In practice, this is not really an issue, is it? We don't hear of Siamese twins being arrested, do we?'

'Perhaps that's because they don't do anything illegal,' suggested Anna. 'If you're a Siamese twin, you know there's always going to be a witness to what you do — always — and so you watch your step.'

That had been the end of the discussion, and now Ulf thought that it did not really help him in his uncertainty as to how to deal with Stig's complaint about police inaction over the outrages in the park. And he was about to say to Stig, 'Let me ask my colleagues in the vice squad about this,' when he heard a loud yelp from a clump of trees. Turning around sharply, he saw Martin engaged in a fight with what seemed to be an invisible enemy, struggling in a confusion of leaves and dust.

'Your dog,' shouted Stig. 'There's something going on.'

Ulf ran towards the trees. Martin had been off the lead and he had been vaguely aware of where he was, but had not been following him closely. Now he saw what had happened — what had been the consequences of his brief inattention.

When Ulf reached the scene of the tussle, the squirrel had already escaped and could be seen clinging to a branch of one of the trees, its tail an electric question mark of bristling fur. Ulf did not spend much time looking up at the branch, though — his attention was focused on Martin, who had been badly bitten about the head, and who was now whimpering at his feet.

A head wound in a human being can result in copious bleeding, and this also applied, it seemed, to dogs. Blood seemed to be pouring from the side of Martin's muzzle and from his nose too, or from where his nose had once been. Ulf gasped in horror as he saw that the soft round bulb of the dog's nose, to all intents and purposes like a small black truffle, had been almost severed. Instinctively he tried to press the nose back into place. It felt like a large crushed blackberry in his fingers and the attempted act of restoration brought a marrow-chilling howl of protest from Martin. For a few moments it seemed as though the dog would shake his nose off altogether, but the sinews still connecting the snout were tough, and the nose remained attached.

Stig had now joined Ulf, and his dog, Candy, tried to lick at Martin's wounds, only to be discouraged by a further unearthly sound — something between a yelp and a howl.

'You'll need to get him to a vet quickly,' said Stig. 'He's already lost a lot of blood.'

Ulf reached down to clip the leash back on to a collar now slippery with blood. He would have carried Martin back, although he was not a small dog, but he could not do so now as any approach to the injured animal was greeted with a baring of teeth and a savage growl. Yet once the leash was back on, Martin seemed keen to get back to the car, parked not far away, on the edge of the park.

'You poor creature,' muttered Ulf as he bundled Martin into the back of the Saab. He was indifferent to the specks of blood that immediately splattered the car's cherished leather upholstery; all that counted now was to get Martin to Dr Håkansson as quickly

12

as possible so that a painkiller of some sort might be administered. Ulf could not bear the thought of animal pain: pain and fear of death were things that we shared with the simplest of animal beings; we had more tricks than they did, but when it came to these basics, we shared that terrain with them, and were as vulnerable as they were.

He set off, and within a block or two encountered a traffic jam. A wedding celebration was taking place somewhere, a colourful ceremony from a distant culture, and the guests had parked inconsiderately. This had led to a build-up of normally free-moving traffic, and at points cars were reduced to walking speed. Ulf looked anxiously in his rear-view mirror at the injured dog. Although Martin's instinct was to lick his wounds, the almost-detached nose and its tiny bond of tissue made this form of self-administered canine first aid impossible. Their eyes met in the mirror, the dog gazing imploringly at his omnipotent master, unable to understand why Ulf, source of all authority, a human sun, should be unable to bid this pain cease.

The silver Saab nosed its way through a cluster of cars, their drivers drumming fingers on their steering wheels, impatient or accepting, according to personal disposition. Ulf craned his neck to get a better view of what was happening ahead, where the long line of cars snaked out as far as a distant junction. It could be half an hour or even more before the tangle of vehicles sorted itself out, and by then it might be too late for Martin. The bleeding had not abated, as far as Ulf could tell, and there must be a point at which the dog's heart would simply give out, as a pump does when it runs dry. How much blood did a dog's body contain? Ulf knew that we had about five litres — a fact that he remembered from forensic medicine lectures at the police college — but he was not sure about dogs. A couple of litres, perhaps; certainly not much more, and Martin must by now have lost a good cupful or two. Then he remembered another curious detail, dredged from memory, not thought about for years. The lecturer in forensic medicine at police college, a desiccated-looking pathologist with a slight nervous tic, had remarked that while we made do with that five litres, an African elephant had roughly fifty times that volume. That was one of the few details that Ulf remembered of those ten lectures from Dr Åström, along with the pathologist's explanation of death by shock — a cause of death he said he had encountered twice in his professional career, with one of the victims being a householder who had opened a cupboard door to find not one but two intruders hiding inside. The intruders had not raised a finger to the householder, but the shock of their presence was enough to cause his heart to fail. The other shock-induced death he had dealt with was that of a lottery winner who had died on realising that he had chosen the exact six figures that would bring him a jackpot of millions. He was a bachelor with no close family, and the millions, claimed on his behalf by his estate, had ended up in the hands of a charity dedicated to expanding public knowledge of coastal geology.

His thoughts returned to Martin, and to the urgency of the situation, and at the same time his eye fell on the detachable blue lamp that he could put on the top of the car if an urgent summons came through. Powered from the power socket of his car, this light would flash intermittently, as might a lighthouse in the darkness. And it worked: seeing the blue light

14

coming up behind them, drivers would slow down and pull in — exactly the course of action recommended in the Highway Code. This would allow Ulf to sail past unimpeded — something that was useful at some points in police work but that was not to be abused — as the Commissioner made clear in his circular on emergency procedures.

'Police vehicles,' he wrote to his section commanders, 'are subject to the ordinary rules of the road, and I shall not countenance any abuse of the occasional — and I underline occasional — licence that we have to break these rules in the interest of a rapid response.'

Ulf hesitated. Was this an emergency of such a nature as to justify a blue light? It was certainly a matter of life and death, even if only canine life and death. And yet why should we distinguish between our lives and the lives of dogs? Dogs were meant to be our friends and felt so many of the things that we felt. Dogs had a sense of self. Dogs understood loyalty and friendship; dogs loved us, and would do anything for us, so why should we not do anything for them?

Ulf retrieved the light. Reaching out of his open window, he placed it on the roof of his car, where its powerful magnet sucked at the metal of the Saab's bodywork. Ahead of him, a driver looked in his mirror and then obligingly pulled over to allow Ulf to pass. On the back seat, Martin bled onto the upholstery, whimpering, puzzled. He had forgotten what had caused his injury — dogs do not remember these things — but he knew that he was in pain and that the epicentre of this pain was his nose — or the place where his nose had once been.

2

I Need to Fall in Love

The blue light made a difference, but, even so, the journey to Dr Håkansson's clinic took half an hour longer than normal. With the usual stoicism of the injured animal, Martin quietened down, his earlier whimpering replaced by a low snuffling sound, probably caused, Ulf thought, by the near detachment of his nose. Ulf kept an eye on him in his rear-view mirror, and although he felt a momentary alarm when he noticed that Martin had become quite still, he was relieved to see a twitching a few seconds later that showed this to be sleep rather than death.

Ulf's thoughts wandered. He assumed that Dr Håkansson's clinic would be open and that the vet would be able to deal with Martin as a matter of urgency. This thought led to more general reflection on how we rely on certain people in our lives and how we tend to assume they will always be there, ready to attend to our needs. And it is in this spirit that we use the possessive my when referring to them. *My dentist, my doctor, my hairdresser* . . . He had to smile. *My dentist* . . . in Ulf's case the somewhat unusual Dr Melker Grahn, whom he saw every six months for his check-up. Dr Grahn was widely appreciated for his gentle touch — a quality that ensures a dentist's popularity. But there was something else that singled him out amongst dentists: his passionate interest in genealogical matters, and in particular his own roots,

16

parlous to the point of unlikelihood, in the Swedish nobility.

Ulf had become aware of Dr Grahn's interest in these matters on the first occasion on which he sat in the dentist's chair, gazing into the bright surgical light above his head. Dr Grahn had commented on Ulf's name — something that many did, or thought of doing until prevented by politeness. 'These wolf-based names are very interesting,' the dentist said, as he probed Ulf's mouth. 'I remember when I was at school there was a boy whose family name was Adolf. That's rare these days, for obvious reasons. But this boy was called Adolf — Gustav Adolf, if I remember correctly.' He paused; the fine pick scratched against the surface of a tooth. 'Which is interesting, because there was, as you probably know, a Gustav II Adolf back in the seventeenth century. But the surname actually comes from *Adalwolf*, which means *noble wolf*. Did you know that? I bet you didn't — not many do.' A further pause. 'You could be *Adalfvarg*, perhaps, which would be much the same thing — were you to think of changing your name, which I'm sure you feel no need to do.'

Ulf listened. Dr Grahn went on and on. He was quite content with his own name, he intoned as he hovered over the dental chair, but had a perfectly legitimate claim to call himself something rather different, were he to pursue the matter. 'I am descended, you see, from a very old family. I don't say that in any boastful way, of course, I merely mention it as a matter of historical interest. There is a family connection, admittedly not close, with a certain distinguished family which, as I'm sure you know, is one of the oldest noble families in Sweden. We — and I feel entitled

17

to say we — go back to the thirteenth century. My connection with the family is through the maternal line, and they take a very limited — unduly limited in my view — position on inheritance through the maternal line. So, too, does the House of Nobles, I'm afraid to say. They have flatly refused to recognise my connection, would you believe it? I have the documentation — screeds of it — and yet they refuse to acknowledge its legitimacy.'

Ulf sighed. He wanted to sympathise, but the instruments in his mouth made it difficult. A sigh would have to do.

'I should be in the *Adelskalendern*, the peerage register, but I am not. I don't care, though, because everybody knows that the *Adelskalendern* is incomplete. That is why I have not bought the latest edition and never — *never* — recommend it to anybody seriously interested in genealogical matters.'

And so it went on — on every visit to the dentist, Ulf would be treated to a lengthy account of Dr Grahn's claims to nobility and to an account of the perfidy of the genealogical establishment. He wondered whether every patient sat through this, but eventually decided that they did not, he being singled out because Dr Grahn knew that he worked in the Department of Sensitive Crimes and might therefore be able to pursue, in some vague and undefined way, cases of genealogical injustice.

Those others who looked after Ulf — his hairdresser, his psychotherapist, the mechanic who tuned and serviced his Saab — none of them was as seemingly monomaniacal as Dr Grahn. Admittedly his hairdresser tended to discuss television shows at greater length than they merited, and his mechanic

18

frequently complained, with some passion, about taxation, but they could talk about other things, and often did. And as for Dr Håkansson — he was the most balanced of all, and the most reassuring in his professional manner. And so, as Ulf drew up in front of his clinic and began the task of gently coaxing Martin out of the car, he knew that Dr Håkansson would do his best to allay his own anxiety and to calm the injured dog.

The receptionist, a fresh-faced young woman who appeared to remember the name of every animal that crossed the clinic's threshold, showed immediate concern.

'Oh, poor Martin!' she exclaimed. 'Look at you, you poor darling. What on earth has happened!'

'A squirrel, I'm afraid,' said Ulf. 'Is Dr Håkansson . . .'

She did not let him finish. 'He's dealing with a cat at the moment, but I shall interrupt him. This is clearly an emergency.'

She left her desk and made her way through a door behind her. In the room beyond, Ulf was afforded a glimpse of Dr Håkansson applying his stethoscope to a struggling bundle of feline opposition. The vet looked up from his task and exchanged a few words with the cat's owner, who nodded, and pushed the cat back into a carrying basket.

Ulf, carrying Martin in his arms, was ushered into the examination room.

'Now what have we here?' asked Dr Håkansson, leaning forward to look at Martin. And then, 'Oh dear. Oh my. Oh goodness me. This is very unfortunate.'

'A squirrel,' explained Ulf.

Dr Håkansson winced. 'Nasty little creatures. I

19

know that people think they're cute, but they have a very efficient set of teeth and they don't hesitate to use them.'

'Of course, Martin probably started it,' said Ulf. 'He's not blameless.'

Dr Håkansson helped to settle Martin. The dog whimpered again, a small drop of blood falling on the dark surface of the treatment table. His tail wagged briefly — a sign, perhaps, of faith in those who were standing about him in this strange place of unusual smells: cat — there had been a cat here, he was sure of it; and disinfectant, and water too, somewhere.

'He'll need a general anaesthetic,' said the vet, placing a gentle hand on Martin's flank. 'I'm going to have to stitch the nose back on. It's a delicate part.' He frowned as he peered more closely at his patient. 'And there are fairly deep lacerations on the muzzle, you'll see. Here, and then here as well. Nasty.'

Dr Håkansson straightened up. 'Leave him with me. We'll probably keep him in overnight. You can collect him on Monday.'

Martin was looking up at Ulf.

'You're going to have an operation,' Ulf said to him. 'Sorry, old boy.'

Martin was deaf. He had been trained to lip-read — and indeed was the only lip-reading dog in Sweden — but he knew none of the words that Ulf now used. But he picked up Ulf's demeanour, which was reassuring, and consequently appeared less frightened. Martin was sensitive to body language — more so, perhaps, than those dogs who could hear what was going on.

The arrangements made, Ulf returned to his car. With his handkerchief he tackled the bloodstains on the back seat, but this only seemed to make them worse. You had to be careful with blood; it responded to immediate attention, but once it penetrated a surface it could be hard to shift. Lawbreakers, Ulf knew, sometimes forgot that, and continued to wear clothing that spoke of assaults they had committed — with bloodstains that had survived the washing machine. Rorschach blots of violence, discernible in certain lights; reminders that what we do stays with us.

He remembered that on the way home he would pass a small garage that advertised on-the-spot car valeting. There was a high-pressure hose that customers could use themselves after placing coins in a slot, but they could stand back and watch while one of the mechanic's sons set about the car's interior with a vacuum cleaner and various sprays. It was run by a family from somewhere up north — the mechanic and his two taciturn sons, one of whom was very short-sighted and wore thick, pebble-lensed glasses. Ulf had called in there on several occasions and the mechanic had admired the Saab. 'Cars today are rubbish,' he said. 'Not like these Saabs.'

He slowed down and saw that the garage forecourt was empty. He drove in and knocked on the office door. 'My car,' he said. 'It needs a thorough clean.'

The mechanic nodded. 'That nice Saab. You want to keep that clean, don't you?'

'The back seat needs a wipe,' said Ulf. 'My dog, you see . . .'

But the garage man had not heard him and was calling out to one of his boys. 'Tomas will give it a good clean,' he said to Ulf. 'You can have coffee. Read the paper, if you like.'

The paper Ulf was offered was not one he would

normally have read. A lurid, inflammatory picture dominated its front page, and the text below it rumbled in apocalyptic terms. He sighed. Was this the way it was going to be? Was this what Sweden was to become — the same as everywhere else? He turned the page and began to read a report about a flying saucer that had been seen over Denmark. Four people — all professionals, the paper said — claimed to have seen the object hovering over a furniture factory. Ulf turned the page. A local politician was being accused of fathering six children by six different women. 'He has expressed surprise at these allegations,' the paper reported, 'but has admitted to two of them.' Ulf sighed again. What did it matter? It was far too late to stop people breeding irresponsibly; it was far too late, in fact, to stop anybody doing *anything*. And yet, that was what he was paid to do. He, and Anna, and Carl were paid by the state, regularly and quite generously, to stop people from doing things that society deemed unacceptable. That was what they did — or were meant to do. But where did one start, given that there was such a tide of wrongdoing? And so much of the wrongdoing was not even covered by any criminal code; it was made up of big, spectacular crimes against the environment: the burning of the Amazon forests, the filling of the seas with plastics, the pumping of toxic fumes into the atmosphere. Those were the crimes that people should be exercised about, but which were not crimes at all in many places. He would hunt those people down if the state asked him to do so. He would rub their noses in the havoc they wrought and say, *Look what you have done*. He would handcuff them, those proud, greedy people, and make them admit to their crimes.

He moved on to the personal columns, where readers advertised for love, for the most part, but sometimes for simple friendship. A man with a caravan was looking for an unattached lady with whom to tour Sweden. He was domestically inclined, the advertisement said, and slightly overweight. A woman who had lived abroad was looking for a man in his sixties who liked opera. She was advertising in the wrong newspaper, Ulf reflected; she might be more successful here if she wanted a man who was interested in flying saucers — or football, perhaps.

Tomas worked slowly and it was almost twenty minutes before he completed his task and sauntered over to speak to his father. Ulf watched as father and son conferred, with Tomas gesturing towards the Saab before looking over towards Ulf. After a further few minutes of delay, the mechanic came over to Ulf to hand over the keys of the Saab.

'All ready,' he said. 'Good as new.'

Ulf put down the newspaper, not without relief, and prepared to pay for the cleaning. The mechanic glanced at the name on the credit card. 'It's Mr Varg, isn't it?' he said. 'Ulf Varg?'

Ulf nodded. He saw the mechanic write something on a slip of paper and then turn to him with a smile. 'Thank you for your custom,' he said. 'Sorry that your car was in such a mess. But I think Tomas has done a good job.'

'I'm sure he has,' said Ulf.

The mechanic hesitated. 'Was that blood all over the back seat?' He wrinkled his nose in disgust. 'Blood. Rather a lot of it.'

Ulf replied that it was. 'My dog,' he said.

The mechanic looked towards the Saab. 'I don't

see a dog,' he said.

'That's because he's not there,' said Ulf. 'He's at the vet's.' He felt a momentary irritation. This was nobody's business but his own.

'A dog,' the other man mused. 'A dog who isn't there.'

Ulf drew a deep breath. 'I am a police officer,' he said. 'Malmö Police.' It was rare for him to mention his occupation; some members of the force were prepared to do so when they needed to intimidate somebody, but Ulf had never approved of that.

The mechanic looked at him disbelievingly. 'A police officer without a uniform.'

'Plainclothes,' snapped Ulf. He felt in his pocket for his police identity card; it was not there, and he remembered that he had put it in his other jacket — the one he usually wore to work.

'Yes?' said the mechanic. 'Looking for something that also isn't there?'

Ulf ignored the taunt. Silently he paid the bill and then walked back towards the Saab, feeling the eyes of Tomas and his father follow his every step. He had no need to put up with this sort of thing; and what, anyway, was this man implying? That he had somehow injured his dog? Was that it?

He got into the car and drove off, a bit calmer now, but still angry over the mechanic's behaviour. There was a time, he reminded himself, when people had showed policemen respect. Now anybody could say anything to anybody, and it made Ulf think: if only we could turn the clock back forty years, if only . . . How peaceful the world was then; how polite were children to their elders; how courteous were our everyday trans-actions; how few cars there were on the road — and

24

most of them Saabs, real Saabs, with leather seats and Swedish instrumentation; how long the summers, and how warm the water in the lakes in which we swam . . . He indulged himself in these thoughts for a few minutes, before privately recanting them. Nostalgia could turn you against your own times, which was of no use to anyone. The past was not golden — it was full of injustice and inequality and silent suffering; whereas the present . . . He stopped himself. Oh well, he thought. Oh well. And there was a name for thinking, Oh well — and that was stoicism. There had been a long article about the resurgence of stoicism in a newspaper he had picked up in the coffee bar — some of it, he recalled, underlined in red ink by an unknown reader. That happened to many of the newspapers and magazines there — somebody was furtively, and selectively, underlining certain things in red.

He parked in his usual place and made his way back to the entrance to his apartment building. As he keyed in the number on its combination lock, the lobby door was opened from within by his neighbour, Mrs Högfors. The widow was carrying a large shopping basket; Saturday afternoon was when she went to the farmers' market a few blocks away. Often, she came back with items she had spotted for Ulf, and he would reimburse her for the purchase. Last week she had bought him a leg of lamb; the week before it had been a string of garlic bulbs and a guinea fowl, plucked and ready for the oven.

She noticed Martin's absence. 'And where is Martin?' she asked, her voice betraying her concern. 'Is he—'

Ulf was quick to reassure her. 'Nothing to worry

about. He's at the vet's, but I shall be picking him up on Monday.'

Mrs Högfors paled. She was particularly fond of Martin, whom she looked after when Ulf was off at work.

Ulf told her what had happened.

She listened, grim-faced. 'I could strangle that squirrel,' she said between gritted teeth. 'It's been taunting Martin for years — for years. Oh, I know which one it is.'

Ulf felt that he had to point out that Martin had been the aggressor. Dogs were almost always responsible for starting any fight they were involved in: that was almost invariably true. Dogs were never the innocent party. 'It's his own fault,' he said. 'The squirrel has always tried to keep out of his way.'

Mrs Högfors was having none of that. 'Squirrels serve no purpose at all,' she said vehemently. 'They dig up bulbs and so on. They're thoroughly useless creatures.'

'They must have their *raison d'être*,' said Ulf. 'Everything has its place — somewhere in the scheme of things.'

'If I get my hands on that creature,' Mrs Högfors persisted, 'I'll show it its place in the scheme of things.'

It was belligerent talk for a middle-aged widow, and although it amused Ulf, it also discomfited him. 'Anyway,' he said, deliberately moving the conversation on, 'Dr Håkansson felt Martin would be all right. He's putting in a few stitches here and there — including around his nose. That was almost detached.'

Mrs Högfors winced. 'But his nose will be saved?'

Ulf nodded. 'I believe so.'

'You'll keep me informed? And I take it I'll be able

26

to visit him when he gets back from the clinic.'

'Of course you can. I imagine he'll be wearing one of those peculiar lampshade things that they put on dogs to stop them worrying at a wound.'

'Poor Martin,' sighed Mrs Högfors. And then she changed the subject. There had been a robbery at a local supermarket — had Ulf heard any details? Were any Russians involved? Mrs Högfors had been deeply alarmed by reports of the Russian use of poison abroad.

'I doubt very much if the Russians are behind that sort of thing,' said Ulf. He wanted to add that he rather liked the Russians he had met, and that the average Russian was probably not all that different from the average Swede.

'I wouldn't be so sure,' she retorted. 'The Russians have always gone in for poisoning.'

'This is a robbery, though,' Ulf said mildly. 'I don't think poison was involved.' He paused. 'But I'll ask one of my colleagues, and let you know if I hear anything.'

Once they had parted company, Ulf went upstairs. The flat was quiet without Martin, and he felt strangely low. He looked out of the window, down to the street below, where a man and a woman were walking alongside one another with the ease and assurance of people who *belonged* together; the man took the woman's arm, and their pace changed: he had her; she had him. That was security; that was completeness. And then two young men came along, walking behind them, and one of the young men suddenly put an arm around the other, and Ulf thought: that is exactly the same thing. He looked away, feeling almost as if he were a voyeur, intruding on the private moments of

27

these people. Perhaps I should get married again, he said to himself. I need to find somebody. I have had enough of living by myself — even if I have Martin for company. Perhaps I need to fall in love.

But then he stopped and thought: but I'm already in love. I'm in love with Anna, and I've been in love with her for years now. Yet I cannot have her because she's married and has two young daughters who are swimming champions, and a husband who's an anaesthetist. And although Ulf thought he was very dull and he did not see how Anna could *really* love such an uninteresting man, it would be wrong to do anything to interfere in that marriage. And anyway, he had no idea whether Anna felt about him the way he felt about her because he had never asked her; there were plenty of unreciprocated love affairs in this world, and the problem was that those who were in them rarely understood that the one they loved did not love them. That was the real tragedy of such relationships: that people should believe in something that simply was not there and could never be conjured into existence. How sad. We had such a short time in this world, this little speck in infinite space, our wobbly little platform, and how wretched were we if we would so love to spend it with one who was unprepared to spend it with us; who would not, or could not — it amounted to the same thing, to the same existential bad luck.

28

3

Selenium, CBD, etc.

The coffee bar could not have been more conveniently placed — directly opposite the entrance to the Department of Sensitive Crimes, two doors down from Carlo's delicatessen, and immediately next door to a newsagent's that sold, alongside a wide selection of newspapers and magazines, those things people needed at odd moments: shoelaces, watch batteries, Swedish–English dictionaries, and assorted birthday cards. It was in the newsagent's that Erik bought his fishing magazines, including *Fish Today* and the English-language *Angling Times*. It was here that Ulf occasionally bought a copy of *Contemporary Art and Artists*, to complement the specialised Scandinavian art magazine to which he subscribed by post.

The coffee bar was popular not only with local police employees, almost all of whom belonged to the detective branch of the force, but also with people working in nearby offices. Some of these Ulf had come to know quite well; others he recognised, and even if he did not know their names, his detective's instinct had enabled him to work out more or less exactly what they did. Those involved in finance gave themselves away with their perusal of the market reports in the newspapers and with the way their demeanour matched the state of the markets. One man in particular, who clearly struggled with his weight, would allow himself a pastry on days in which the stock

29

markets plunged for whatever reason — comfort eating, Ulf decided. Another sold insurance to farmers, as he would occasionally come in with a client whose ruddy complexion gave the game away. Then there were two women who were something to do with fashion modelling, as they would from time to time bring in the models — lanky young women whose eyes darted about the room, looking to see who was looking at them, or broad-shouldered young men with improbably chiselled chins and with cashmere sweaters tied casually about their waists. Working out to which world somebody belonged was second nature to Ulf — and to Anna, too, who was even better at it than he was. Not that they were self-conscious about it — it was a simple concomitant of being a good detective.

Now, on that Monday morning, Ulf was at his usual table in the coffee bar a good half-hour before he was due in the office. He had the morning paper with him, and had settled into this over a generous cup of latte when Anna arrived. She was not as regular a customer of the coffee bar as was Ulf, as she often had to drop her girls off at school before coming into work, but she still enjoyed calling in when she could. It was a good time for both of them, as they could talk without involving the colleagues with whom they shared the office. At the same time, there remained a frisson of anxiety about their meetings in the coffee bar — these were by no means assignations, but Ulf remained conscious of the fact that he was in a coffee bar with another man's wife, and even if nothing had ever been said, there was an undercurrent of danger in the situation. These were innocent meetings of two colleagues — not much different from a meeting in a staff canteen — but the fact remained that Anna had Jo and that he, the loyal husband, was not there with them but was at the head of an operating table, manipulating his gases, keeping lungs inflating and consciousness at bay. Did Anna tell him that she regularly met Ulf for coffee, or did she say nothing? Would he object, or would he take the view that it was perfectly natural for colleagues to meet over a pre-work cup of coffee? More importantly, did Dr Jo Svensson have any inkling — any inkling at all — that there was another man who felt this way about his wife; who even, rather regularly — and Ulf felt deep shame about this — dreamed about her in a way he could not possibly admit to, even to his therapist? Of course, one could not be held accountable for one's dreams, but they revealed one's inmost wishes, they laid out exactly what one really wanted to do. And what one really wanted to do constituted, in a sense, one's deepest self, for which, surely, we were all responsible — at least to some degree. Or were we? Could we make our character better than it was? Was it realistic to expect us to banish unwelcome or illicit desires with just a little more moral effort? Ulf had once raised this question with a friend from university days, now a Catholic priest. The friend had listened to the question, thought for a few moments, and then said, 'Yes, that's what Catholicism is all about. That's our daily struggle.' Ulf had smiled, and said, 'Cold showers and prayer?' And the priest had looked at him reproachfully and said, quite simply, 'If necessary.'

Having collected her double espresso from the counter, Anna joined Ulf at his table.

'Another week,' she remarked.

31

Ulf smiled. 'Monday,' he said.

Anna took a sip of her coffee. 'I've never had difficulties with Monday. Jo doesn't like Mondays, but I don't mind them too much. Thursday depresses me, for some reason. I have no idea why.'

Ulf asked why Jo, Anna's husband, felt as he did.

'I suppose it goes back to schooldays,' she said. 'You enjoy yourself over the weekend, seeing all your friends, and then along comes Monday, and you have to return to the classroom. Something like that.'

'I don't like February,' said Ulf. 'I'm indifferent to the various days of the week, but I have strong views on months. I don't like November too much because one thinks, Yes, this is the winter coming now — it's unavoidable. December is fun — parties and Christmas and so on — and January is a bit of a welcome end to all that — the excesses, that is — but then February drags terribly. It's all been going on too long by that stage. You yearn for light.'

She looked at him. 'You yearn for light,' she muttered, and added, 'Don't we all?'

'We do,' he said. He raised his eyes and met her gaze. She looked away.

'And I suppose that's the lot of so many,' Ulf continued. 'They look for light — and warmth — and love too, when all is said and done. People just want to be loved — somehow — anyhow. They want the world to love them. Or somebody to love them.'

Anna toyed with her coffee cup. 'Yes, you're right. Love makes people complete. Or people hope it will.' She paused. 'Do you think it does? Or is that a fond illusion?'

'Sometimes,' said Ulf. 'Sometimes.'

'Sometimes is a good answer to anything, isn't it?'

32

'Sometimes.'

They both laughed, and the moment of tension passed. Anna now said, 'While you were out of the office on Friday, we had a call. Somebody wanted an appointment with you. He said it was urgent, and he was quite insistent. So I told him he could come this morning at eleven. Is that all right?'

She was apologetic. There was an understanding that, as far as possible, people would be discouraged from coming to the office on their own instance. On occasion they might have a good reason for wanting to discuss a complaint on police premises, but in ordinary cases it was far better for the Department of Sensitive Crimes to interview people in their home or a business setting. There was much to be learned from seeing people in their own surroundings — personal possessions, décor, demeanour: these were all factors that an observant detective might pay attention to on meeting a complainant. And then there was the problem of those who arrived in the office and dug in, enjoying the sheer luxury of a listening presence in which to spill out their issues, imaginary or otherwise, rooted in reality or grossly paranoid.

Ulf assured her that he did not mind. 'I'm not going anywhere,' he said. 'What's it about?'

'It's an Anders Kindgren. Very well spoken.'

'Kindgren?'

'Yes, do you know him? He said he had met you somewhere, but then people phoning up for an appointment often say that.'

They did. And the meeting might have been five years ago, at a cocktail party with sixty others. And yet on such a tenuous basis might attention be claimed, might favours be requested.

Ulf had met Anders Kindgren before, but did not know him at all well. 'I know his work, though. I've read Kindgren.'

'He's an author?'

'Yes. Not an author author, so to speak — he doesn't write novels or plays or anything like that. He writes about art.'

'Ah.' Anna was bemused by Ulf's fascination with art history. She was no philistine, and enjoyed the occasional trip to a gallery or museum, but she had never been able to understand the appeal of the detailed study of paintings and painters. Surely the interest in a painting lay in how it made one feel, or perhaps how it made one think about something. What did it matter whether the artist had been influenced by this painter or that painter? What did it matter that he had been commissioned to paint something by this or that wealthy patron, or that a painting had been mentioned in a marriage contract or a will? And as for aesthetics, what could one say about that other than that one liked what one liked and disliked what one disliked?

She had occasionally picked up one of Ulf's art magazines from his desk and perused it over her lunchtime sandwich. She liked looking at the photographs, or at least some of them: she could not see the point of the installations that some artists created. Why stack six boxes one on top of one another, slap white paint over them, and then call the whole thing *Containers of Innocence*? Where was the art in that? And where was the art in the collection of abandoned domestic heaters on which vivid sunflowers had been painted? That particular installation — described in the text as a 'statement' — was entitled *van Gogh no!*

34

Was she missing something? She looked for an explanation in the text accompanying such works, but it failed to enlighten her. *In his practice, this artist is striving to distance himself from pressure applied to artists to bear witness to what people falsely see as beauty . . .* What did that mean? And why should even the humble lay public, unversed in art theory, not have an idea of beauty?

Ulf told her about Kindgren. 'He's written several books,' he said. 'I have two of them, but I think there are more. He's an authority on Nicolas Poussin. But he's also done a lot of work on earlier artists — Piero di Cosimo, Botticelli — he wrote books on both of them, I think. I read something he wrote on Primavera.'

'So he's something of an expert?'

'Definitely. He has something that most scholars would give their eye teeth for — an international reputation. Academics would commit murder to be described as an international authority. They're very vain people — or they can be.'

'Is he — this Kindgren — vain?'

Ulf confessed that he did not know. And now that he thought of it, he felt that perhaps he had been slightly uncharitable in his assessment of professors. Some of them were vain, but others were modest about their achievements. His own professors, he recalled, had been in the modest camp — for the most part. Now he wondered what could be prompting Anders Kindgren to seek a conversation with the Department of Sensitive Crimes. Could it be an artistic forgery? Ulf rather hoped that it would be: he had been hoping for an opportunity to investigate art crime, but had not yet been given the chance. The last major art

35

theft had been claimed by the Division of High Value Property Crimes, a rival department that took a condescending view of humbler echelons, amongst which they clearly numbered Ulf's own department. It was typical of them to hold on to that particular art theft, which had involved a painting from the collection of a high-profile fashion designer. They had leapt at the chance of hobnobbing with those flashy people, even though the Commissioner himself had expressed the view that the case in question might have been referred to Ulf in view of its undoubted sensitivity. They had not done so, and then they had failed to handle the negotiations for the painting's return in a satisfactory manner and it had ended up being destroyed. A Klimt, of all things: burned to a cinder by the thieves once they felt the net was closing in on them and they had to destroy the evidence. Ulf could have told his colleagues that they were going about it in entirely the wrong way — that art theft was more akin to kidnapping than to a property crime. Art thieves would be interested in a ransom for the painting's return as its value in the market was virtually nothing. People spoke about wealthy art collectors in South America who liked to adorn their walls with stolen masterpieces, but nobody had ever proved the existence of such people. Ulf thought it highly unlikely that a collector would pay a large sum for a painting and then be unable to show it off to friends. People who collected usually had an eye on what their collection would say about them — and their wealth — not only to their friends but also to their rivals. If you had three Picassos, you would want to boast about it — while striking a modest pose, of course. *Just little Picassos, actually — I'm rather fond of them. I love the colours.*

He thanked Anna. 'I'm glad you arranged this,' he said. 'I can think of a whole lot of people I would not like to see. But I rather look forward to meeting him.'

'Meeting him again, you mean.'

Ulf shrugged. 'I'm surprised he remembered meeting me. I had a reason to remember even a casual meeting with somebody like him — having read his books. But why would he remember meeting me at some gallery opening or whatever?'

Anna thought for a moment. 'Because he doesn't ordinarily meet detectives at gallery openings? Could that be it?'

Ulf was not sure. 'I usually don't tell people I'm a detective. I don't see how he would have known.'

'Or your name,' suggested Anna. 'You have an unusual name, Ulf. He might have thought: here's somebody called Wolf Wolf — how interesting. Not that . . . ' She trailed off. People were sensitive about their names and she had never discussed Ulf's with him. She knew that there were people on the force who teased him — that silly young man from supplies, for instance, who would sometimes howl like a wolf if he spotted Ulf in the car park — and she would not want him to think she found anything comic in his name.

Ulf was unperturbed. 'Possibly. But I don't think so.'

Anna smiled. 'Or you said something particularly interesting, and he remembered. That happens, you know. We remember odd things that people have said — sometimes years after the event. It might have been that.'

'Oh?' He looked thoughtful. 'I doubt if I said anything that somebody like Anders Kindgren would find memorable. Most of what I say is . . . well,

37

unremarkable, I'd have thought.'

Anna shook her head. 'You have plenty of interesting opinions, Ulf,' she said. 'I know how modest you are, but you shouldn't undersell yourself.'

He was touched by her reassurance. 'You're being very kind. But frankly, when I think of what a transcription of what we say each day would look like, I shudder. All the inconsequential things. All the trite observations. All the radio noise.'

Anna was thinking of Blomquist. A smile played about her lips. 'Blomquist,' she said.

Ulf knew what she meant. Blomquist went on and on about his pet interests. Vitamins. Diets. Exercise regimes. Origami. His mind could be relied upon to dart off into the most curious byways — and dwell there for hours, exhausting the possibilities of whatever subject it had alighted upon.

'I was in the car with him the other day,' Ulf said. 'It was a thirty-minute journey and he didn't draw breath.'

'What was it?'

'The benefits of hemp extract. Blomquist has trouble getting a good night's sleep, he says. Apparently he talks in his sleep a lot — and wakes up at odd hours too.'

Anna burst out laughing. 'I can just imagine Blomquist mumbling away about vitamin supplements — all while fully asleep. What a trial for his wife.'

Ulf agreed. 'Poor woman. She has the patience of a saint, I'm told.' He remembered the conversation in the car. 'He says that his pharmacist recommended that he take something called CBD,' he continued. 'Cannabidiol, to give it its full name. It's derived from

38

the hemp plant, but it's not the stuff that makes you high. They take the THC out. Blomquist explained the distinction — in pharmaceutical detail.'

'I've seen it in the shops. And of course there were those court cases over it. The government was digging in, but—'

'Governments who dig themselves in,' said Ulf, 'usually dig a hole for themselves.'

Anna was sceptical about supplements. Blomquist had given up on her: 'Much as I admire Anna,' he had once confessed to Ulf, 'it seems to me that she has a closed mind. And surely that can't be a good thing in detective work, can it? You have to keep your mind open to all sorts of possibilities. Preclude some, and you may be missing the solution.'

Now Anna said, 'I don't take anything. No vitamin C, no vitamin D, no selenium supplements. Nothing.'

'Selenium,' mused Ulf. 'You may need to watch that. We've mined our soil so much that the average diet doesn't contain the selenium we need to protect ourselves against oxidative damage. And for thyroid health.' He stopped himself. What he had said was pure Blomquist; he would need to be careful. But he felt a sudden tug of concern. He did not want Anna to be selenium-deficient; and that, surely, was a sign of love. We want those we love to get enough selenium — of course we do.

'I eat a couple of Brazil nuts a day,' Anna went on. 'That gives you as much selenium as you need, I'm told.'

'Good,' said Ulf. 'I do too.'

'Mind you,' Anna continued, 'you have to be careful not to eat too many Brazil nuts. Apparently, there's a condition that goes with getting too much selenium.

Selenium poisoning. Your nails become brittle; your hair falls out; and you experience abdominal pain. There are some places in China where there is too much selenium in the soil and as a result people get too much in their diet. They become quite sick.'

Ulf thought that selenium had been exhausted — as a topic, as well as a trace element. 'This CBD stuff,' he said. 'Blomquist swears by it. He said that he doesn't like taking the serious sleeping pills you get from the doctor, and that this CBD has a real effect on sleep. It makes you less anxious, he says, and as a result you get a much better night's sleep.'

'And the evidence?' asked Anna.

'He said there was some research — somewhere — that backed this up.'

Anna looked doubtful. 'Jo says that you have to have proper evidence for these claims. You have to have papers in reputable medical journals. Copper-bottomed stuff. Large sample groups — placebos and all the rest — double-blind studies and so on. You can't just have some report from the internet somewhere.'

'I'm not defending CBD,' said Ulf. 'I'm just saying what Blomquist told me.'

'I wouldn't listen to him,' said Anna.

Ulf said nothing. Blomquist had accused Anna of having a closed mind, and here she was saying that she would not listen to him. If one wanted to keep an open mind, then surely one had to be prepared to listen to what other people had to say, even if you were minded to disagree with it.

He looked at his watch. Although the Department of Sensitive Crimes worked flexible hours, they tried to keep these hours as regular as possible. That meant he should be at his desk at nine every morning, ready for whatever the working day brought: ready to deal with the unusual ways in which people could infringe the rights of others, could threaten the glue of society with their selfishness, could engage in inconsiderate or malevolent behaviour because they were inconsiderate or malevolent people. That was why he and his colleagues went into the office each morning: to do battle against the tide that threatened to wash away society's foundations. Or so he sometimes thought. At other times he thought that what he did was exactly the same as what everybody else did: put in time, as conscientiously as possible, until that distant, scarcely imaginable day when he came in for the last time before retirement.

'We must get into the office,' he said, pushing his chair back from the table.

'Another day, another krona,' sighed Anna.

He looked at her. He loved her wit. He loved her high cheekbones. He loved her eyes, which seemed to him to change colour, depending on the light. Was that unusual? Did his eyes change colour like that? He stopped. What about his own eyes? Did they always look the same?

On impulse, he said to Anna, 'What colour are my eyes at the moment?'

She looked at him in surprise. 'The same as they've always been.'

'Which is?'

She stared at him. 'Nondescript, I'd say.'

Ulf tried to smile. But he felt hurt. *I love your eyes, but you don't love mine.* His brother, Björn, liked to strum the guitar from time to time and sing countryish songs. These tended to be about unfaithful girlfriends and broken hearts; about dogs and vans; about male

41

unhappiness — all delivered in American-accented Swedish. Björn might do something with that line — *I love your eyes, but you don't love mine / And now I think it's really time / To see you just as you see me . . . Und so weiter*, as the Germans said; usw, three letters capable of conveying predictability every bit as effectively as etc. and osv — *och så vidare.*

Anna saw that she had offended him. 'Sorry, I didn't mean to say nondescript,' she said. 'I meant to say 'indescribable'. That's different, Ulf. Believe me: completely different.'

4

English Shoes

Ulf looked at Anders Kindgren. The art historian was seated in the interview room, his chair pushed slightly out from its normal position so that the two of them were not facing one another across the table. That gave the encounter a less formal feel — enhanced by the tray of coffee and biscuits that Ulf had provided. The Department of Sensitive Crimes, unlike other police departments, had good china: cups with saucers, rather than the mugs in which police coffee was served elsewhere. This china had been given to them by a wealthy woman after the department had quickly and efficiently dealt with an extortionist who had been attempting to extract eighty thousand kronor from her bank account. She had proposed a more personal gift for each member of the department involved in her case, but the rule against accepting gifts had stood in the way of that. Welfare gifts — donations to police charities or gifts designed to help the police do their work — were in a different category, and so the china coffee service had been duly approved by the authorities.

Ulf was glad they were using the good china, as everything about Anders Kindgren spoke of cultivated elegance, of quiet good taste. This was a man who would appreciate the difference between bone china and a ceramic mug, particularly one with a message. The department's kitchen had several mugs with the symbols of well-known football clubs embossed on them, and a milk jug in the shape of a fish. That belonged to Erik, of course, and was generally used only by him, although it did occasionally make an appearance when the interview room was being used.

Ulf noted every detail of his visitor's clothing. Firstly, there were the shoes, which were English Oxfords. Other people made Oxfords, of course, but nobody made them in quite the same way as the English did. These, he thought, were Joseph Cheaney & Sons rather than Church's. Church's shoes were all right, of course, but he slightly preferred those made by Mr Cheaney and his sons.

Then there were the trousers, which were linen and tailored, rather than bought off a rack. That was a detail that most people would miss, but Ulf picked it up from the angle of the pockets and the size of the turn-ups. These were about half as generous again as ordinary turn-ups, not that most off-the-peg trousers gave one the option of turn-ups at all any more. Then the shirt — Egyptian cotton, made by a shirtmaker, probably in Jermyn Street, London, because of the ample room it provided: Italian shirts were as elegant, possibly even more so, but were tighter in their fit. And finally, the jacket, a blazer with dark blue buttons — dyed bone, Ulf thought, not plastic.

He poured Anders Kindgren a cup of coffee.

'We have met before, of course,' Ulf said, handing his guest the cup.

'I know,' said Kindgren. 'Four years ago. It was at an opening of the Joseph Claesson retrospective. You told me that you had recently been to St Petersburg on holiday and had visited the Yusupov Palace. You made me want to go and see it — which I have not

44

done yet. Perhaps some day.'

Ulf could not conceal his astonishment. He recalled meeting Kindgren, but he had no recollection of their conversation. 'Your memory's very impressive,' he began. 'How do you do it?'

Kindgren shrugged. 'It's just the way it is,' he said. 'I find it easy to remember. Forgetting is the hard part — for me, at least.'

'You would be an ideal witness,' said Ulf, smiling.

Kindgren sipped at his coffee. 'I remember that you said something about the Yusupov Palace being a crime scene. And that stuck in my mind — the thought of a detective, like yourself, going to visit a museum and being interested in the crimes committed there. I'm not saying that you would not be interested in the furniture and the paintings, but the basement, I think, particularly attracted your attention.'

Ulf shook his head in wonderment at Kindgren's power of recall. 'It was where Rasputin was murdered,' he said. 'Prince Yusupov invited the monk to tea and served him with cyanide pastries and cyanide-spiked wine. He believed that Rasputin had too much influence with the Tsarina and was imperilling the Romanov dynasty: he had to go. But Rasputin seemed to be utterly unaffected by the poison. So he shot him — there and then. Through the heart.'

'What a thought,' said Kindgren.

'And then Yusupov shot a dog,' Ulf continued, 'so that there would be an explanation for the blood on the scene. He obviously felt he had to do something to cover his tracks.'

He remembered the blood on the seat of his Saab, and for a moment he felt a stab of anxiety. What if those slow-witted people at the garage decided that his Saab had been some sort of crime scene? He put the thought aside. There was no point in worrying about things like that; they could be easily cleared up, if they ever went any further — which was highly unlikely.

'What happened then?' asked Kindgren.

'At the Yusupov Palace? Prince Yusupov returned a little while later to shift the body and found that Rasputin was still alive. He shot him again, but Rasputin got to his feet and ran down a corridor. One of Yusupov's friends then shot him again — twice. Then they stove in his skull with an iron bar, wrapped him up in a carpet, and tipped him through a hole in the ice of the canal. The body was found the next day in the Neva.'

Kindgren winced. 'He was not exactly the most co-operative victim, was he?'

'The interesting thing,' Ulf went on, 'is that the post-mortem revealed water in the lungs. So he was still alive when he went into the water.' He paused. 'And the coroner's verdict was — would you believe it — death through hypothermia.'

Kindgren laughed. 'The Yusupovs were very influential, weren't they? And rich.'

Ulf nodded. 'The rich are very rarely convicted. I don't like to be cynical, but there's some truth in that.'

Ulf offered Kindgren more coffee, but the offer was declined. 'I have to watch my caffeine,' said Kindgren, holding a hand above his cup.

'Now,' said Ulf, 'you wanted to speak to me about something.'

Kindgren dabbed at the corners of his mouth with a handkerchief. 'I did. I hope you don't mind my approaching you directly. I don't really know anybody in the police and what I have to say is . . . well, it's a bit delicate.'

Ulf held the other man's gaze. 'You can speak in confidence,' he said, but then added, 'However, I must point out that any disclosure of criminality — on any-body's part — will need to be investigated.'

'I understand that,' said Kindgren. 'And I hasten to point out that I haven't come here to confess any-thing. I've come here as the victim.'

Ulf inclined his head. 'That's what I imagined,' he said.

'And I chose you,' Kindgren continued, 'because I know you to be interested in art, and this touches on art — or may touch on it.'

For a few moments, Ulf said nothing. Then, 'I'm listening.'

Kindgren settled back in his chair. 'It's been going on for six months now,' he said. 'The first incident was in January. January the twelfth. I had driven off to see my sister-in-law in hospital. She was having an orthopaedic operation and was going to be in for some weeks. My wife had asked me to take her some reading material and one or two other things that she needed. I delivered it all to the ward and after a brief chat with her — about twenty minutes or so — I returned to my car. And that's when I smelled it.'

'What?'

'Fish. Rotten fish. Somebody had deposited four or five stinking fish on the bonnet of the car — pushed into the air vents. The smell was indescribable.' Kind-gren wrinkled his nose at the memory. 'Are you familiar with the smell of rotten fish, Ulf?'

Ulf was. 'When I was a boy, my brother and I left some fish in our father's cool box. We forgot about

47

them until they became only too noticeable. We were unable to get the smell out of the box and it had to be thrown away. We tried everything: pure alcohol, bleach; we even tried—'

Kindgren interrupted him. 'Your brother? That's Björn Varg, I take it? The politician?'

Ulf nodded. He was used to people asking about Björn, but he did not particularly like it. As leader of the Moderate Extremists, Björn's politics were very different from his brother's. Ulf was an old-fashioned centrist: wary of extremism and intolerance whether it came from the right or the left. Björn, by contrast, was happy to throw incendiary comments into the national political debate and then, point by point, qualify them. He was a controversialist, with that streak of mischievousness that such people often have. Ulf was glad that his brother would never be in power, or remotely close to the exercise of power. 'He's the worst government we never had,' he once said to a friend. 'I know he's my brother, but I would never vote for him. *Never.*'

'I do enjoy listening to him on the radio,' said Kindgren. 'He speaks his mind, your brother.'

Ulf nodded again — sadly this time. 'I'm not sure if that's an altogether good thing,' he said. 'There are too many tinder kegs waiting to be ignited. We don't need politicians getting people worked up about things.'

Kindgren thought about this. 'We Swedes tend to wish our problems away, I think. We want the world to be like us — cool, rational, unemotional. But it isn't. And we don't like conflict, do we?'

'Hence our traditional neutrality,' said Ulf.

Kindgren looked away. 'Yes,' he said doubtfully. 'Although we did provide Nazi Germany with our

48

iron ore.'

'Yet we sheltered the Danish Jews,' said Ulf. 'And we had very little room to manoeuvre. Germany would have invaded us — they very nearly did. Think what that would have done to the country.'

'Yes,' said Kindgren. 'But let's not get bogged down in those difficult years. I'm left feeling a bit ashamed about it, frankly. I don't think we come out of it as well as we might have done.' He paused. 'Where were we?'

'Fish,' replied Ulf. 'You found rotten fish on your car?'

'It was the most appalling experience. I took them off, of course, but there were bits that had got into the ventilation system, and so when I switched on the engine, the whole car was permeated by this unbearable odour. I was retching all the way home — it was that disgusting.'

Ulf shook his head. 'A very horrible bit of vandalism.'

'If it *was* vandalism,' said Kindgren. 'Which I don't think it was. Vandalism tends to be random, doesn't it? This was targeted.'

Ulf suggested he might simply have been unlucky enough to be in the wrong place at the wrong time. 'There are youths who go around scratching people's cars, letting their tyres down, and so on. Rotten fish may be a new departure, but who knows what goes through the heads of these kids?' He wondered about the car: was it the sort to give rise to envy? 'If a car is very expensive, it may be damaged out of envy. That happens, I'm afraid.'

'A Volvo,' said Kindgren. 'Absolutely standard.' Then he added, 'And it wasn't random. There was another thing that happened round about the same time. A few days later I had a telephone call at two in the morning — nobody there, of course; not even heavy breathing. Just silence. But somehow it was a *threatening* silence, if you see what I mean.'

Ulf looked out of the window. The fish incident was clearly intentional — and sinister — the other one might just have been a coincidence. People dialled numbers by mistake and were sometimes struck dumb when the wrong person answered. He was about to suggest this when Kindgren went on to describe a more worrying series of developments.

'What really tipped the balance,' he said, 'was two very damaging incidents. These were quite unlike the earlier ones, but had potentially much more profound consequences. I have a professional reputation, you see, and if that is damaged — well, my livelihood will be at stake.'

Ulf waited.

'By way of background,' Kindgren began, 'I'm often consulted by art dealers and the auction houses. If a painting is being put on the market, the seller wants to have as much support as possible when it comes to attribution. You'll probably know all about that.'

Ulf nodded. 'I've read a bit about it. It can be life and death for a painting, can't it?'

'Oh yes. If you have a strong attribution, it makes all the difference to the price. If the world authority on Degas, for example, says that a particular drawing is by Degas, then it's by Degas. No argument.'

'But if he expresses doubt?'

'That's another matter altogether. Value can be wiped off a painting with a single word from the experts. Like that.' Kindgren clicked his fingers; a somewhat incongruous gesture, Ulf thought, for one of his urbanity. 'There can be de-attribution — where a painting is taken away, so to speak, from an artist. If you're a collector and some expert publishes a piece in one of the art journals that your Renoir is not actually a Renoir, then you stand to lose a lot of money.'

'So a lot is at stake?'

'It is. But I wasn't going to burden you with any of that — I just wanted to explain that I am considered an expert for these purposes.'

'I'm sure you are,' said Ulf.

'Thank you. And I'm regularly approached by a particular auction house here in Sweden: Christina Berks — you know of them?'

Ulf did. The only picture he had ever bought at auction — a small watercolour of an island scene — had been at Christina Berks. It had not been expensive, as nobody else in the room was particularly interested in it, and Ulf had got it with his second bid. He was proud of the picture and enjoyed it until, three years later, he went off it. He gave it to Mrs Högfors, who had often admired it, saying that it reminded her of the island on which she and her husband had spent their honeymoon.

'Christina Berks got in touch about a painting that had been brought into their saleroom. Extraordinary things can turn up out of nowhere in the art world — suddenly somebody discovers a Matisse under the sofa or a de Chirico in the attic. You'd be surprised.

'I was called in by Christina Berks because the painting was a Gaspard Dughet, a painter closely associated with Nicolas Poussin — a passion of mine. In fact, Gaspard was Poussin's brother-in-law, and

51

his pupil — he even changed his name to Gaspard Poussin. He was a landscape painter and his skies are very Poussinesque. He has always been popular with collectors, although his paintings reach a fraction of the price a Nicolas Poussin can command.

'I looked at the painting. Its provenance was weak, and so we got no support there. It bore on the back the signature of the chief restorer of the Hermitage Gallery in the middle of the nineteenth century, and so we know it was in Russia. But there were no links in its ownership that would give us a useful provenance, and so I had to go on style.

'It was Dughet all right. There were a number of very typical Dughet passages in it, and so, after not too much agonising, I was able to give the painting the thumbs up. The auctioneers were pleased. They passed on my report to the owner, who took the painting back and said that he would let them know when he had made his mind up about selling. That he did two weeks later, sending the painting in once more and formally consigning it for auction.

'The catalogue was printed. There was a picture of the Dughet in it and underneath was an excerpt from my report. I gave it a firm attribution: Gaspard Dughet (also known as Gaspard Poussin). I wrote 'This fine example of a mid-career Gaspard Dughet . . .' I used the words *fine example*. What could be clearer?

'There was a lot of interest in the auction, and even more, including press coverage, when, two days before the sale, a visiting curator from a museum in France happened to look at the painting in the auction preview. He spent a couple of hours in front of it, apparently, and then went straight to Christina herself and announced that the painting being sold as a

Dughet was no such thing, but was an inept copy. It transpired that this man had written a scholarly volume on Dughet and knew what he was talking about. In fact, I was familiar with his work and set great store by it myself.

'I was horrified. I had been so sure about my attribution that I decided to ask for a meeting with Christina and the Frenchman. We met in the Berks boardroom, and they brought the Dughet in for us to examine. I remember the porter coming in with the young man who carried it in. He was an intern with Berks, and I remember that he was grinning about something — some secret joke shared with the other young man who was hanging about at the time. There was something between them, I think, but I'm not sure what it was. He was wearing white gloves — the sort that picture-handlers always wear — and he lifted the painting onto an easel. And I looked at it and thought: this is clearly a fake. It wasn't the same painting I had examined. It was the same scene, down to the last detail, but it was by a different hand.'

Ulf was intrigued. 'So you told them that?'

'I said — and I remember my exact words — 'This is not a Dughet.' And the Frenchman looked at me and said, 'I told them that.' So I said, 'But the one I looked at was by Dughet. I'm absolutely sure of it. This is a different painting.'

'Christina was clearly embarrassed. She said, 'But Anders, this painting is the same one that was brought in for identification. We have a photograph of it.' She showed me a photograph, and the paintings looked identical — in the photograph itself.'

Kindgren paused. The narration of the uncomfortable scene had caused his colour to rise. Now he looked angry. 'It was obvious to me that the French-man did not believe me. He gave one of those Gallic shrugs that the French are famous for — a sort of insouciant, superior dismissal. Christina was looking everywhere except at me, and I realised then, at that precise moment, my professional reputation had taken a massive hit.'

Ulf frowned. 'Might it not have been seen as an understandable mistake?'

Kindgren was adamant. 'No. Anybody should have been able to tell that the painting that had been brought to the sale was not a genuine Dughet. And yet there it was in the catalogue, with my attribution below it.' He paused before continuing, 'But it was not the same Dughet that I had examined.'

Ulf expressed his puzzlement. 'But the same person brought the painting in on each occasion?'

'I don't know for certain, but I assume so.'

It seemed so obvious to Ulf. 'Then couldn't they have gone back to him for an explanation?'

Kindgren's smile was rueful. 'If they knew who he was.'

Ulf's eyes widened.

'Yes,' continued Kindgren, 'you'd think they would know. He gave a name — and an address — but both proved to be false. The gallery sent somebody round to check on the address — not there. And a few questions to people in the area revealed that nobody had heard of him.'

Ulf asked whether Kindgren had been sure about his attribution of the first painting.

'Oh, yes,' came the reply. 'I'd stake my reputation — or what remains of it — on that. It was definitely a Dughet, painted when he was working in

54

Poussin's studio in Rome. The view had elements that Poussin himself had used — Dughet was, in fact, an influence on his master when it came to landscape.'

Ulf began to think an explanation was emerging. 'Actually, doesn't this amount to a simple art fraud scheme?' He paused to consider it further. Yes, it was really quite straightforward. 'Let's imagine that somebody has a valuable painting –a Dughet, for example — and he needs a bit of money. One of those unexpected expenses — tooth implants, for instance.' He grinned at the unlikely example; Björn had recently had trouble with his teeth and had been told by his dentist what tooth implants would cost. 'Those can be extremely expensive, as you probably know.'

'Oh, I know all about that,' said Kindgren. 'My brother-in-law needed three implants. Even with the state subsidy we can get now, it's pretty expensive here in Sweden. He went abroad.'

'I've heard of people doing that,' said Ulf. He felt the back of his teeth with his tongue. They seemed reassuringly solid. It must be disheartening to have to worry about whether one's teeth might fall out. Did selenium deficiency have anything to do with that? The thought crossed his mind briefly, and for a moment he imagined Blomquist standing before him, considering this question, and about to give his opinion.

Perhaps this was his visitor's 'Blomquist button'; he seemed keen to prolong the discussion. 'He decided to go to Thailand,' Kindgren continued. 'He thought about India initially. In fact, he looked very seriously at India, as there was a clinic down in Kerala that a friend of his had gone to. That city there . . . '

'Trivandrum?'

'Yes, but it has a new name now. Thiruvanan . . . something.'

'We could look it up,' suggested Ulf.

Kindgren shook his head. 'No matter. There was a large clinic there that offered very competitive prices, but he decided against it. He wanted somewhere quieter. Indian cities are usually very busy. All that traffic; people rushing about. And they have a major problem with air quality now, don't they? Living in Delhi, apparently, is the same as smoking forty cigarettes a day. Just think of that. Children, too.'

Ulf winced. 'I've seen photographs of their smog. Such a pity.'

'So he went to Thailand.'

'Bangkok isn't exactly quiet,' Ulf remarked. 'Or unpolluted.'

Kindgren laughed. 'It certainly isn't. I went there once, a few years ago. We stayed at a hotel on the river. You have to stay on the river in Bangkok. It was very restful, in spite of being in the centre of this vast urban sprawl.'

'I wonder if they do teeth?' mused Ulf.

'Not that particular hotel,' said Kindgren. 'He found a place further south. It was on one of those islands they have. Koh Phi Phi, it's called. There's a dental clinic there that's part beach hotel, part dental clinic. You can have your dental care in the morning and then spend the rest of the day lounging on the beach, under a palm tree, listening to the waves.'

'There are worse ways of having a tooth implanted,' said Ulf. He wondered, now, whether they might get back to the subject. His theory was now clear in his mind and he wanted to put it to Kindgren. 'But, going back to the—'

56

Kindgren was not finished. 'His dentist — the one who was doing his implants — was quite a large man, by Thai standards. They're rather neat people. Neat and compact. This man was bulky — my brother-in-law showed me a photograph of him. They still correspond occasionally. The dentist sends him pictures of his son, who wants to study aeronautical engineering. He thinks Sweden might be the place for him to do it.'

Ulf shrugged. 'Possibly. There's Saab, of course. Linköping University's the place for that, isn't it?'

'So I believe. They teach that sort of thing in English, so he'd be all right.' Kindgren paused. 'The dentist was a body-builder, apparently. My brother-in-law said that he saw him in the gym at the hotel. Or clinic, I suppose. But in spite of that, when it came to dental procedures, he was extremely gentle. Odd, that, but then very strong people are often very nimble in their movements. Large people too. Look at a fat dancer — they move almost daintily. It's not what you expect, but they do.'

Ulf made another effort. 'This person — this person I was talking about. He has to raise money — not necessarily for a dental implant — that was just an example I came up with—'

'A very interesting one,' Kindgren interrupted.

'Possibly,' Ulf conceded. 'But he doesn't want to sell the original, which he likes, and so he gets a copyist to make a copy — after he has had the attribution from the auction house and its expert. He lays the ground in advance. The auctioneer is expecting the real thing — with its attribution — and doesn't look too closely at the painting that subsequently comes in. The painting goes up for sale and in view of the

57

authoritative attribution it has, somebody is keen to buy it. The original owner is then in the enviable position of getting money for a painting that he still possesses. Fraud — pure and simple.' He paused. 'Unfortunately, there is some collateral damage when the whole thing is unexpectedly thwarted — and that is to the reputation of the expert — in this case, I regret to say, you.'

Kindgren looked up at the ceiling. Ulf saw that he had nicked himself just underneath the chin — a shaving cut, he decided. That meant Kindgren used a manual razor rather than an electric one. This did not surprise Ulf: the blazer, the shoes, the Egyptian cotton shirt — these were marks of one with an old-fashioned aesthetic. Such a man would use sandalwood shaving soap and a badger-hair brush. But with such an aesthetic went the risk of occasional cuts; unless, of course — and here Ulf's detective training intruded — somebody had scratched him. That was a distraction, and was dismissed. One could easily become too suspicious in this job, he thought.

'That's quite possible,' Kindgren said. 'And taken in isolation, I would be inclined to agree with you. But the problem is that this incident did not occur in isolation; it came on the heels of those nasty little events. However, most significantly — if you ask me — it was followed by another attempt to destroy my reputation.'

'How odd,' said Ulf.

Kindgren lowered his gaze from the ceiling. 'Yes? You're surprised? Well, so was I. A couple of weeks after this auction affair, I had an article published in the *Swedish Art Review*. You may know the publication.'

58

Ulf replied that he did. It was a bi-monthly, and although he did not subscribe to it, he read it from time to time when he called in at the library.

'It's published in hard copy,' Kindgren said, 'and also online. More people read it online than in printed form these days — that's increasingly the case, I think.'

'And this article?' Ulf asked. 'What was the subject?'

Kindgren waved a hand dismissively. 'Nothing important. There had been a discussion about Italian artists at the Swedish court. It was a storm in a teacup, as the English say, but a certain group in the Swedish art establishment was taking it very seriously. A real troublemaker — one of these maverick scholars who turn up from time to time — had published an appallingly badly researched piece refuting the generally accepted view of the matter. That set the cat among the pigeons. My piece wasn't about that controversy at all, but I alluded to it in a lengthy footnote. The gist of what I said was that there was no basis to the radical theory that this troublemaker had put forward. The only problem is that when my article was published online, my footnote had been changed. I now endorsed what he had said. I supported him strongly.'

Ulf drew in his breath. This was malice, without a shadow of doubt.

Kindgren spread his hands in a gesture of defeat. 'What could I do? The damage was done. I got in touch with the editor. He accepted that there had been a change in my original text, but he was at a loss to explain it. He swore blind it had nothing to do with him — and I accepted that. But how had it been done, then? My first thought was for the copy-editor

59

or the person in charge of putting the journal online. I spoke to both of these, and they denied all knowledge of the change. I drew a complete blank.'

'Another blow to your reputation,' Ulf mused.

Kindgren nodded. 'Yes. Almost a *coup de grâce*. Some of my friends phoned me to check that I had not gone mad. They could not believe that I would have endorsed the absurd theories that man had put forward. And of course I did not, but somebody — this unseen enemy of mine — was determined that I should be made a laughing stock.'

Ulf felt a strong surge of sympathy for this man before him. He tried to convey this now, assuring him that he would treat the case as a matter of priority. 'I can see how you feel,' he said. 'And I am very sorry about it. You are being subjected to serious harm.'

Ulf's recognition of his distress seemed to mean a lot to Kindgren. 'It's such a relief to be believed,' he said. 'I was worried that I would not be taken seriously.'

'I assure you there's no danger of that,' said Ulf. He reached for a pad of paper and took a pen out of his jacket pocket. 'I shall need a few details, if you don't mind. I know who the auction people are and can get in touch with them, but I need the name of the editor at the *Swedish Art Review*. Also, I would find it very useful if you were to give me the names of anybody — anybody at all — who you think may harbour ill-feeling towards you. Your enemies — if you have any. Your rivals. People whom . . .' And here Ulf faltered. This bit was always difficult. 'And the names of people whom you think you may have wronged.'

Kindgren raised an eyebrow. 'I try my best not to wrong anybody,' he said quietly.

'I'm sure you do,' said Ulf. 'But we don't always succeed in doing the things we'd like to do, do we? We all fall short from time to time — all of us.'

As he said this, he thought of himself, and the respects in which he fell short of the standards to which he aspired. He knew he had faults: he knew that he had to do something about his diet — he was not overweight, but he would need to watch that he did not go the way of so many men at his stage in life; he rarely achieved the exercise goals he set for himself: the ten thousand daily steps — in his case the total was often under six thousand; learning a foreign language — he had been trying to learn Italian, and had let that slip for months now; he fully intended to use dental floss every day, but he seemed to forget to do so on more days than he remembered; and so it went on — little failure after little failure.

Lost in thought, Ulf suddenly realised that Kindgren was talking.

'I suppose I should start with my wife,' the art historian began. 'She is bored with me, I think. And she's having an affair with a man called Linus Wallin. He teaches philosophy, but I suspect he knows very little about the subject. He published a book on Kierkegaard that I saw referred to as the worst book on Kierkegaard ever. Hah! And his shoes . . . You should see the shoes he wears. Narrow shoes with sharpened toes. Women's shoes for men, I call them.'

'You clearly don't like him,' observed Ulf. 'But we're looking for people who don't like you.'

'Oh, he can't stand me,' said Kindgren. 'He thinks I show him up — which wouldn't be hard.'

'I see,' said Ulf. And then he added, 'Anybody else?'

'My mother,' said Kindgren.

Ulf was silent. Kindgren looked shamefaced.

'I shouldn't say that,' he said. 'But I find it so hard. I love my mother, of course, but she won't stop interfering with my life. She doesn't like what I do. She never has.'

Ulf remained silent.

'She always wanted me to study medicine,' Kindgren continued. 'Her father was a surgeon and she had this idea that I would be one too. When I said I wanted to study the history of art, she was devastated. She thinks it an unsuitable occupation for a man — she really does.'

Ulf smiled. 'Some mothers are old-fashioned.'

'She accepts that I can't be a doctor now, but she has a plan B, which is for me to go into the family firm — my father's side of the family, that is. They are property developers on a fairly large scale. My father used to be the chairman of the company — now it's my cousin, Max. He says I could be his deputy if I wanted to be. But I have no interest in that at all.'

Kindgren sighed. 'All I want is to lead a quiet life doing what I want to do, which is looking at art. I'm not harming anybody. I've got enough money — more than enough, and so I can be independent.' He sighed again. 'Anyway, on a positive note, would you care to come to dinner at my place next week? We're having a few people round and you might enjoy them — or some of them, shall I say.'

Ulf was hesitant. In general, it was best to draw a clear line between professional duties and one's social life, and yet there were occasions on which a social engagement might provide information unobtainable elsewhere; perhaps flexibility was the best policy.

And now it was as if Kindgren had sensed the

reason for Ulf's hesitation. 'All the guests will be friends,' he said, but then added, wryly, 'Or so I like to think.'

Ulf accepted.

'Will you be on your own?' Kindgren asked tentatively.

'Yes,' said Ulf.

Kindgren was watching him.

'I lost my wife,' said Ulf. 'Some years ago.'

'I'm so sorry.'

Kindgren hesitated. Then he said, 'And you haven't met anybody?'

'No. I suppose I'd like to, but . . . ' But what? Why had he not met anybody else? Because he had not bothered to look because of his ridiculous longing for Anna. It was this that was holding him back; freezing his emotional life in a state of unsatisfied longing. I should admit that, he told himself. I should have the courage to face up to it.

Suddenly, and without thinking it through, he decided to confide in Kindgren.

'The truth of the matter is that I have a thing for somebody,' he said. 'She's married, and I don't want to do anything to compromise her marriage.'

Kindgren listened. His expression was grave.

'I know it's hopeless,' said Ulf. 'But how do you fall out of love? Can you tell me how you do that? Is it even possible?'

'You forget about the other person. You don't try to reassess her. You don't try to persuade yourself that you don't really love her. You make an effort to forget.'

'I suppose so,' said Ulf.

'And you find somebody else. Falling in love with

somebody else cancels out the earlier feeling. That always works. I don't think it's possible to be in love with two people at the same time. Not *fully* in love.' Kindgren was looking at him in a bemused way. 'Perhaps you should let somebody introduce you to someone,' he went on. 'It's not always easy to meet the right person.'

'I'll think about it,' said Ulf. He did not want to talk about himself any more — not in this setting. And so he brought the encounter to an end by accepting the invitation to dinner at the Kindgren house the following Wednesday.

'Informal,' said Kindgren. 'Smart informal. Or, rather, informal smart.'

Ulf smiled. 'I know what you mean,' adding, 'I think.'

5

You're a Very Kind Man, Ulf

Ulf had arranged with Dr Håkansson that Martin would be dropped off with Mrs Högfors when he was ready to be discharged. He had been keen to collect him himself, but commitments in the office made it impossible for him to drive out to the vet's clinic. Dr Håkansson had an assistant, though, a young woman hoping to qualify as a veterinary nurse, who was happy to drive Martin round in the small white van that served as the clinic's ambulance.

When Ulf got home that evening, he went straight to his neighbour's flat and rang the bell. Normally when he did that, if Martin was in the flat, the sound of the bell would trigger a bout of enthusiastic barking — the shrill frequency of the bell being one of the few sounds that Martin could actually hear. Rather contrary to Dr Håkansson's expectations, the dog's hearing had recently changed — for the better — and he now seemed able to pick up a few high sounds: Mrs Högfors' doorbell, the Queen of the Night aria from Mozart's *Magic Flute*, and the high-pitched buzz emitted by Ulf's battery-operated egg timer. Apart from that, Martin's world was one of silence.

Now, though, there was no barking, and Ulf decided that Martin had not been delivered as planned. There was a moment of concern: had something gone wrong during the operation? Dr Håkansson had assured him

65

that it would be quite straightforward, but there was always a risk with a general anaesthetic. Ulf had lost an aunt that way: she had gone in for the extraction of a wisdom tooth and had not survived the anaesthetic. Anna's husband had explained to him that this sometimes happened, and that it was a good idea to make your will before you submitted to general anaesthesia — not that anaesthetists were encouraged to give that advice to their patients before they went under. 'People became anxious,' he had said, 'and so I've stopped giving that advice. Pity, really.'

Mrs Högfors' demeanour allayed Ulf's concerns.

'He's through there,' she said, smiling and gesturing towards the living room behind her. 'He's been quite drowsy ever since they brought him back. But I don't think he's in any pain.'

Ulf followed her into the living room. Martin was sleeping on a blanket laid out on the floor, his protective lampshade round his neck.

'That peculiar thing looks awfully uncomfortable,' said Mrs Högfors, 'but the young woman who brought him round assured me that he'll soon get used to it. I think she's right — he seems indifferent to it now.'

Ulf bent down to speak to the dog. As he did so, Martin blinked, and then opened his eyes wide. He looked up at Ulf and slowly raised his head, his tail thumping on the blanket behind him.

Ulf reached out to pat Martin's head but withdrew his hand when he saw the criss-cross of stiches across the muzzle. He saw, too, that there were stitches around the nose and little crusts of blood where the wounds were beginning to heal.

'The young woman said the nose became completely detached in the clinic. They've had to sew it all the way round. You see there? You see that line of stitches?'

Ulf peered at Martin's snout while the dog gazed up at him, uncertain as to what might be expected of him. There was something odd about the nose, although Ulf could not quite decide what it was. Perhaps it was swollen; perhaps the trauma of the original injury, coupled with the impact of the surgery, had taken its toll on the delicate ball of moist, black flesh; perhaps that was why it looked rather different; Ulf was not at all sure.

He turned to Mrs Högfors. 'Have you had a close look at his nose?' he asked.

She joined him, adjusting her spectacles. 'Poor boy,' she muttered. 'Poor Martin.'

Ulf pointed at the front part of the nose. 'Do you think it's just because it's swollen? Does it normally look like that?'

Mrs Högfors looked more closely. 'The nostrils are a bit enlarged,' she said. 'That could be the drugs.' But then she said, 'No, there's definitely something different. I think . . .' She did not finish.

'Do you think it's upside down?' asked Ulf.

Mrs Högfors drew in her breath. 'I see what you mean,' she said. 'Yes, you may be right. The nostrils used to point down — now they're pointing upwards.'

Ulf stood up straight. 'I'm going to phone Dr Håkansson.'

He dialled the vet's number. After a few rings, he heard Dr Håkansson answer.

'I'm with Martin,' Ulf began. 'And I've been looking at his nose.'

'It was a very delicate procedure,' Dr Håkansson said. 'The nose became detached, I'm afraid, and

67

we had to sew it back on. I hope it's getting an adequate blood supply.' He paused. 'It was complex surgery — most demanding.'

Ulf hesitated. By nature, he was not given to complaining, and he was reluctant to find fault with the vet's efforts. And yet if the nose had indeed been sewn back on upside down, it would be important to raise this in order to allow remedial steps to be taken — should any be available.

'It looks a bit strange,' Ulf said. 'I don't like to criticise, but I wondered whether it is, in fact, now upside down. I'm not saying that it is — not definitely — but I just wondered.'

There was a long silence at the other end of the line. At Ulf's side, Mrs Högfors looked at him anxiously.

At last Dr Håkansson spoke. 'I very much doubt it.'

'But the nostrils,' said Ulf. 'They're pointing upwards now. They used to point downwards — I think.'

Mrs Högfors nodded vigorously.

'They can't be,' said Dr Håkansson.

'They are, I'm afraid,' Ulf insisted.

There was silence. Then Dr Håkansson asked whether Martin was breathing normally. Ulf glanced at Mrs Högfors, who bent down to listen to Martin's breath. She made a gesture to suggest that all was normal.

'His breathing appears to be fine,' said Ulf. 'As far as we can tell.'

Dr Håkansson sounded relieved. 'Well, that's good. If he's breathing normally, it means that the airways are open.' He paused. 'And even if there has been a slight misplacement of tissue, as long as it's not affecting respiration, I don't think we need to worry.'

68

Ulf frowned. 'But—' he began.

He did not get any further. 'Let sleeping dogs lie,' said Dr Håkansson firmly. 'Often we have minor imperfections after surgery, but you make matters far worse if you try to correct them. I'll take a look when you bring him in to have his stitches out, but I imagine that we won't want to do anything. Nature heals herself most of the time.'

Ulf did not argue, but thanked the vet and brought the call to an end. 'I'm not entirely happy,' he said to Mrs Högfors as he tucked his phone back in his pocket.

'I'm not surprised,' she said, glancing back at Martin. 'He's going to look very peculiar. Mind you, do dogs mind how they look?'

Ulf raised an eyebrow. 'Their owners do.'

'Yes, but from the dog's point of view, it doesn't matter, does it?' She paused. 'You see some ridiculous-looking dogs in the park — Pekingese, those Tibetan dogs with their hair in ribbons . . .'

Ulf smiled. He knew that there were things of which Mrs Högfors disapproved strongly, and affectation of any sort was one of them. Her disapproval was often presented as though through the eyes of her late husband — what he felt or might have felt had he still been there to take a view. Sure enough, his views on fancy dogs were now expressed. 'Högfors never liked to see dogs with dog waistcoats on. Even in winter, he thought that dogs shouldn't be dressed up by their owners. He once saw a Swedish Vallhund with small knitted boots on. He did not like that at all — and he had a word with the owner. Högfors spoke his mind, you know.'

Ulf made a noncommittal remark. He was still

69

thinking about Martin's nose.

'You know something, though, Ulf? I think there's some Vallhund in Martin. I know that he's much bigger than they are, and he doesn't have their short legs, but his ears are typical Vallhund ears, and I think you can see it in his coat. He has that soft coat underneath the outer layer.'

'Oh yes?'

'Yes,' she continued. 'Although I also see a bit of Spitz in him. I think there's Lapphund in there, you know.'

'And wolf, of course,' said Ulf vaguely. 'All of them come from wolves originally. Although with some dogs — you mentioned Pekingese — the connection with wolves is surely only aspirational.'

As this conversation took place, Martin appeared to go back to sleep. Ulf was wondering whether he should wake him up to take him back into his own flat when Mrs Högfors made her suggestion that it might be better to leave him where he was overnight. She was often up in the course of the night, she said — not being a very sound sleeper — and she could keep a close eye on him. 'You need your sleep, Ulf, with all that demanding work you have to do in the Department of Sensible Crimes.'

He corrected her gently. She often got that wrong. 'Sensitive Crimes.'

'Of course. Sensitive Crimes, or whatever. You need to get a good night's sleep. I'm just a widow and it doesn't matter so much.'

Ulf felt a surge of sympathy for his neighbour; he almost felt that he wanted to put an arm around her shoulder, to embrace her. *I'm just a widow* . . . What a sad reflection that was on the way we ordered our

70

affairs, that anybody should feel that they were *just* something. Everybody was significant; everybody was as valuable as everybody else. If we stopped thinking that, then any attempt at morality would be built on sand. He knew, of course, that widows could feel unsure about their position; for some people, their status, their whole *raison d'être*, was connected with that of their spouse, or the fact that they had a spouse at all. And when the spouse died — and this seemed to apply most strongly to women — they felt uncertain as to where they fitted in. What a shame that was, he thought; what a shame.

He turned to Mrs Högfors. 'You mustn't say that, you know. You are not just a widow. Your sleep is as important as anybody else's. It's certainly as important as mine.'

She looked at him and smiled. 'You're a very kind man, Ulf.'

He shook his head. 'No, I'm not. I'm just—'

She stopped him. 'You were about to say exactly what you said I mustn't say. You said *I'm just* . . .'

Ulf made a gesture of acceptance. 'I wasn't thinking. I suppose I'm a bit worried about Martin.'

She reached out to touch him, laying a hand briefly on his forearm. 'I know. I feel that too. And that's because we both love him. Having a dog, especially a dog like dear Martin, is like having a child, I sometimes think. We give our hearts to these creatures.'

They agreed that Martin would stay where he was. Ulf would look in the following morning and, if Martin was well enough, might take him for a brief walk.

'Not in the park, though,' warned Mrs Högfors. 'That might be a bit traumatic for him. It might revive painful memories.'

Mrs Högfors insisted on making Ulf a cup of tea before he left to go upstairs to his own flat. It was while she was in the kitchen doing this that Ulf noticed the gun on a side table, next to her television set. No attempt had been made to conceal it: it was there, for any visitor to see, a small air rifle with a polished wooden stock. He blinked as he took in the sight. A gun on Mrs Högfors' table?

She came back in before he had the opportunity to examine the weapon.

'I see you have a gun,' Ulf said, as he took the teacup she proffered to him. He tried to sound unsurprised.

She followed his gaze towards the table, but he was watching her. She had forgotten about it, he decided. And now, as she replied, he could tell that she was not telling him the truth.

'Oh that. Yes, that's an air rifle, you know. It's not a proper gun.' She laughed, but the laugh was forced. 'I suppose you, being a policeman, might find it a bit odd that I have a rifle in my flat. But it's not mine, you see. That is not my air rifle.'

As a policeman, Ulf knew that's what *everybody* who has an illicit weapon says. It's not mine.

He waited for her explanation.

'My nephew. I think you've met him. Åke. The one who's training to be a chef.'

Ulf had met Åke on several occasions. The young man, who was an apprentice chef in a large hotel, was fond of his aunt and often brought her dishes he had cooked for her in the hotel kitchens — technically stolen food, of course, Ulf told himself, but well intentioned and not something one would pursue.

'Åke must have left it here when he came to see me. He goes target shooting with his friends. I think

72

he's a very good shot — a marksman, in fact. Like his father.'

Ulf moved towards the rifle. 'Do you mind if I take a look?' he asked.

'No. Please do.' Mrs Högfors laughed nervously. 'I don't know one end of a gun from another, but I'm sure you do.'

'He should be careful where he leaves it,' said Ulf, as he picked up the weapon. 'You can't walk around with an air rifle without causing alarm. It should be kept in a proper case — under lock and key.'

'I'll tell him that,' said Mrs Högfors. And then, in what seemed to Ulf like an attempt to change the subject, she said, 'I heard Björn on the radio this afternoon. He was being interviewed by that stupid man who knows nothing about anything. You know the one? He's always interrupting.'

Ulf was examining the rifle. It was of a small enough bore not to be a serious weapon, but even so, a pellet could do a surprising amount of damage. Velocity was the important factor, and the smaller rifles usually had limited compression and therefore sent their pellet out at a lower speed.

'Your brother was talking about traffic congestion,' Mrs Högfors continued. 'I'm no expert on these things, but it seemed to me that he talked a lot of sense.'

Ulf hummed. He did not. Björn did not talk sense — or very rarely.

'He said that the traffic problem was caused by there being too many cars,' Mrs Högfors said. 'I thought there was a lot to that. I thought he'd hit the nail on the head.'

'Oh yes?' said Ulf, replacing the rifle on the table.

73

'And what was his solution? Fewer cars? It hardly takes a genius to come up with that.'

'Oh no,' Mrs Högfors interjected. 'Fewer driving licences. He said that if we rationed driving licences, then there would be fewer drivers, and therefore fewer cars on the road.'

Ulf rolled his eyes. 'Is that his party's position? Is that what the Moderate Extremists say about the traffic problem?'

Mrs Högfors said that she believed it was. 'Not everything they say goes down well with everybody, but I think this particular idea has possibilities. He said that licences could be allocated on the basis of—'

'On the basis of ability to drive?' suggested Ulf.

'No. Not that. He said that it should be on the basis of need. People who couldn't come up with a good reason to drive would not be allocated a licence. They would have to use public transport.'

Ulf sighed. This was typical of the Moderate Extremists: an impossible policy, dressed up in Utopian language, and destined — if not actually calculated — to antagonise at least one large segment of the population. 'Or stay where they were,' Ulf remarked.

'Yes.'

'I don't think that would go down well,' Ulf said, taking a sip of his tea. 'I think some would feel it rather unjust if they did not get a licence and others did.'

'People are very difficult to please,' said Mrs Högfors. 'They really are.'

She held Ulf's gaze. She had brought up the subject of Björn in order to distract Ulf from the air rifle. But she could see that it had not worked — he was still puzzling over it — and she could also tell that he

74

knew that she knew.

'Oh well,' said Ulf, giving the rifle one last glance. 'Time for me to get back upstairs.'

Mrs Högfors breathed a sigh of relief.

6

You're Björn Varg's Brother?

The next morning an unfortunate, unexpected and disturbing thing happened.

Ulf went downstairs to check up on Martin shortly before eight o'clock. He knew that Mrs Högfors was an early riser — in the summer she was often up, she had told him, by five in the morning — in order to catch the best part of the day. And so, when he rang her bell, she soon answered it, with Martin by her side.

'The patient is on very good form,' she said. 'He's had his breakfast, and I'm happy to report that he ate every scrap. Licked the bowl clean.'

Martin seemed pleased to see Ulf. Gazing up at his owner, he wagged his tail enthusiastically. It was Martin's metronome, Ulf thought, and now it was moving rapidly from side to side — *prestissimo*, in 12/8 time.

'Do you think he's up to a walk?' asked Ulf, bending down to pat Martin's head in its curious lampshade cover.

Mrs Högfors replied that she was sure he would like that. 'I was about to take him myself,' she said, 'but I'm sure he would prefer to go with you.'

Martin's lead was fetched, and together he and Ulf made their way down the street. Ulf had decided not to go to the park, as he did not want Martin to become anxious, and so a shorter walk was planned — a couple of times round the block would suffice. This route led along a leafy side street on which Ulf often parked his Saab, if the parking places outside his apartment block were all occupied. That had been the case the previous evening when he had returned from work, and so the Saab was waiting for him a few yards along the street — and beside it was a drawn-up police car.

It took Ulf a moment or two to realise that two policemen were peering into the back of his car. Ulf's first thought was that his car had been broken into. Perhaps somebody had broken one of the windows and the policemen, driving past, had noticed the shattered glass. He felt the immediate anger of one who has been the victim of a senseless crime.

He increased his pace, and was soon at the policemen's side.

'Is there a problem?' he asked.

One of the policemen, the older of the two, dark-haired and with a moustache, turned to face him. Ulf knew many members of the uniformed branch, but this young man was a stranger.

'Is this your car?' asked the policeman.

Ulf nodded. 'Yes. Has there been—'

He did not get the chance to finish. 'And your name is Varg?' asked the policeman.

Again Ulf nodded. 'That's me.'

The younger policeman joined in. 'We need to take this car in, sir.'

Ulf frowned. 'I don't understand,' he said. 'It's legally parked. I'm not infringing any regulations — as far as I know.'

The senior policeman drew him aside. He lowered his voice. 'Look,' he said, 'we know who you are. You're in the Criminal Investigation Department, aren't you?'

77

'Sensitive Crimes,' Ulf said. 'I'm departmental head, in fact.'

The policeman looked apologetic. 'I know that. We were going to call round at your place and talk to you about this. But since you're here . . . '

'I really don't understand what the problem is,' said Ulf. 'You say that you need to take my car away. What for? And take it where?'

The policeman's discomfort became more apparent. 'I'm sorry about this, but the car has to be handed over to the Forensic Unit.'

Ulf was at a complete loss. 'I don't understand,' he said.

The policeman pointed to the back of the car. 'We have to examine the back seat. Would you mind opening the vehicle.'

Ulf took the key from his pocket and opened the driver's door. Access to the back seat was gained by pushing the driver's seat forward, and he did this now, as the two policemen watched over his shoulder.

'Don't touch anything,' the senior one said, his tone suddenly becoming officious.

Ulf stood back up. 'Don't touch anything? What is this? A crime scene?'

The two policemen glanced at one another. The older policeman said, 'Possibly,' and the other added, 'That's why it has to go to Forensics.'

Ulf felt his patience wearing thin. 'Look,' he blurted out, 'this is ridiculous. I have co-operated so far, but frankly this is getting beyond a joke.'

The older policeman thought for a moment. He placed a hand on Ulf's shoulder — a friendly hand, still, but Ulf moved away, resenting the gesture. 'I'm trying to make it easy for you,' the policeman said.

'But the truth of the matter is this: we received information that there was a substantial amount of blood on the back seat of your car. Allegations were made that there were signs of a struggle. And now, looking at it, I can see there are, in fact, some red stains there.'

Ulf listened in open-mouthed astonishment. He thought, the mechanic and his son: they were responsible. They had been to the police. Shaking his head, he blurted out, 'My dog! That blood comes from my dog. He was attacked by a squirrel, you see, and—'

The policeman interrupted him. 'By a squirrel?'

'Yes,' said Ulf. 'You see, there's a squirrel in the park round the corner. He's been taunting Martin for a long time.'

'Martin?' asked the younger policeman.

'My dog. That's his name.'

The younger policeman wrote something in his notebook.

'What are you writing?' asked Ulf.

'Your dog's name.'

Ulf laughed. 'Is he a suspect now? Assault on squirrels?'

The senior policeman looked disapproving. 'This is a not a joke, Varg.'

'All right,' said Ulf. 'Take the car. Here are the keys.'

★ ★ ★

He did not tell Mrs Högfors that the Saab had been taken away. The situation was too complicated, he decided, and there was no point in burdening her with a problem that would very quickly be sorted out. She had enough to do looking after Martin, for which he told her, as he often did, that he was most grateful.

'He is like a son to me,' she said. 'You don't have to be thanked for looking after your own son.'

He called a taxi to take him into the office. On the journey, the slow-moving morning traffic gave him time to think about what had happened. At first, he felt a simmering anger over the fact that the mechanic or his son had gone to the police, but then, on reflection, he reminded himself that this was exactly what the police encouraged responsible citizens to do. And so he sighed and mentally forgave them, and even managed to smile at the speed with which they had reached their fanciful conclusion.

His thoughts were interrupted by the radio broadcast to which the taxi driver was listening. It was a chatty news programme and Ulf realised, with a jolt, that the person being interviewed was his brother, Björn. He closed his eyes. He did not want to listen to Björn — whatever he was talking about. Björn. Björn. He was ruining the name Varg with his ridiculous, self-centred political career. The Moderate Extremists were his creation, and their main point, as far as Ulf could make out, was to further the political fortunes of their founder. This was not conviction politics; unless, of course, it was the conviction that Björn Varg should progress as far as possible up the slippery political pole.

Ulf opened his eyes.

'Tired?' asked the taxi driver, glancing at Ulf in his rear-view mirror. 'Busy day ahead?'

Ulf looked at his hands, folded on his lap. He stared out of the window, at the rain that had started to fall. He looked at the building they were passing — shuttered for some reason, in need of paint. A large *For Sale* sign had been plastered on one of the shutters.

Behind it, Ulf thought, lay some story of economic woe, some casualty of the seismic economic shifts that were disrupting the lives of the hard-working majority. In the background, Björn's voice droned on. Too much attention was being paid to people's rights, he was saying. What about their duties? Why was there no charter of social duties?

Ulf looked back into the mirror — into the taxi driver's eyes. Something within him made him want to unburden himself.

'My brother,' he said. 'That guy on the radio is my brother.'

The taxi driver reacted with interest. 'You don't say! Björn Varg? You're Björn Varg's brother?'

Ulf nodded. 'Yes, I am. And sometimes I think—'

He was not allowed to finish. 'He's the man, all right,' said the taxi driver. 'You want to know something? I've joined his party. The Moderate Extremists. You're already a member, I take it.'

Ulf shook his head. 'I don't belong to any party.'

'You should,' enthused the driver. 'Especially the Moderate Extremists — what with your family connection. If they were in power, well, you can imagine what it would be like.'

Ulf pursed his lips. He could imagine it.

'They've got the right ideas about just about everything,' said the driver. 'You have to look at it from my perspective: we taxi drivers see a lot, as you can imagine. We get everybody in the cab — and I mean *everybody*. We see everything, and you know what? Sometimes it's really hard to keep our mouths shut. We see things and we know what the answer is, but nobody seems to want to listen. Except your brother, of course.'

81

Ulf said nothing.

'And, unlike other politicians,' the driver went on, 'he's ready to change his mind if he gets it wrong. Will he admit to making mistakes? He will. I've heard him.'

Ulf remained silent.

'The other day he changed their policy on education,' the driver continued. 'It was some issue about schools — I forget what it was. Björn withdrew what they had said the previous week. He mis-spoke. He admitted it. He came right out and said 'I mis-spoke'. How's that for integrity?'

Ulf winced. He did not like the expression 'mis-spoke'. What did it *mean*? Did it cover lying? Did it cover the withdrawal of ill-thought-out outbursts?

'Your brother had the guts to cancel. He just said, 'No, we're holding a different position now.' He didn't attempt to cover anything up.'

'He's certainly changeable,' said Ulf.

They were nearing the end of the journey. Björn's interview was coming to an end, just as the taxi driver turned up the volume. 'Say hello to him from me,' he said. 'Tell him he's got our vote — every time.'

'I shall,' said Ulf. 'He'll be pleased to hear it.'

Ulf walked the final block. The day was proving disastrous. There was the ridiculous business with the Saab. There was Björn on the radio. There was the taxi driver and his unwanted opinions. Could anything else go wrong?

He looked at his watch. He was later than usual, and his colleagues would already have been at their desks for twenty minutes or so. They would not say anything, of course, but he knew that his tardy arrival might be commented upon. Not by Anna, of course: he could not imagine her criticising him, but Carl would probably mutter something about there being one rule for detectives and another for filing clerks — not to Ulf's face, but loudly enough for the others to hear.

The day had started so badly that he decided he would treat himself to a quiet half-hour in the coffee bar before going into the office. It always had a calming effect, sitting there at his preferred table at the window with a copy of the morning paper and the smell of coffee wafting up from the cup before him. His conscience was clear: he worked far longer hours than those required under his contract of employment — and he never claimed the overtime payments that so many of his colleagues relished. If he took the occasional half-hour off, then the scales were still heavily weighted in favour of the department, and he could justify himself should anybody in authority get round to asking.

He was pleased to see that his preferred table was unoccupied, and so, his coffee ordered, he settled himself with the newspaper. The front page was dominated by news of another Russian submarine that had been detected in Swedish waters. Ulf thought of Mrs Högfors: this news would inflame her, fuelling her strong belief that Russia was plotting to take over the country. 'They've wanted to do it for centuries,' she said. 'They haven't changed.'

He turned to the less explosive contents of page two. A student had become stuck in a washing machine during a party and had been rescued by the local fire brigade. 'These young people think it's funny to climb into washing machines,' said the local fire chief. 'And then they get stuck, and we have to come and

83

get them out.'

Ulf had to smile. Of course students thought it funny to climb into a washing machine: everybody aged nineteen, or whatever age they were, would think that funny.

He turned the page. Moderate Extremists Warn of Serious Consequences, announced a headline. Ulf rapidly went on to the next page. He had had enough of his brother's politics for one day. Now there were letters from readers, and he had started to peruse these when his coffee arrived. And so did Blomquist.

Ulf liked Blomquist, but then he liked most people with whom he worked, and, if pressed on the matter, he would even admit to liking most people whom it was his duty to arrest. Blomquist might have been treated well by the Department of Sensitive Crimes, but he had been cold-shouldered by the wider Criminal Investigation Department when he was seconded to their strength from the uniformed branch. As a result, he very much appreciated Ulf's courtesy and warmth. Yet, like many of those who go on at excessive length about subjects of interest to them, Blomquist knew that some people found him annoying. And like many in that situation, he was unable to stop himself from sharing his enthusiasms. People's eyes might glaze over as he told them, for example, about the latest dietary research he had unearthed, but he was confident they would go away, think about it, and perhaps act accordingly — and then they would be grateful. People needed to be told, even if many seemed indifferent to what they so clearly needed to know.

Ulf, thought Blomquist, was different. He listened, and every so often he asked a question that showed he was taking things in. He was not sure how far Ulf followed his advice — he suspected he had not taken the issue of vitamin D supplementation as seriously as he might — but he had at least thought about it. So it was that when Blomquist heard the news that he was about to impart to Ulf, he had felt a hollow sense of regret. Of all the people to whom this sort of thing should happen, Ulf was the least deserving. It was, Blomquist felt, simply outrageous. But then, he went on to think, life is never fair. If it were, then people would not get away with bad diets as some now seemed able to do, eating unhealthy food with impunity, never becoming ill and living to a ripe old age. There had been a highly publicised case of this recently, Blomquist recollected, when a well-known poet, who had died in his early nineties, was revealed in his obituary to have drunk two bottles of wine a day, eaten steak and eggs for breakfast every single morning for fifty-two years, and been an enthusiastic user of mentholated snuff. There seemed to be no justice in such a career path, which Blomquist believed could only be explained by quirky DNA; and DNA, as everybody knew, was as indifferent to justice as was any other sequence of acids.

Now Blomquist, coming into the coffee bar in the hope of finding Ulf there, approached the table in the window with a heavy heart. Ulf looked up at him. Suppressing a sigh — Blomquist and the reading of a newspaper did not mix — Ulf greeted his colleague politely and invited him to join him. 'I just thought I'd snatch a quick coffee before going in,' he said. 'I've had one of those mornings, I'm afraid.'

Blomquist signalled his order to the young man behind the counter. He would have the same as Ulf. 'Oh, I know mornings like that,' he said. 'They usually start with me cutting myself while shaving.'

Ulf smiled. 'I use an electric razor. Cuts are a thing of the past.'

He immediately realised the mistake he'd made in raising a matter like this, but it was too late. Rather than impart the news it was his duty to report, Blomquist seized the opportunity of an excursus on the subject of shaving soap. He had recently ordered a tube of Italian shaving cream and was very pleased with it. 'Of course, if you use an electric razor, then you don't need shaving cream, do you? Mind you, there are those waterproof ones that allow you to have a wet shave, but I'm not sure how they work with thick shaving cream. Probably not very well. Do you know, Ulf?'

It made Ulf feel tired just to think about it. He shook his head.

'I like the feel you get from using a razor,' Blomquist continued. 'You know those Turkish barbershops you see everywhere these days? They use cut-throats.'

Ulf grimaced. 'Those things make my blood run cold. Just the sight of the blade.'

'And yet they never cut their customers,' Blomquist said. 'They have very steady hands.'

'Just as well.'

'It's a wonderful feeling, you know,' Blomquist went on. 'I had a Turkish shave a couple of weeks ago. They use hot towels and they slap astringent lotion on your face. It's very invigorating. And you feel very pleased with yourself afterwards. It's like having highly polished shoes. You know how pleased that makes you feel.' He paused, and as he did so, his face fell.

Ulf could tell that something was wrong. He looked expectantly at Blomquist.

86

'I'm afraid there's bad news,' Blomquist blurted out.

Ulf froze. Anna. Something had happened to Anna. He was sure of it.

'You've been suspended,' said Blomquist.

This came as a relief. This had nothing to do with Anna, and although the word *suspended* was a bit of a shock, it was nothing that could not be sorted out. He knew the reason, of course, even before Blomquist could tell him. This was to do with the ridiculous mis-understanding over the blood on the seat of the Saab. The powers that be would look foolish once that was explained.

Blomquist was staring at him. 'You don't seem sur-prised,' he said.

'Not really,' said Ulf. 'It's to do with my car, you see. They came for it this morning.'

It was clear to Ulf that Blomquist knew nothing beyond the fact of the suspension, and now he reas-sured him that although the situation looked serious, in reality it was merely an administrative over-re-action to an unfounded report by a member of the public. Such things were usually cleared up within a few hours, or a day or so at the most.

'It's really very simple,' Ulf said. 'My dog, Martin, was attacked and rather badly injured by a squirrel. I took him to the vet in my car, and he bled over the seat. I then called in to have the car valeted, and the people who did that got it into their minds that it was human blood. They obviously reported me. They must have taken the car's registration number and passed that on.'

Blomquist frowned. 'I don't think it's that,' he said.

'But it must be,' said Ulf. 'They came to take my

car away this morning. It'll be at Forensics as we speak. They'll soon discover it's not human blood and they'll look pretty foolish when they bring it back to me. I won't crow, of course, I'll just—'

He did not finish. Blomquist was shaking his head. 'It's not that, Ulf. It's something quite different. I heard from a friend in Internal Discipline. He likes you and he was pretty upset by it. He didn't want to process the matter, but the instruction, I'm afraid, came from the very top.'

'The Commissioner?'

Blomquist sighed. 'You know what he's like. He gets these bees in his bonnet. One of them is using the blue light for personal purposes.'

Ulf hesitated. If the issue of blood on the seat of the Saab was easily resolved, this was different. In this case he was potentially in the wrong. He waited for Blomquist to say more.

'You've been called to see Lund at two this afternoon.'

Ulf gazed out of the window. Lund was in charge of Internal Discipline. Everybody dreaded him.

'Of course you'll be able to explain,' said Blomquist. 'I know — well, everybody knows — that you would never abuse the blue light to get through traffic . . . ' His voice slowed down. He had noticed Ulf's expression. 'To get through traffic inappropriately.' It took Blomquist a long time to say 'inappropriately', and by the time he got the word out of the way, he realised the matter was not going to be as simple as he had hoped.

'I might have some difficulty doing that,' said Ulf.

Blomquist winced. 'You did it?'

'Yes and no,' said Ulf.

Ulf explained the circumstances: 'It was the same occasion — after Martin had been attacked. I had to get him to the vet as quickly as possible, and I found myself in a traffic snarl-up. I used the blue light to get past the other cars purely to get to the vet's in time.'

Blomquist looked immediately relieved. 'So it was life or death. You had a good excuse.'

Ulf was not so sure. He did not think it would be that simple. 'It depends what you mean by life or death. I think they'll say that only *human* life or death counts. I don't think that a veterinary emergency would have the same weight.'

Blomquist considered this. Ulf was right, he feared: these rules were always interpreted narrowly — especially in the light of the Commissioner's sensitivities on the subject. 'You could argue the point,' he said. 'And a lot of people would agree with you.'

'But they aren't Lund and his friends,' Ulf pointed out. 'Remember when those two local policemen ate sausage rolls that had been part of a crime scene — there had been a break-in at a bakery. The sausage rolls would have gone off if they were kept, and so they ate them. They were accused of destroying evidence.'

'Ridiculous,' said Blomquist. 'Mind you, they did themselves no good eating the sausage rolls. Those things are full of goodness knows what. Carbohydrates for one. Preservatives, too.'

Ulf, not wanting to prolong this line of conversation, said nothing. And his thoughts were bleak. Lund, as one might expect of a man in his position, was stern to the point of humourlessness. A more relaxed figure might be expected to take his concern for Martin into account — might excuse a brief breach of the regulations, or at least a liberal interpretation of them. But one could not expect this of the legendary Lund.

Blomquist had an idea. 'Why don't you say that you were following a speeding motorist? That's a perfectly good reason for using the blue light. Perhaps that's what you should do.'

Ulf stared at him. 'Are you serious?'

Blomquist nodded. 'Yes. Lund won't be able to disprove it. He'll have to accept what you say.'

'But it's not true,' said Ulf quietly, but with an unmistakeable firmness.

'He doesn't know that,' was Blomquist's riposte.

Ulf looked down at his empty coffee cup. He liked to believe that, by and large, his fellow detectives were honest, that they did not tell lies. He *had* to believe that, he told himself, because if he did not, then he would be unable to believe anybody, and the world would be a house of lies, one on top of another. Now, he said as mildly as he could manage, 'It's not a good policy to lie, Blomquist. Sorry.'

'Oh, I wasn't *suggesting* you lied,' protested Blomquist. 'I was merely raising it as a possibility. I didn't say you should do that.'

That itself, thought Ulf, is a lie. Blomquist was lying about lying, which, of course, was what happened when you started to lie. The first lie required a second — for consistency's sake — and then a third and a fourth. Soon you would end up living in a vale of lies, where even the fact that it was night or day would be uncertain because the position of the sun could be denied if you so desired.

Blomquist lowered his gaze. 'I am ashamed of myself,' he said, suddenly. 'I am thoroughly ashamed of what I have just said. I urged you to lie to get

90

yourself out of trouble. I should not have done that, and I apologise.'

Ulf looked at the man before him. In his eyes, Blomquist had just redeemed himself. The real Blomquist was a man of integrity — and clouds of useless information, of course, but a man who did, after all, know the difference between right and wrong. He had simply been misled by his sympathy for a colleague in trouble, as any of us might be. He had merely given in to a passing idea, before he'd had the time to evaluate what he wanted to say.

Ulf reached out a hand. 'Don't worry, Blomquist. I knew you didn't mean it.'

That was a lie, of course: Ulf did not really believe what he had just claimed to believe, but it was a completely innocuous lie, an instance of the social hypocrisy we all must show from time to time if we are to get on reasonably well with our fellow beings. We cannot be *too* truthful if we are to avoid giving offence to those about us. We admire their new shoes when we secretly dislike them intensely and think, I would never wear those. We tell them they look as if they've lost weight when their belts are clearly straining on the last hole. We tell them they look well when in reality we think they are unlikely to be long for this world. That sort of lie: the lies coined to encourage the weaker brethren.

'I try to tell the truth,' said Blomquist, still looking down. 'I really do.'

'I know that,' said Ulf quietly. 'I've seen it.'

Blomquist seemed cheered. 'It's just that I think it really unfair that a good officer like you should be bullied by somebody like Lund when ... when there are numerous things, really serious things, that some

91

other officers are doing — and they get away with it.'

'I shall have to bear the consequences of my action,' said Ulf. 'He won't fire me for that.'

'No, but you'll get a censure. That'll go on your record.'

Ulf acknowledged that this might happen. 'I only hope the good points outweigh the bad. That's all that one can hope for when one thinks of one's record.'

They got up from the table. Ulf found himself feeling a bit better after this conversation with Blomquist.

'Are you going home now?' asked Blomquist.

'No, I need to get into the office,' said Ulf, without thinking. 'I have things to do.' Then he remembered. 'But, of course, I'm suspended. I suppose there'll be an official note to the effect on my desk.'

'You could sit here and read the paper,' suggested Blomquist. 'I could go and tell Anna that you're here. I'm sure she'd want to come and speak to you.'

Ulf looked away. He was unsure whether Blomquist knew. Perhaps he did. But for all of Blomquist's keenness to talk about vitamins and antioxidants and the rest, he was not one for gossip. If he knew Ulf's secret, he would be likely to keep it to himself.

Blomquist left, and Ulf sat down again. The newspaper was before him, but he found that he could not concentrate on it. It seemed to be concerned with such petty, transient things. Ulf was thinking about Anna, and how lucky he was to have her, not in the sense that lovers and spouses have one another, of course — as compass points, fixed saliences in their world. He did not really have her in that sense; but he knew what he meant. I am a lucky man, thought Ulf. Lund could not take Anna away from him. Nor Sweden. He had Sweden. And his Saab. And Martin, and the help and support of Mrs Högfors, bless her. And that of Blomquist too, whose friendship shone through all the radio noise of healthy-eating tips and drifting anecdotes. I am a fortunate man — a suspended, but fortunate man.

His phone rang. It was Anna.

'Ulf,' she said. 'Lund wants to see you immediately.'

Ulf drew a deep breath. 'Tell him to wait,' he said. 'I'll be with him in half an hour.'

The silence at the other end of the line was one of shock. Then, 'Do you really want me to tell him that? Those exact words?'

'Yes,' said Ulf. 'I'm about to have my second cup of coffee, and I've hardly started the newspaper.'

'You're amazing,' said Anna.

Or very foolish, thought Ulf.

7

The Love of Dogs
Is a Shared Thing

Lund's office was on the top floor of the building next door to the Department of Sensitive Crimes. It was of a size that befitted his seniority, and was furnished with items that were of rather better quality than the usual police issue. A large desk, in two sorts of wood, occupied the central space, while underneath it was a modern rug, certainly not one taken from the pool of drab, functional rugs available to more senior officers. On the wall behind Lund, framed in a silver-painted wooden frame, was a copy of Manet's famous painting depicting the execution of the Mexican Emperor Maximilian. Ulf's eye was drawn to that first, and then to the painting above the filing cabinets — a print of the martyrdom of Saint Sebastian.

Lund was a thin, rather ascetic-looking man in his late forties. He had slicked-down dark hair, rather like that of a ballroom-dancing teacher of forty years ago, thought Ulf, and was wearing a pair of fashionable horn-rimmed spectacles. As Ulf came into his office, he looked up impassively, although Ulf saw the anger in his eyes.

'Sorry I'm a bit late,' Ulf said as he took the seat to which Lund had gestured. 'One of those mornings, I'm afraid. You know what they're like.'

Lund cleared his throat. 'I was expecting you earlier.' His voice was precise, the words emerging with a

94

careful, chiselled feel to them.

'Well, I'm here,' said Ulf, adding, 'As requested.' He looked about him. 'Nice pictures,' he said. 'That's Manet, isn't it?'

Lund had clearly not expected this: most of the recalcitrant policemen who sat before him awaiting sanction were indifferent to Manet and failed to see in the painting an allegory of their own plight. 'Yes,' he said, almost resentfully; almost as if he felt he *blamed* Manet for the execution of Maximilian.

'And that over there is Saint Sebastian, of course. Poor man. It's obviously Italian. Let me guess. No, I can't, really. There are so many martyrdoms of Saint Sebastian, aren't there? Everybody painted one.'

In spite of himself, Lund's eye wandered to the depiction of the unfortunate saint.

'It's interesting that both of the pictures you have up on the walls involve punishment,' said Ulf. 'I'm not reading anything into that, of course. It's just an observation.'

Lund opened a file on his desk. 'You know that you've been suspended?'

Ulf nodded. 'I found the note on my desk.' He looked again at Saint Sebastian. 'Of course, some artist might even have painted something called *The Suspension of Saint Sebastian*, mightn't he? After all, we can imagine that the saint was suspended first before they moved on to execution.'

Lund affected to ignore this. 'The incident in question is wrongful use of a blue light and consequent breach of the relevant provision of the code of conduct.' He looked at Ulf across the table, and adjusted the horn-rimmed spectacles. 'The evidence is that you were seen by a member of the traffic squad, who

95

observed that there was nobody in the car with you. It is also noted that there was no record of an emergency call being routed to you that morning.'

'But my car wasn't empty,' said Ulf. 'I had my dog with me.'

Lund frowned. 'I would advise you not to make light of this, Varg. This is a serious matter.' Then he paused. 'What sort of dog do you have?'

'He's a bit nondescript,' Ulf answered. 'He has Vallhund ears, but he doesn't have those short legs they have.'

Lund nodded his agreement. 'Far too short. Useless in snow.'

'Yes,' said Ulf. 'My neighbour says that she sees a bit of Lapphund in him. I think I know what she means.'

'I had a Lapphund when I was a boy,' said Lund. 'He was called Sven. A wonderful dog.' He paused. 'The dogs we have as boys are very important. You never have a better dog than the dog you had as a boy.'

'Do you have a dog now?' asked Ulf.

Lund sat back in his chair. 'Yes, we do, as a matter of fact. We've just acquired a West Highland terrier. They're a Scottish breed. You will have seen them. Very attractive little dogs. Spirited.'

Ulf agreed.

'Mind you,' Lund continued, 'they have a problem with their diet.'

Ulf thought of Blomquist.

'They can be allergic to certain things, Varg. They're also prone to skin conditions. It's all genetic.'

Ulf nodded wisely. 'It's all in the genes, isn't it?'

'Except crime,' said Lund, and smiled — for the first time in their meeting. 'We're not meant to say

96

that about crime, but it runs in families. You and I know that, but do the politicians? They do not.'

'Of course that might be environment rather than genes,' Ulf suggested.

'Pah!' said Lund. He looked out of the window. He wanted to carry on their conversation about dogs. 'I have a wonderful book I could pass on to you — if you haven't already seen it. It's about how dogs think — how they see the world.' He paused. 'Do you know it?'

Ulf shook his head. 'I'm behind with my reading. I read the reviews and make a mental note to get hold of the book, but I never do.' He glanced at the Manet. 'I read a lot about art. I get a monthly magazine and I buy books about painters.'

'I read a lot about dogs,' said Lund. 'I find that it calms me down.'

'There are worse things to read about,' said Ulf. He was puzzled: he had come here to be reprimanded — at the very least — and yet the atmosphere had completely changed. Lund had visibly relaxed and seemed to be getting into his stride with this conversation about dogs. Did people misjudge him simply because he had the misfortune to be the force's disciplinary officer? Was the real Lund quite different from the unforgiving martinet of office gossip?

'I like art too,' said Lund. 'But I must say that I read far more about dogs than about paintings.'

Ulf waited.

'I can thoroughly recommend this book,' Lund said. 'I can't recall the name of the author — nor the title, unfortunately. It's been translated into Swedish now, although I read it when it first came out — in English. Horowitz. That's the name of the author. I remember now. She's a psychologist, and I suppose that means she knows what she's talking about. Or should do. I'm not saying every psychologist falls into that category, but that's another matter. I suppose you have to use psychology in that department of yours — the Department of Sensational Crimes.'

'Sensitive Crimes,' said Ulf politely. 'The Department of Sensitive Crimes.'

'Of course. Please forgive me. I meant to say *sensitive*. Department of Sensitive Crimes. You have that rather charming woman there, don't you? Anna Something-or-other. Her husband's a doctor, I believe. Very charming — and an accomplished detective, I'm told.'

Ulf was noncommittal. However benign Lund might seem, Ulf did not want him to be party to any of his secrets. But he need not have worried: Lund was not interested in Anna, or in Ulf's relationship with her; he wanted to get back to dogs.

'There's a very interesting chapter in this book,' Lund explained, 'on communicating with dogs. There's a discussion of a German dog that is able to recognise over two hundred different words. They've experimented with soft toys — giving a soft toy a name and then asking the dog to find such-and-such a thing. He gets it right, apparently.'

Ulf told Lund of Martin's deafness. 'My dog wouldn't be much good at that,' he said. 'Unfortunately, he's deaf. He can hear a few very high-pitched sounds, but many sounds he doesn't pick up at all. I've taught him to lip-read.'

Lund let out a whistle of admiration. 'To lip-read!' he exclaimed. 'That's wonderful, Varg. I don't think I've ever heard of a dog who can lip-read.'

'I think he may be the only one in Sweden,' said Ulf proudly. 'I don't know if there are any anywhere else. I don't think so.'

Lund shook his head in wonderment. 'That's a major achievement, Varg — a major achievement.' He hesitated, dragging himself back to the matter in hand. 'You had the dog in the car with you, you say?'

'Yes,' said Ulf. 'I had to get him to the vet. He had been attacked by a squirrel and his face was fairly badly torn. There was a lot of blood. Actually, I thought he might die.'

There was a silence as Lund digested this information. Then, eventually, he said, 'So that was why you used the blue light?'

Ulf nodded. 'Yes. The traffic was very bad.'

'And that,' Lund continued, 'would explain why there was blood on the back seat of your car?'

'It does,' said Ulf. 'It's not human blood. A young man at a garage became very suspicious. I think he must have been the one who reported me.'

Lund confirmed this. 'It's easy to get the wrong end of the stick. At least he was vigilant.'

'Yes,' said Ulf. 'I wouldn't condemn him for doing his civic duty.'

'I was worried about that side of things,' said Lund. 'Using a blue light inappropriately is one thing; murder is quite another.' He paused. 'I'd say that's that, Varg. I would never blame you for an errand of mercy. If blue lights can't be used for this, then what can they be used for?'

Ulf smiled gently. He felt nothing but warmth, now, towards Lund. Not only was the allegedly fierce officer not fierce at all, he was a dog-lover too. And here he was being more than understanding about

Ulf's dilemma.

It became even better. 'What you did,' Lund said, 'is exactly what I would have done in the circumstances.' He looked at Ulf as if he was waiting for some confirmation. Ulf responded.

'That's good to know. Sometimes . . .' Ulf made a gesture of hopelessness. 'Sometimes it's difficult to know what to do. We have protocols, we have procedures; but some situations are marginal, so to speak.'

This went down well with Lund. 'Liminal spaces,' he said. 'The space in-between. Liminal.'

'A very nice word,' said Ulf. He muttered it himself: 'Liminal.'

'The concept comes from anthropology,' Lund explained. 'Perhaps you know that.' He looked again at Saint Sebastian. Ulf followed his gaze. The saint was in a liminal space, perhaps — halfway between life and the death that the arrows would inevitably bring.

'It's where you aren't quite one thing or the other,' Lund continued. 'It usually arises in the context of a rite of passage. It's a bit like being a teenager.'

Ulf smiled. 'That can be unpleasant.'

Lund agreed. 'We have a teenage daughter. She's just sixteen, and . . .' He gave Ulf a look that seemed to be a plea for sympathy.

'Not a good age for anybody,' Ulf offered.

Lund rolled his eyes. 'Exactly. It's definitely liminal. In fact, perhaps we should call them 'limagers'. How about that? A neologism that you and I have coined right here and now.'

Ulf studied him. Who would have thought that this would happen, he asked himself. An interview with Lund, an event that the entire Criminal Investigation

100

Department believed to be the worst thing that could happen to you, was proving to be a rambling discussion of dogs and teenagers. He corrected himself: if one had a new word, one might as well think it, even if one did not use it. Dogs and limagers.

'She — our daughter — has a boyfriend. Oh my God, Varg . . . This youth . . . One makes all the necessary allowances, of course, but we are sorely tested. It's not just his clothes — you know, those jeans with rips across the knees, in his case so extensive that the lower part of the trousers have to be attached to the top part with safety pins. Safety pins, Varg! He's held together by safety pins. Anyway, we have great difficulty in understanding anything he says — when he condescends to talk to us, which is not all that often. I think he's speaking Swedish, but I can't be sure. It sounds a bit like Swedish, but the words are very unclear and he runs them all together. Some of them are new to me. I asked him what he meant by something and he replied in equally unintelligible terms.'

'Foreign background?' asked Ulf.

'No. Entirely Swedish. His father's a Lutheran pastor.'

'Ah,' said Ulf. 'Rebellion.'

'I'd say so. But I wish he'd rebel elsewhere.' Lund paused. 'Do you have any children, Varg?'

Ulf shook his head. 'I'd like to,' he said.

He was about to say something more, but he stopped himself. Why had he said that he would like to have children? He had not given the question of children much thought. Of course, there were moments when you saw other people delighting in their children, and you thought: That could be me, but those did not occur all that often. If you had children, you had to

101

have somebody to have children with, and Ulf had nobody.

I have nobody. It was such a bleak admission, even when made entirely to oneself. *I have nobody.* And yet, if you had somebody, you gave a hostage to fortune. There were people who sensed that, and deliberately held back from human involvement because they did not want to experience loss. Was he like that? No. He wanted involvement, but it simply had not come his way. He knew with whom he wanted to be involved, there was no doubt about that, but that simply could not be.

Lund was staring at him. 'You look sad,' he said. 'Are you feeling sad because you'd like to have children, and you don't?' And then, immediately, he apologised. 'I'm sorry: I shouldn't be prying into your private life. Please forgive me.'

'There's nothing to forgive,' said Ulf. 'You haven't asked me anything I wouldn't want you to ask me.'

'It was your look of unhappiness,' said Lund. 'I know that we detectives are meant to be a troubled bunch — or at least, that's the way we're portrayed. All those television series in which we're shown as having drink problems, matrimonial problems, problems with virtually everything. It's not really like that, is it?'

Ulf was not sure how to answer. Perhaps they were right, these television directors; perhaps that's what it was like to be a Nordic detective — to be depressed, to be melancholy, to be having therapy. He should speak to his therapist about it. Perhaps there was some deep, Jungian archetype that governed the lives of detectives, condemning them all to the same angst, the same unfulfilled dreams, the same . . . liminality.

102

Perhaps life really is a Bergman film in which we have no choice but to occupy this uncomfortable territory of doubt and indecision.

Lund was tapping his desk with a finger. 'I think we should have a cup of coffee,' he said. 'Then I can let you get back to the office.'

Ulf raised an eyebrow. 'My suspension?'

'Oh that,' said Lund. 'That's rescinded. And I'll get your car back. I'll even get them to valet it for you. By way of apology.'

Ulf thanked him, but declined the valeting. He declined the coffee, too, on the grounds that he had already had two cups that morning.

'I have decaf,' said Lund. 'It would be no trouble.'

'In that case . . . '

They drank their coffee together. Lund seemed thoughtful. 'I'd like you to meet my wife,' he said. 'And young Alvar.'

Ulf looked puzzled.

'Our West Highland terrier.'

'Of course. I'd like to meet them both.'

Lund looked pleased. 'Come round for dinner sometime. We can fix up a day next month, perhaps.'

'That would be very nice.'

Lund drained the last of his coffee. 'And I hope that your dog makes a full recovery.'

They shook hands as Ulf left. He felt Saint Sebastian's eyes upon him, resigned, but still reproachful, and he knew then why Lund chose to have that picture on his wall. It was his job: that was his martyrdom. Every day must be part of a sentence. He would have liked to have been able to say something, but he could not think of the words. 'I understand' might have done, but the moment passed, and there is always a very precise moment for words like that to be uttered; then it passes and it is too late. Just as the moment for words like *sorry* or *I love you* is a brief one, fleeting and irreplaceable; a moment of liminality, perhaps.

8

He Has an Eye

Ulf had done his homework by the time he went with Blomquist to the Berks auction house that afternoon. He had intended to go alone, but had felt sorry for Blomquist who was standing in the corridor directly outside the office saying, half seriously, half in jest, 'I wish I had something to do.'

Ulf had stopped and met Blomquist's gaze. 'No reports to write up?'

Blomquist shook his head. 'All done and dusted.'

'Claim forms?' asked Ulf.

Again this was met with a shake of the head. 'No investigations, therefore no expenses.'

Ulf sighed. 'Correspondence? Couldn't you send a memo?'

'I can't think of anything to send a memo about,' he said. 'And anyway, there was that memo we got the other day telling us not to send too many memos.'

They both smiled at that. It was a classic piece of self-defeating bureaucracy: 'There are far too many memos,' the memo had said. 'Please show restraint.'

Ulf's natural kindness came into play. This was not really the sort of case in which Blomquist would have anything to offer, he thought; this was a sophisticated inquiry, to be conducted in the higher echelons of the art world. Blomquist would be a fish out of water in such circles; poor Blomquist knew nothing about art — not that there was any fault involved in

105

that, but it was, alas, the case. And then, suddenly, he felt ashamed at this thought. He was worried that the sophisticates he would be interviewing would judge him by the professional company he kept. They would see him as a sort of Blomquist, promoted from the realm of mundane crimes and out of his depth in the art world. That was what he was worried about, and it was shameful. If those people were going to be snobbish, then he should not join in with their unkind attitudes. Blomquist was his colleague. He was a good man, and if other people failed to see that quality in him, then it was their loss.

'Actually, Blomquist,' Ulf said, 'I'm pleased that you don't have any correspondence or memos or whatnot. I have a rather interesting case on the go, and I was hoping you might be able to give me a hand.'

Blomquist beamed with pleasure. 'Me?' he asked.

'Yes, Blomquist, you. Are you up for it?'

He did not hesitate. 'I certainly am,' he replied. 'When do we start?'

'Now,' said Ulf. 'We'll go in my Saab. It's outside.'

They went downstairs and out into the car park.

'I love your car,' said Blomquist, as they climbed in. 'I know I've said it before, but these are the most beautiful cars ever made.'

Ulf was pleased, and thanked Blomquist for the compliment. But he had to express his reservations about the comparative standing of the 1960s Saab. 'Ever made in Sweden, perhaps, but there are many other very beautiful cars. Many.'

He continued on this theme as they drove out into the traffic. 'Earlier Saabs have superb lines, but there are other cars that are perhaps even greater works of art. The old Hispano-Suiza, for instance, with silver exhaust pipes coming out of the side. That's a very fine car. Some Bugattis. Even the Citroën DS — you remember that one, the car that General de Gaulle drove about in? The suspension had to inflate before you could drive off. Or the Citroën Traction Avant. That was a great car.'

Blomquist had seen those in French films. 'Inspector Maigret had one. Remember?'

'So he did,' said Ulf. 'So he did.'

'We couldn't use them in the department,' Blomquist observed. 'We would be too conspicuous. Suspects would get advance warning.' He hesitated before continuing. 'There's even a case for not using a Saab like this. You're hardly anonymous in the streets of Malmö. The criminal fraternity probably say, 'Look out for Varg — you'll see his car coming a mile off.'.'

Ulf did not comment on this. He wanted to give Blomquist a brief summary of the case before they arrived at the auction house. He did so. And at the end Blomquist said, 'Somebody has it in for him. That's obvious.'

'Yes,' said Ulf. 'I'd rather concluded that.'

'Except,' Blomquist went on, 'except that this Anders Kindgren might be trying to get at somebody else. What if he has a grudge against this auction woman — what's her name?'

'Christina Berks.'

'Yes, her. This business can't be good for *her* reputation, I would have thought. People might think that she, at least, should have spotted a fake.'

It was typical of the unexpected points that Blomquist occasionally raised. It was easy to dismiss them, but Ulf had learned from experience that Blomquist's points were sometimes very helpful — in a curious way.

'We should keep that in mind,' Ulf said. 'But for the time being, let's assume that Kindgren is the wronged party. We can always revise our position if we need to.'

They were approaching the auction house. It was in a quiet suburb of large mercantile villas, most of which had been converted into business premises, including a number of galleries. The Auction House Otto Berks was the last house on the street. Beyond it was a riding school with an indoor dressage ring.

'I know that place,' said Blomquist. 'There was some funny business going on there a few years ago. It's in different hands now.'

Ulf wondered what funny business might be conducted in a riding school. Of course, funny business could go on anywhere, and did, even in the most unlikely places. There had been that funny business in the Vatican, for example, involving banks and secret societies. If there could be funny business in the Vatican, then surely there could be funny business anywhere.

They parked at the side of the building, next to a black 1980s Mercedes coupé.

'That'll be hers,' said Ulf to Blomquist. He was good at linking cars to owners. This was just the car that Christina Berks, from what he had read about her, would be likely to have.

Ulf had found out a lot about Christina Berks. She had inherited the auction house from her father, Otto, who had himself been left it by his own father, Joseph Berks. Joseph had been born in 1905, the son of a successful Berlin psychiatrist, a regular visitor to Vienna, who moved in the fringes of Freud's circle

108

and had co-authored a paper with Jung. Dr Wilhelm Berks was a German patriot — and Jewish. He had brought Joseph up to be proud of German achievements in science and the arts, and when the Nazis began to flex their muscles, he had found it inconceivable that the Germany he knew and of which he was so proud, the Germany of Goethe and Schiller, would allow these street bullies to overwhelm the institutions of state. How could the jurists and philosophers allow such a thing? How could they allow people of substance and reputation to be humiliated and stripped of their assets? It was impossible, and yet it had happened. Wilhelm eventually realised that it would be safer for Joseph to follow his friends who were escaping abroad. He himself felt too old and too tired to move.

'They won't bother about somebody like me,' he said, 'a retired doctor harming nobody. But you must go.'

Joseph managed to get into Sweden in 1940, having spent the previous three years in Denmark. He was then thirty-five years old, a qualified accountant. A kind Swede gave him a job in his fertiliser business, and he worked at this until the end of the war. Then, having married a Swedish woman, he was taken into his wife's family auction business. He had greater ambitions than to sell household effects, and the auction house began to specialise in art. By his death in 1970, it was established as one of the main art auction businesses in Scandinavia, operating a tier or two below the large international auction houses, the Christie's and Sotheby's of this world, but doing well enough.

Joseph had two sons. One became a chest physician,

the other went into the business. That was Christina's father, Otto, who ran the business until his death in a boating accident. Christina was only twenty-five at the time of Otto's death, but she had been brought up with art and auctions and moved seamlessly into the role of managing director. She was destined for the role: at the age of eight she had conducted her first auction — of a collection of antique dolls, being sold for a children's charity — and had been featured in many of the papers as Europe's youngest auction-eer. She had a brother, Bobby, who was a musician in Stockholm and who had no desire to be involved in running the firm. She bought Bobby out and assumed sole control of the business. Christina was now thirty-five, and both well known and well liked in artistic circles. She was also, Ulf read, a prominent member of a women's professional organisation and the founder of a self-help initiative for recovering drug addicts. She was unmarried.

The articles that Ulf had unearthed online usually featured Christina's photograph — she was photogenic by any standards — but he was unprepared for the sheer glamour of her appearance in the flesh. As he and Blomquist were shown into her office by her secretary, a rather prim, middle-aged woman, they were greeted by an elegant, fine-looking woman wearing a red trouser suit and a large art nouveau brooch. The brooch was on the verge of being too big, but just avoided that. Similarly, her shoes, if even moderately more pointed and modestly more crocodilian, could have tipped over into bad taste, but they did not.

Ulf studied Christina's features. She had high cheekbones and a broad forehead; her eyes were somewhere between hazel and green, and were intense in their stare. She was not one who would fail to make an impression. She was, he decided, very beautiful — like a rare porcelain object, a Meissen statuette. And there was about her the same brittleness of that sort of precious object, as if she might break if too roughly handled.

He tried not to show his reaction to her appearance. He knew, though, that people like Christina would know that they made an impression on those who met them. Good-looking people, in Ulf's experience, were usually only too well aware of how they made others feel, whether resentful and envious, or charmed and enticed. And like so many good-looking people, she had about her that confident self-assuredness that goes with not caring about the light in which one is surveyed nor the angle from which one is regarded.

'Ulf Varg,' she said, offering her hand for a handshake. 'I'm happy to be able to help you.'

Ulf had phoned in advance to make the appointment and had explained why he wanted to speak to her.

'It's more a question of helping Anders Kindgren,' said Ulf, and then turned to introduce Blomquist. 'This is Blomquist. He's a member of my team.'

Christina glanced at Blomquist. She did not offer her hand, and quickly turned back to Ulf. 'Are you any relation of Björn Varg?' she asked. 'It's an unusual name. That politician — you know who I mean. The Moderate Extremist man.'

Ulf sighed, but only inwardly. 'I'm afraid so,' he said. 'Björn is my brother.'

He thought he saw a smile play about her lips.

'We can't always choose our siblings' politics, I suppose.'

111

Ulf had not expected this. People were usually more circumspect about their attitude towards Björn, at least when Ulf was about: Christina was being direct.

'No,' said Ulf. 'We have good relations — as brothers — but we are not political allies.'

'Good,' said Christina. 'That increases my confidence in you.'

That rankled — but only slightly. Björn was his brother; he could be as rude as he liked about his own brother, but he was not sure that he wanted others to run him down.

'He goes on a lot about law and order,' Christina went on. 'But did you see that his own treasurer was arrested for assault the other day. He hit somebody with a cucumber.'

Ulf was about to laugh, but checked himself. A cucumber? He looked at Christina quizzically. 'That's a bit odd,' he said.

'Very,' she replied. 'But we live in strange times, I suppose. Nothing would surprise me any longer.'

Ulf made a mental note to look into that. A cucumber: perhaps it was just a coincidence . . .

Christina invited them both to sit and buzzed her secretary for a pot of coffee and three cups.

'Let's get down to it without delay,' she said. 'You've come to see me about that unfortunate Dughet affair.'

'We have,' said Ulf. 'We've had a complaint from Anders Kindgren. He believes that somebody has been deliberately trying to damage his reputation.'

Christina smiled. 'You could say that again. It was a dreadful mistake.'

'Was it?' asked Ulf. 'I'm not sure that his original attribution was mistaken.'

112

Christina looked at him in a manner that Ulf could only think of as haughty. 'He examined the painting. He doesn't deny it.' There was an angry note in her voice. 'It did us serious harm, you know. It was all over the newspapers and I know that colleagues in other houses were putting it about that we couldn't be trusted to identify things correctly. That sort of thing can be the kiss of death for a business like mine.'

Ulf waited a few moments. The self-assured, he thought, were often the most easily deflated. He spoke tentatively, in the tone of one who was only exploring a remote possibility. 'It could have been another painting, though. It might not have been the one that was then brought in.'

Christina stared at him. She looked confused, but only momentarily. Now she recovered her poise. 'I don't think so. It was the same subject and it was brought in following a direct approach to us. That makes it frankly unlikely that it was a copy — or an attempt at a copy.'

Ulf did not further explain his theory. Rather, he asked her why she thought Anders Kindgren had made such a clumsy mistake.

Christina shrugged. 'People develop preconceptions. They may want a painting to be something, and they persuade themselves that it is. In reality, it may not be that at all, but the power of suggestion is such that they convince themselves.'

Blomquist had said nothing so far; now he joined the conversation. 'Psychosomatic,' he said. 'It's the same with symptoms. You think that you have something, and the body plays its part by showing the symptoms.'

Christina had paid no attention to Blomquist; now

113

she looked at him as if for the first time since his arrival. 'Interesting,' she said, and turned her attention back to Ulf.

But Blomquist had not finished. 'And the same thing happens with vision, you know. The eye can be tricked into reading what you think is there rather than what is actually on the page. So 'Pope hopes' may become 'Pope elopes', which is somewhat different, as you can readily imagine.'

Christina glanced at Ulf, as if expecting him to explain this extraordinary man.

'The Pope would never elope,' said Blomquist, grinning. 'I don't think we need have any fear of that.'

Christina was unsmiling. 'No,' she said. 'Very reassuring.'

Ulf intervened. 'So you think he just didn't look hard enough — or, if he did, he did so with preconceptions?'

'Precisely,' said Christina.

Ulf had a final question. 'If it were the case — and this is pure hypothesis — if it were the case that somebody did, in fact, exchange the real Dughet for a copy — and a rather amateur copy at that — and if we were to imagine that this was done to cause embarrassment to Anders Kindgren, then who do you think might do such a thing? Do you know if he has any enemies? Any rivals, perhaps?'

Christina looked thoughtful. 'I'm not sure about enemies — I don't think he's the sort of man who attracts them. I don't know him all that well, of course, and I may be wrong about that, but I shouldn't think he's done anything to incur the wrath of others. As to rivals, well, that's different.'

Ulf was interested. A rival would obviously benefit

114

from the fall of Anders Kindgren. There could not be a great deal of business in the world of attribution, and thinning the field would no doubt help somebody somewhere. 'He could be the object of professional jealousy?'

Christina fiddled with a piece of paper on her desk. She was weighing her words, Ulf decided; she was working out whom to incriminate.

'There are a couple of possible candidates,' she said. 'There's a professor in Lund. Originally from Hamburg, I think. Hans-Dieter Kaufmann. In the past he was used by some of the bigger houses — Sotheby's and so on. Then he fell out of favour. I believe he's trying to re-establish himself.' She paused. 'But he's too gentlemanly to do anything like . . . like what you're proposing.'

Ulf nodded to Blomquist, who wrote down the name. 'And there's another?'

'A far more likely possibility,' said Christina. 'There's Marlene Johansson. She trained in Rome and thinks she knows everything there is to know about seventeenth-century Italian art.' She gave Ulf a conspiratorial look. 'But she doesn't. I'm pretty sure she's jealous of Anders. And she's just the sort to try to slip into his shoes.'

Blomquist made another note.

'Where is she?' asked Ulf.

'Here in Malmö. Her husband has an engineering business here. He has pots of money, so she doesn't have to work, but she does occasional teaching at the university and she writes a little. Very dull stuff — virtually unreadable.'

'Would she go so far as to seek to harm Anders?' asked Ulf.

115

Christina laughed. 'She'd stop at nothing, that woman.'

Ulf waited to see if she had anything to add, but it became clear that Christina had said all she intended to say. Now he asked, 'Did you have any dealings with the man who brought the painting in? I gather he gave a false name.'

'He did. And in answer to your question as to whether I had any dealings with him, no, I didn't. He came in when I was on holiday in Italy. Umbria. We were away for three weeks and so the staff were in charge. There are three full-time people, apart from me, and two interns. We take postgraduate students — people doing PhDs in art history, that sort of person. They come as interns and we do our best to place them somewhere in the art trade at the end of the year they spend with us. But we give them lots of responsibility — they're usually pretty competent.' She paused. 'It was one of our interns who spoke to the person who brought the painting in. He's called Ivar, and you can speak to him if you like — he's here right now.'

Ulf accepted the offer. Then he asked, 'He conducted the whole transaction?'

Christina clearly struggled to keep her voice even. Why should that be? Ulf wondered. 'He did. He's very good at his job. He understands, and, most importantly, he has an eye. If you have an eye in the art world, then that's half the battle — if not the entire campaign. Ivar has it.'

'Having an eye means what?'

'It means that you can spot a painter's style. It means you know in your bones what is genuine and what is not. It means you just *know* things.'

'So this intern — Ivar — he should have known if

116

the Dughet that was brought in was the real thing?'

Christina hesitated. 'Possibly.'

'But then why didn't he see it as a fake? After all, he referred it to Anders for attribution.'

Christina shrugged. 'Maybe he had an off day. Maybe it wasn't too obvious a fake.'

'The Frenchman thought it was.'

'He's entitled to his opinion,' said Christina curtly. She rose from her desk. 'I'll take you to see him — that would be better than my speculating as to what he thought. Ask him yourselves.'

She led them out into a corridor, and then into the large room in which the auctions were held. On each of the four walls, paintings were hung at various heights. A few visitors, catalogues in hand, were inspecting these.

'There's a viewing on at present,' Christina said. 'We're selling these paintings on Friday. Scandinavian art — our special annual sale. People come from abroad for it. We have a lot of American interest in this one.'

They were walking past a small oil painting of a man and a woman sitting in a kitchen. The kitchen walls were festooned with copper saucepans. Christina stopped and drew their attention to the painting.

'Lovely,' said Ulf. 'Mina Carlson-Bredberg?'

Christina stared at him in astonishment. 'As it happens, yes. How did you . . . ' She stopped, and blushed with embarrassment.

'I'm interested in Scandinavian art,' said Ulf.

'He knows a lot about it,' added Blomquist.

Christina raised an eyebrow. 'So it would seem.'

Ulf was modest. 'Not really. I read a bit, I suppose.'

'A lot,' said Blomquist.

117

'It's her style,' said Ulf quickly. 'I find her very like Vuillard. Or at least her interiors are. I'm very fond of Vuillard and Bonnard. I love the intimacy.'

'Is she dead?' asked Blomquist.

'Very,' snapped Christina. 'And I suppose you're going to ask me who killed her.'

It was all that Ulf could do not to gasp. Quickly he sought to cover up the cutting remark. 'She died in the early 1940s,' said Ulf. '1942, I think.'

Christina corrected him. ''43, actually.'

Ulf peered at the painting on display. 'This is a very charming example of her work.'

'It's likely to go to Minneapolis,' said Christina. 'They've been asking a lot of questions about it. They're going to be bidding, I think.'

Christina looked across the auction room. On the other side, standing in front of a large, ornately framed landscape painting, a young man was finishing a conversation with an elderly couple. He caught her glance and responded to her signal to join them.

'This is Ivar,' Christina said to Ulf, as the young man joined them. 'Ivar, this is Ulf and ... and ...' She looked to Ulf for assistance, but it was Blomquist himself who helped her out.

'Blomquist,' he said.

Ulf gave Christina a reproachful glance. If there was one thing that irritated him above all else, it was the ignoring — by the articulate, the powerful, the influential — of those they considered their inferiors. That was compounded by the forgetting of their names. It would have been different had Christina forgotten Ulf's name too — that would have been a forgivable *lapsus memoriae* — but this was not that — this was a *lapsus liberalitatis* — a failure of civility.

9

He Moved with Feline Grace

Christina had to deal with a client. She excused herself, suggesting that Ivar should take Ulf and Blomquist to the staffroom for a cup of coffee; they could talk there without being disturbed by people viewing the auction lots.

'I shall say goodbye before you go,' she said, 'but in the meantime, Ivar is at your disposal.'

Ivar caught her eye. 'So to speak,' he said.

As the intern led them to an airy, well-lit room at the back of the auction hall, Ulf made his usual assessment of clothing and demeanour. The young man was tall, about the same height as Ulf, and therefore half a head taller than Blomquist. His hair was just on the brown side of blond and was cut short. He was wearing formal dark jeans and an open-necked shirt in Bengal stripe. His wristwatch was discreet, but clearly expensive — perhaps even Patek Philippe, although Ulf had difficulty in identifying it under the cuff of the shirt. A young man in his very early twenties did not buy a watch like that. A gift, then? Which raised the question: a gift from whom? Lastly, he noticed the shoes: leather trainers — soft Italian leather.

The intern's bearing was more or less as expected. There was a certain languor to his movements — if one could divide humanity into dogs and cats, then this was definitely cat, thought Ulf. There was a feline grace to the way he walked, to the way he opened the door for Ulf and Blomquist and smiled as he ushered them through. And there was a certain detachment, a distance: cats did not care; they kept their emotions to themselves; dogs were all externals — wagging tails, smiles, slobbery licks. A phrase came to Ulf's mind: 'a good conceit of himself'.

Ivar fetched them coffee.

'You wanted to talk to me?' he said as he sat down at the table. His tone was friendly, but not too familiar. He thinks we're clients, thought Ulf.

'We're from the police,' Blomquist said.

Ivar had been looking at Ulf; now he spun round. His eyes widened.

That was a shock, thought Ulf. It was always the same — always. The innocent might react with surprise if they learned that the police wanted to speak to them; the guilty always reacted with dread.

'Police?' said Ivar.

Blomquist nodded. 'The Department of Sensitive Crimes.'

Ivar swallowed hard. Ulf saw the movement of his Adam's apple; it was one of the most revealing of organs — along with the nose, which, Ulf had learned, contained erectile tissue. Telling lies could activate that, he had read; they called it the Pinocchio effect.

Ulf took over. 'We need to ask you a few questions about a painting that was offered for sale here recently.'

Ivar looked away. His voice was strained. 'A painting?'

'That's what you sell, isn't it?' Blomquist interjected.

Ivar fumbled with his answer. 'Yes, I suppose so; I mean yes, we do. Paintings. Yes.' He collected himself. 'I hope none of our lots has been stolen. We're careful about title.'

'No, nothing like that,' said Ulf.

The young man seemed to relax. 'Oh well, that's a relief.'

Ulf fixed him with a gaze. 'A painting by one Gaspard Dughet.'

There was a silence. Now Ivar looked at the floor before slowly raising his eyes to meet Ulf's. 'That,' he said, 'was very unfortunate.' He paused, and his voice became anxious. 'But selling something that has been wrongly attributed isn't a police matter, is it?' And then he added, 'And we didn't sell it anyway. It was withdrawn from the sale. There was no fraud or anything like that.' The confident manner was over-come by a supplicant look. Ulf realised that charm was being deployed now. 'We'd never offer anything in bad faith. We really wouldn't.'

Ulf reassured him. 'Nobody has suggested that.'

'Then why—'

Blomquist interrupted him. 'The inspector doesn't need to explain himself.'

Ivar bit his lip. He became silent.

Ulf was grateful to Blomquist. He was finding this young man a bit precious — a bit too pleased with himself; Blomquist had exerted their authority. 'I'd like you to tell me what happened with this painting — this Dughet. I'd like to know who brought it in. I'd like to know what happened subsequently.' He paused. 'Take your time. And tell me everything — I . . . we'll decide what's relevant.'

Ivar began with the arrival of the painting. There had been no prior arrangement, he said, the owner had simply appeared and said that he had an interest-ing painting in his car. Ivar went out with him to the car park and saw the Dughet in the back, wrapped in a threadbare blanket.

'He said that it had been in the family for years. He said that he had inherited it jointly with his brother and sister. He kept it in his house, but the understanding was that in the future, they would share, and might take turns to hang it in their homes. That sometimes happens with family pictures, you know — and it can lead to complications if one person wants to sell and others don't.'

'I can understand that,' said Ulf.

'I was not unsure about it,' Ivar continued. 'I thought it was a seventeenth-century painting — French or Italian. Probably the latter, but I was not sure about the artist. Dughet crossed my mind, and so I arranged for Anders Kindgren to look at it. He does attribution for paintings like that — Christina's used him a lot.

'I called him up and told him about it. He was very interested and came around the next day — the owner having left the painting with us.'

'And did you know who he was?' asked Ulf.

'He gave me a name and address,' replied Ivar. 'That was all I knew.'

'I see.'

'Anyway, Anders came and looked at it and gave it a firm attribution. He liked it. He said it was one of Dughet's better paintings — he was very popular, apparently. I had told the owner to come back the following week — he seemed unwilling to give me a telephone number.'

'But he came back?' asked Ulf.

Ivar nodded. 'Yes, and I gave him the good news. I told him what Anders had said and the valuation he had put on the painting. He seemed pleased enough with this and said he'd discuss it with his brother and sister. He took the painting away with him. I told him that we would have to know within five weeks if it was to be included in our next Old Masters. Exactly ten days later he called to say that the family had decided to go ahead and offer the painting for sale.'

'So you prepared the catalogue entry?' asked Ulf.

Ivar said that he did, although he sent it first to Christina, who signed it off. 'She was in Italy, you see.'

'She told me,' said Ulf. 'Umbria.'

'And then,' Ivar continued, 'a week before the sale, it was delivered back to us. It was done up in bubble-wrap and I put it in the storeroom, in one of the racks.'

'Wait a moment,' said Ulf. 'Delivered?'

'Yes,' said Ivar. 'I didn't see who it was. The porter took it. I assumed it was the owner — the man I spoke to.'

Blomquist corrected him. 'Part-owner.'

Ivar shrugged. 'Whatever.'

'And the porter?' asked Ulf. 'Could he tell us who handed it in?'

Ivar looked away. 'I asked him. He said he didn't see. Somebody came in and left it beside his desk.'

Ulf said that he was surprised that security was so slack. 'You have valuable paintings coming in — surely people should be a bit more careful.'

Ivar admitted they might. 'But I'm just the intern,' he said defensively.

'All right,' said Ulf. 'So it was brought in. Then you stored it in one of the racks — is that correct?'

'Yes. I stored it safely.'

'And it remained there?' asked Blomquist.

'Of course — until the Frenchman saw it.'

Ulf was keen to establish that the painting had been undisturbed. 'Nobody else saw it between its arrival, then, and the point at which it was shown to the French curator?'

'Nobody,' answered Ivar.

'And you yourself took delivery of it when it was brought round?'

Ivar hesitated. Then he frowned. 'No, I just told you. The porter did. Then he handed it to me — wrapped, as I said.'

Blomquist looked puzzled. 'Shouldn't you have opened it before you stored it?'

The question hit home, and Ivar was embarrassed. 'Maybe. In fact, yes, I suppose I should have.' He added lamely, 'We're quite trusting in this business.'

'Maybe too trusting,' muttered Ulf. He sat back in his chair and then addressed Blomquist. 'You said you'd like to take a look at the lots.'

Blomquist looked puzzled.

'Out there,' said Ulf, nodding in the direction of the auction room. He was not sure if Blomquist would take the hint, but he did, and rose to his feet in compliance.

'I'll finish my coffee here,' said Ulf. 'I'll join you in ten minutes, Blomquist.'

Ivar rose to his feet too, preparing to go. 'I don't think I can add much,' he said.

'I wasn't going to question you,' said Ulf, signalling for him to stay. 'I thought we could chat for a few minutes.'

The young man sat down again. Ulf sipped at his coffee. 'It's a nice job you have here,' he said. 'I imagine these internships are hard to come by. Everything is, these days, I suppose.'

Ivar agreed. 'There are very few openings in the art world. Everybody wants in.'

'I can imagine,' said Ulf. 'What could be better than to be around art all day — and be paid for it. I'd love it.'

'But you enjoy your job,' said Ivar, adding, 'Don't you?' He gave Ulf a sideways glance. 'Or are you one of those detectives who have issues? The type we see on television?'

Ulf chuckled. 'Those films are very unrealistic. The people I work with are not like that at all. We're very ordinary, you know.'

Ivar looked thoughtful. 'But you have to do some pretty unpleasant things, don't you? You have to arrest people. Put them away. Doesn't that make you feel bad?'

Ulf pointed out that the police never put people away — that was for the courts to do. 'And we just get on with our job,' he said. 'We don't have sleepless nights over it. We can't afford to.'

He changed the subject, asking about how Ivar had become interested in art. There had been a teacher at his school, Ivar said, who had inspired him. And then he had been taken at the age of fourteen to Florence and he had spent days in the Uffizi. 'That was it,' he said. 'I knew that was what I wanted to do. I just knew.'

'And then?' asked Ulf.

'Uppsala. I did art history there, and then a master's at the Courtauld in London. Then I came back to Sweden and started a PhD. I'm taking a year out from that, doing this internship.'

'A nice thing to do,' said Ulf.

'Two hundred and sixteen other people thought so too.'

Ulf whistled. 'You were very lucky.'

Ivar hesitated. He seemed to be weighing up whether to say something. Ulf waited.

'I don't think I got it on merit,' Ivar said. 'I wish I had.'

Ulf raised an eyebrow.

'Christina is—' He broke off, as if he regretted having started. But then he sighed. 'She's my father's lover.'

'I see. Well, that's the way things are, I suppose. But I can see that you might feel awkward about it.'

'She doesn't know I know,' Ivar blurted out.

'I see.'

'And nor does he — my father. He obviously spoke to her and fixed it up for me.'

Ulf said nothing. He was not sure why this young man was opening up to him in this way, but in his experience it was not unusual. People often had nobody to talk to about their anxieties, so they unburdened themselves to a taxi driver or a policeman — to anybody they found themselves with. He had had numerous witnesses or complainants suddenly reveal their life secrets in the course of an interview — they seemed to need to talk. He would let Ivar tell him about this. It would have nothing to do with the investigation, but it would make him feel better and he was in no hurry.

'I hate her,' Ivar said suddenly.

'Who?'

'I hate Christina. She's been seeing my father for two years now. My mother knows that he's having an affair, although he likes to think she doesn't. But she

126

knows all right, and it's wrecked her life.'

Ulf made a sympathetic noise. 'These things can be very hard on the other person.'

It was what Ivar wanted to hear. 'Yes, they can — and I'll tell you something: a few weeks ago, I was in the house — I have my own flat, but I spend quite a bit of time at my parents' place — and I happened to hear my mother in the living room. She didn't know I was there in the house and she didn't know I could hear her. She was weeping — just weeping. It was horrible.'

'Yes,' said Ulf gently. 'It must have been.'

'And I've seen her sometimes just sitting, staring into space. She never used to do that. She's a fantastic person — really lively, really kind. But now her whole life has been wrecked by . . . by this other woman.'

Ulf waited a few moments before he spoke. 'Affairs are difficult. They involve two people, remember . . . '

'Oh, I blame my father too,' said Ivar. 'But not as much as I blame Christina. My father's weak. He's a weak rich man who's had everything he wants, all his life. Everything. He hasn't had to work for anything at all. And he's never done anything for anybody, you know. He's mean with his money.'

'I see.' Ulf's eye went again to the wristwatch. It was Patek Philippe.

'And Christina . . . She loves the fact that he's wealthy. She loves rich people because they buy art. And she doesn't care about how my mother might feel; she doesn't care about wrecking somebody else's life.'

Ulf was thinking. This conversation was painful to him not only because of its intensity, and the obvious suffering of this young man, but also because it brought into stark relief the contours of his own situ-

127

ation. He had been through much the same thoughts himself; he had weighed his feelings for Anna against the survival of a marriage, and the marriage had won. He could not have Anna, even if she agreed to have him. She belonged in a family that he could not be instrumental in breaking up. He was destined, then, to love without reciprocation: his companion was to be Himeros, god of unrequited love, rather than Eros himself.

'I'm sorry to hear about all this,' Ulf said.

Ivar shook his head. 'I shouldn't have told you. I'm sorry.'

'No,' said Ulf. 'I don't mind at all. There are some things it's better to get off your chest. And if talking to me has helped, then I'm glad.'

Ivar was looking at him with unconcealed gratitude.

'The only thing I'd say,' said Ulf, 'is this. You mentioned that you hated Christina. Be careful of that.'

Ivar's eyes narrowed; a sign, Ulf thought, that advice would not be welcome. But in spite of this he continued, 'I've come face to face with hate a lot in my career. And it has a very ugly face, believe me. It can take over. It can be like a weedkiller that spills over — it can kill the things you'd like to grow. Bear that in mind.' Ulf stood up. 'I'd better join my colleague,' he said. 'I've enjoyed talking to you, Ivar.'

Ivar stood up too. Ulf's advice, it seemed, had not been rejected out of hand. Now it seemed that he wanted to please Ulf — to give him something. 'There's one thing,' he said. 'Or two things, actually. One is about the man who brought the painting in: he gave a false name, but I can tell you what he looked like.'

Ulf waited.

128

'You know that actor?' Ivar said. 'You know the one who was in that film that won all those awards last year. He was in all the papers.'

Ulf thought. He was bad on actors' names, but he thought he might know this one. 'Lennart Solander?'

'That's him,' said Ivar. 'Well, he looked a bit like him.'

'Nothing else?'

'No, that's all I can say about him — apart from the second thing.'

'And that is?'

'When he came around that first time, he asked me . . . ' Ivar hesitated. Ulf thought he saw him colour. And he knew immediately what it was.

'He was — how shall I put it — interested?' Ulf suggested.

Ivar looked down at the floor. 'He asked me whether I'd like to go for a drink. It was six in the evening, you see, and we were about to close. He said there was a bar nearby and could he buy me a drink.'

'Which bar?'

'The Divine Apollo.'

Ulf smiled. The Greek gods were still with us, after millennia, casting their shadow, present in our language, in the names of our bars, in our dreams, interfering in our affairs. 'I see. I know the place.'

Ivar looked momentarily confused, but he quickly recovered.

'I said no. I thanked him, of course, but I said I had to meet some friends. He just shrugged and said, 'Maybe some other time.' I said maybe. And we left it at that.'

129

10

The Lion Shall Lie Down

Mrs Högfors was being very solicitous. She would have kept the dog with her until Ulf's return had it not been for her having been called to visit her sister, who suffered from a lung condition and occasionally needed help with her oxygen cylinders. So Martin had been delivered back to Ulf's flat, where a note, laboriously typed on an ancient manual typewriter, was left on the kitchen table. *Martin has had a good day. His nose seems to be healing nicely and he has stopped trying to scratch his wounds. I think he is feeling more cheerful.*

Ulf decided that he would not take Martin out until after he had had his dinner. He had lamb chops in the fridge and there was a tray of baked aubergine to accompany them. That had been bought at Carlo's delicatessen, the source of most of his provisions. The aubergine bake was one of his favourites and was set aside for him each Monday when fresh supplies of home-made pasta and other prepared dishes were delivered. Ulf would eat the lamb chops and aubergines while reading the latest issue of the art magazine to which he subscribed. This contained an article on *Peaceable Kingdom* paintings that he was looking forward to reading: 'The Lion Shall Lie Down with the Lamb' — and there it was, as envisaged by Edward Hicks, who painted over sixty of these paintings, all very much the same, and all making the same point. Ulf gazed at the reproduction of one of the best-known of these paintings, spread across an entire page of the magazine, and sighed. Not only did a lion stand benevolently by, but a leopard and a panther similarly showed indifference to the presence of sheep, fattened pigs and grazing calves. The Quaker ideal, the article explained, and yet the yearning was wider than that: co-existence was what we all wanted — peaceful co-existence. Yet that was the very thing that continued to elude us. The world was a vale of tears — of conflict and competition, of injustice, of unkindness and exploitation. And he had to deal with a small corner of all that, all day, every day; that was the furrow he was expected to plough. Why? Why was he a detective rather than something else? What had happened to those great ambitions he had had when he was a youth? The world lay before him in those days, infinitely promising and accommodating. He could have been a healer of some sort; he could have been a doctor or a dentist, or even a psychotherapist, soothing the pain of others. He could have been something creative: a painter or sculptor, or carpenter working with wood — somebody who at least *made* something. But he was not; he was a functionary in the Department of Sensitive Crimes investigating why somebody should have dumped rotten fish on somebody else's car; why somebody should have sought to destroy another's professional reputation; why somebody should be inclined to harm another in any of the inventive ways we have of making others unhappy. He was an avenger of minor nastiness, a provider of anodynes and sticking plasters for imperfect and incorrigible humanity — nothing more than that.

Art was the opposite of all that. Art was all about the finer feelings of life. Art was about feeling and

131

passion and the understanding of beauty. An artist left something behind; he would leave nothing, not a trace — unless one counted those files on which Carl would have stamped 'Case Closed'. That was a legacy of sorts, Ulf supposed: a minor resolution in the affairs of men, and there were many whose work did not even involve that.

He finished his lamb, gnawing at the bones to get at the last scraps. That came with being single, he told himself. One did things that one would not do if there were others about; one stopped caring. So he gnawed at the bones when he had lamb or chicken; he sometimes licked his plate to get the last drops of a particularly tasty gravy; he blew his nose on the paper napkins he used at the table rather than fetch a handkerchief from the bedroom or a tissue from the bathroom. And why not? Manners were for the comfort of others, and if there were no others present, then why bother?

He sometimes wondered what would happen if he were to live with somebody again. He would have to change — he accepted that. He would have to stop singing tunelessly in the shower; he would have to put crockery away rather than let it dry on the side of the sink; he would have to stop hanging his shirts over the bath once he had washed them. He would do all that for Anna — that and more, far more. He allowed himself to think of Anna being with him; he imagined her at the table with him, talking about their day, discussing their plans for the weekend — dinner out, perhaps, a walk in the country, time together doing nothing in particular, building up memories of the ordinary moments of life that they would be able to share years from now, and laugh about; the secrets of lovers who have spent the years together.

That was territory into which he should not stray; he knew that. He had erected a wall between himself and any vision of that and he knew that he should not breach it, however appealing the prospect on the other side of the barrier. That was a barrier of morality: it was as simple as that. It was the same barrier that prevented us from helping ourselves to the possessions of others, that stopped us from speaking our mind when we knew that our words would cause offence or hurt, that made us show restraint in a hundred different contexts when our nagging ego would rail against the constraints of reason. Anna was out of bounds, and although it made him want to cry out in frustration at the unfairness of life, that was where she would have to remain. So find somebody else, he told himself; the best cure for one lover is another — that cynical, seemingly heartless advice is absolutely true, of course it is.

He cleared the plates away and rather than stack them in the sink, as he often did, he washed them and put them in the rack to dry. Then he sat down in his living room to watch the second half of a football match, broadcast from Rotterdam. Sweden was playing against the Netherlands and one section of the stadium was a sea of blue flags, marking the place where the Swedish fans were seated. There were waves of sound from the crowd, collective gasps and roars, and an excited stream of words from the Swedish commentator. Sweden was doing well, and the blue flags fluttered with renewed vigour. Ulf was not really interested. He wanted Sweden to win, of course, but it seemed that they were doing so already, without his support or encouragement. And as for the football itself, he acknowledged that it was balletic, but he could not work himself up over this artificial contest, nor feel anything but impatience, or even distaste for the adulation lavished on these single-minded young men.

The game came to an end with a Swedish victory. The camera showed a group of ecstatic young Swedish fans, tears of joy streaming down cheeks otherwise unsullied by age or disappointment. 'Our boys played thoughtfully,' said the Swedish manager. 'Strategy pays off.'

Yes, thought Ulf, strategy paid off. You could go through life without a strategy — as so many did — and you would get nowhere. Strategy paid off, and he should devise one.

He looked at his watch. He was feeling tired, as he had woken earlier than usual that morning. If he took Martin for his final walk of the day, it would be time to go to bed when they returned. He might read for a few minutes before dropping off.

'Martin,' he said. 'Walk?'

Martin was dozing, his eyes half closed, so he did not lip-read *walk*. Ulf got up and crossed the kitchen floor to where he was lying on his blanket. The dog looked up expectantly as he saw Ulf approach. Now Ulf leaned forward and articulated the word *walk*, making sure that Martin could see his lips.

The effect was immediate. Martin gave a high-pitched bark, rose to his feet, and jumped up in an attempt to lick Ulf's face. The protective shield around his head — the horizontal lampshade, to all intents and purposes like an exaggerated Elizabethan collar — bumped up against Ulf, while Martin's tongue, moist and pink, hung uselessly out of his mouth. Ulf

134

laughed, and Martin, who interpreted human lips in laughter as a good sign, gave another bark. The lead was fetched and they set off.

It was later than usual, and the streets were quiet. The park was kept open at night, a place of shadows and quiet corners as appreciated by those on romantic trysts as by those engaged in clandestine dealings. For the most part, though, the park's nocturnal visitors were, like Ulf, local people taking their dogs for their evening exercise. Ulf did not see anybody when he first entered the park and slipped Martin off his lead. 'Don't go too far,' he said as Martin shot off into the undergrowth.

Ulf began to tread his usual route around the park's perimeter. He had not gone far before he saw a figure emerging from a small clump of trees. Ulf tensed: there were occasional robberies in the park, perpetrated, for the most part, by drug addicts or opportunistic thieves, but his policeman's instinct quickly told him the figure approaching him was entirely innocent. And it was: it was Stig, the man whom he saw here from time to time, the doctor who had witnessed with him the unfortunate meeting of Martin and the aggressive squirrel.

'It's you,' said Stig, as he came out of the shadows. 'Where's Martin?'

Ulf pointed to the bushes. 'Somewhere in there. And Olav?'

Olav was Stig's dog. 'Back there,' said Stig, with a toss of the head towards another cluster of shrubs.

'Martin's recovering very well,' said Ulf. 'There was damage to his nose.'

'Ouch,' said Stig.

'Yes, but the vet — '

'Håkansson?' enquired Stig.

'Yes. Dr Håkansson said that he should be all right.' Ulf paused. 'The surgery was successful — up to a point.'

'Oh yes?' enquired Stig.

'His nose was almost completely detached,' Ulf explained. 'Håkansson had to sew it back on.'

'Tricky.'

'Very. And although he got it back on, it seems to be . . . well, it seems to be upside down.'

Stig showed his surprise. 'What?' he exclaimed.

'The nostrils used to point down,' said Ulf. 'Now they point upwards.'

'Can he breathe?' asked Stig.

'He breathes just fine,' said Ulf. 'I don't think it makes any difference to him.'

Stig thought for a few moments. 'What about in the rain? What if he's running about in the rain? Won't the water go down into the nostrils?'

Ulf had not thought of this. 'I suppose it might,' he said. 'On the other hand, if he's swimming, it'll be as if he has a tiny snorkel.'

Stig laughed. 'I doubt if it matters much to him.' He looked over his shoulder and lowered his voice. 'Actually, Ulf, I'm rather glad you turned up. There's something going on back there. Somebody's lurking in the bushes.'

Ulf followed his glance. In the unlit park, the trees and bushes were no more than dark shapes, bulky and clumped in clusters. At night one kept to the path and did not venture into these dim zones.

Ulf felt vaguely uncomfortable. Stig probably wanted him to investigate, and yet there was a limit to what any policeman could do. If you saw a crime

136

being committed, of course, you would do what it took to stop it, but you couldn't do everything. 'Probably harmless,' he said. 'Teenagers smoking weed. That sort of thing. It's hard to stop them.'

Stig kept his voice lowered. 'No, it's not kids. I didn't get a proper look, but I think it's somebody with a weapon of some sort — a stick or spear.'

Ulf sighed. He could not ignore this. It was highly unlikely that anybody would be lurking in the park with a spear, but he could soon find out.

'I'll go and take a look,' he said.

He had not intended to ask Stig to accompany him, but when the doctor offered to do so, Ulf accepted. If anybody was up to no good in the bushes, then two people would be safer than one.

They made their way quietly in the direction in which Stig had pointed, and were soon surrounded by the foliage of various large shrubs. In the darkness, the size of the trees and bushes was exaggerated, as was the shadow the plants threw in the wan moonlight. Ulf shivered — this was a perfect spot for somebody to lie in wait for a victim. A quick movement, a thrust of a knife, and the victim would fall unseen by any witness, to be found by a morning walker, long after the assailant had made good his escape. This was how murders happened: quickly, darkly, when there were no eyes to see what was happening. He stopped himself. It was ridiculous to think in those terms. Nobody was going to murder anybody.

Suddenly there was a cry. It was a shriek, really, and it could have issued from a man or a woman. It was a cry of surprise, tinged with terror.

Ulf spun round. The noise came from behind them. He bumped into Stig, who was turning round too, and who now said, 'Over there, Ulf!'

A figure burst out of a clump of bushes and was upon them before they had time to react. It was a man, and he pushed Stig aside before colliding with Ulf. Shoulder met shoulder, and Ulf, unprepared, was taken off balance. He fell to the ground, the softness of leaf mulch breaking his fall. Stig shouted out something he did not quite catch, but that sounded like 'You!' or 'You there!'

Ulf was clambering to his feet when they heard a sharp popping sound. Then out of the shadows came another figure, a smaller one, carrying the weapon that Stig had seen. But it was not a spear — it was a rifle, and the popping sound had been the sound of its being discharged at the fleeing man who had knocked Ulf down.

The second figure stopped, and Ulf saw who it was. It was Mrs Högfors.

She came up to Ulf. 'It's you, Ulf! Are you all right?'

Ulf's astonishment was such that he struggled to speak. Eventually he managed, 'Yes, it's me. And you . . . What are *you* doing here?' He gestured to the rifle. 'And that?'

Mrs Högfors lowered the rifle. 'That man,' she said, 'approached me with a cucumber.' She paused for her words to sink in. Then she repeated, 'A cucumber!'

Ulf shook his head. 'Extraordinary,' he said. 'But what were you doing here with that?' He pointed at the rifle.

Mrs Högfors shifted from foot to foot. 'I was taking a walk.'

Stig interrupted. 'That's the man,' he said. 'That lunatic with the cucumber.'

'Possibly,' said Ulf.

138

'Definitely,' said Stig. 'There won't be more than one man going around threatening people with cucumbers.'

'He certainly threatened me,' said Mrs Högfors. 'But then he saw my air rifle and he took flight. I managed to get one shot at him, but I'm not sure if I hit him.'

Ulf reached out to take the rifle from his neighbour. 'You can't wander around with an air rifle,' he said. 'And you certainly can't fire it at people.' To this he added, as if by way of afterthought, 'This is Sweden.'

'Even if they threaten you with cucumbers?' challenged Mrs Högfors.

'Even then,' said Ulf. 'And what were you doing with it in the first place?'

Mrs Högfors was silent.

'You have to tell me,' said Ulf, his tone becoming firm. 'I'm asking you now as a police officer. I'm not asking you as my neighbour.'

The effect of this warning was dramatic. Mrs Högfors started to explain herself, but stumbled after the first few words. Then she started to cry. 'You mustn't be cross with me, Ulf,' she sobbed. 'You mustn't arrest me.'

Ulf immediately relented. The firm tone was replaced by one of concern. 'Nobody's going to arrest anybody,' he said.

'That's the problem,' muttered Stig. 'Nobody gets arrested these days.'

Ulf ignored this. 'But you must tell me,' he continued, 'why you were carrying this rifle. I just want to know.'

Mrs Högfors extracted a handkerchief from her coat pocket and blew her nose loudly. 'I was dealing with the squirrel,' she said. 'The one who attacked Martin.'

Ulf stared at her in complete astonishment. 'You were going to shoot a squirrel?'

'Not *a* squirrel, Ulf — *the* squirrel. The one responsible for Martin's injuries.'

Ulf took a deep breath. 'You can't take the law into your own hands,' he said. 'That's vigilantism. It's not allowed. And besides, firing an air rifle in a park is an offence.'

Stig joined in. 'It's as well she had it, though. If she hadn't, then that lunatic could have . . . well, heaven knows what might have happened.'

Ulf sighed. 'I think we all need to get home,' he said. 'These things are better discussed in the clear light of day.'

He did not hand the rifle back, but tucked it under his arm as he called to Martin. Then, once the dog was back on the lead, he escorted Mrs Högfors back to her flat.

'I'm keeping this rifle,' he said to her at the door.

She did not object, and said goodnight in a cheerful way, as if nothing at all had happened. Ulf returned to his own flat, where he had a shower before settling Martin for the night and retiring to his bed with the unfinished article on the *Peaceable Kingdom* theme. He did not read much, as he was tired, and he nodded off with comfortable images in his mind of the lion and the lamb, the wolf and its prey, the tiny bird and the proud eagle — each pair a metaphor for what, in a much better world, might be.

11

The Gardens of Childhood

The following day, Ulf had an appointment shortly after lunch with his therapist, Dr Svensson. The therapist was a natty dresser, and the moment Ulf entered his consulting room, he noticed Dr Svensson's shoes. This was the second pair of fine English shoes he had encountered within a week. There had been that pair of Oxfords worn by the elegantly dressed Anders Kindgren, and now here was a pair of tobacco-coloured half-brogues, once again of a characteristic English cut, sported by Ulf's therapist. He would need to take a closer look to identify their maker, of course, but that was difficult to do discreetly. Shoes, Ulf felt, spoke volumes: no shoe was silent when it came to making revealing statements about its owner.

Dr Svensson followed his gaze. He might not have had Ulf's ability to read shoes, but he was adept at reading eyes. What the eyes did in a few seconds, Dr Svensson once wrote, tells you more than many hours on the couch.

'You're interested in my shoes,' the therapist said.

Ulf looked up, embarrassed. 'I'm sorry. I was staring.'

'Nothing wrong with staring,' said Dr Svensson. 'Indeed, we should stare more, rather than less. We need to dwell on our surroundings a bit more, rather than taking them for granted.' He paused. 'I like my shoes.'

141

Ulf wondered how many people *disliked* their shoes. There were, he supposed, many who had to make do with shoes that they would not choose to wear, had they the choice — people who were too poor to own anything but the humblest shoes, people who were obliged to wear hand-me-downs — people who had no shoes at all. We sometimes forgot about poverty in our sated societies.

'You're thinking about shoes?' asked Dr Svensson.

Ulf admitted he was. 'I was thinking about how there are people who have to make do with inadequate shoes. There must be many — not here in Sweden, but in poorer countries.'

'There undoubtedly are,' said Dr Svensson. 'And even in Sweden there'll be some parents who don't have the money to buy their children shoes that fit. We're rich — but not that rich.'

'And supportive,' added Ulf, 'but not that supportive.' He sighed. There were people who did not have papers; people on the margins for one reason or another. No society on earth, it seemed, had solved the problem of poverty; and the image of *The Peaceable Kingdom* came to him, and he looked away in sadness.

Dr Svensson, though, was still thinking of shoes. 'I've always longed to have a pair of made-to-measure shoes,' he said, a note of wistfulness creeping into his voice. 'They make lasts just for you — exact models of your feet. They build the leather around them and the shoes fit perfectly. It's like walking around with gloves on your feet.'

'Very nice,' said Ulf.

'But expensive,' added Dr Svensson.

'Nice things often are.'

That was true, said Dr Svensson, but one should not fall into the trap of thinking that material things could be the solution to the pain of living. 'People talk about shopping therapy,' he said. 'And there's a scintilla of truth in it — but just a scintilla. Treating yourself to some longed-for purchase provides a very passing hit — a brief boost to the pleasure centres of the brain, and then, *pouf*, it evaporates. You might feel better for about ten minutes, and then you're back to where you were before, or even in a worse place. The pleasure centres may be clamouring for more, and it becomes a vicious circle.'

'I don't care much for shopping,' said Ulf. 'I buy things I need, and I don't take much pleasure in buying them.'

Dr Svensson smiled. 'I think we should get back to your relationship with your brother,' he said. 'Last time you were here, you mentioned that you were going to see him. I sensed a degree of reluctance on your part — a certain dread, in fact.'

Dread, thought Ulf. There was indeed dread. He dreaded going to see Björn because he always came away feeling so annoyed. Try as he might, he could not control the irritation that his brother caused him. This was in spite of every effort on his part to ignore the inflammatory statements Björn so delighted in making, knowing full well how much they annoyed Ulf. He tried, biting his tongue metaphorically and, at times, literally, as Björn waxed eloquent on the latest policy proposals of the Moderate Extremists.

'How did the visit go?' asked Dr Svensson.

'Not very well.'

Dr Svensson settled back in his chair. 'That doesn't surprise me,' he said. 'And I take it that you weren't

143

surprised either.'

'I was not,' said Ulf. 'I know exactly how a visit to my brother will end. We have a script, you see.'

This appealed to Dr Svensson. 'Ah yes, a script — how many of our relationships in this life proceed along the lines of a script. The play's all there, stage directions and all — we merely say the lines.'

'Really?' asked Ulf. 'We can't write our own parts?'

Dr Svensson thought for a few moments. 'To an extent we can,' he said. 'But most of us seem to prefer a predetermined script in so many of our relationships. It's easier that way — and perhaps that's the reason why we do it.'

Ulf said nothing. Dr Svensson was almost always right, he found. He *understood*.

Now the therapist asked whether Ulf would like to work on his relationship with his brother. 'Perhaps you're tired of the script,' he said. 'Perhaps you want to talk to him in a different register.'

That was possible, thought Ulf, but it was difficult given the confrontational nature of Björn's world view. 'I don't think he'd allow me to press any reset button,' said Ulf. 'Our conversation travels along the same lines every time we meet. He says something outrageous; I try to ignore it. He says something more controversial in order to goad me into a response, and I invariably rise to the bait. Then he smirks.'

'That's because he's got you where he wants you,' said Dr Svensson. 'It's a power game. And it stems from the dynamics of your childhood. He sees you in a certain way because that is how he saw you when you were small boys. I'd venture a guess that you were the responsible one; that you were the one who gained the approbation of the adults. That you were the one

144

who kept your nose clean and never got into trouble. Am I correct?'

Ulf nodded. That was how it had been.

'And he was the maverick, the one who liked to challenge authority?'

'Yes. He was always getting into trouble.'

'Precisely. And what is he doing now? Why has he chosen to join these . . . these so-called Moderate Extremists?' As he uttered the name of the party, Dr Svensson wrinkled his nose in distaste.

Ulf pointed out that Björn had not just joined the Moderate Extremists — he had founded them. 'It's all his creation,' he said. 'Take him out of the equation, and what are you left with? A rag-bag of eccentrics and obsessives.'

'And people who are unhappy,' said Dr Svensson. 'Lost souls who think their unhappiness will be cured by being part of some movement.' He paused. 'And sometimes it will, you know. It gives them the sense of identity they've been missing all along. They feel they're nobody and then, suddenly, they're some-body.'

'My brother's not unhappy,' said Ulf. 'He's actu-ally rather pleased with himself. He was full of a new policy he'd cooked up to tackle obesity. He's been concerned over the effects of rising levels of obesity and thinks that this might be tackled by imposing higher taxes on overweight people.'

Dr Svensson laughed. 'The King of Tonga went on a diet not all that long ago. He needed it. But he put the whole country on a diet with him.'

'The Moderate Extremists think this is a vote-win-ner,' said Ulf. 'But frankly I think it's absurd. It's tactless and unfair. Many people can't help their

145

weight — it's not something you should blame them for.'

'I agree,' said Dr Svensson. 'It's the same with smoking. You can't blame people for smoking because smoking is not the result of a free choice. The first cigarette may involve free choice — made in ignorance, perhaps, of the addictive power of nicotine — and thereafter you can't help yourself. You are trapped as firmly as is any innocent who walks into an opium den thinking it's a sauna. The craving may be too strong.' He returned to the subject of Björn. 'Have you discussed your childhood with him?'

'Often,' said Ulf. 'It comes up all the time.'

'That's very significant,' said Dr Svensson. 'That suggests that it's a live issue for him. That explains why he's still fighting the battles of childhood.' He looked at Ulf with the air of one explaining an inevitable and immutable physical process — the movement of the planets, or the effect of gravity. If Björn was fighting a battle, that battle was an ancient one, as eternal as the movement of the tides. 'You do know, don't you, that siblings will always have a very different view of their shared childhood? Sometimes the differences are so profound that they could be talking about different families altogether.'

Ulf thought about this. It was true: Björn's recollections of what had happened in their childhood was often quite different from his own. Now he remembered something: Bergman films.

'You're right,' he said.

Dr Svensson inclined his head. Of course he was right.

Ulf smiled. 'The other day, you know, he was on the radio. A phone-in programme.'

146

Dr Svensson said that he often heard him on the radio. 'They like interviewing him. They like him to say things that get the public phoning in.'

'Yes,' said Ulf. 'It's often his supporters who call. They're a sort of Greek chorus that follows him round.'

'Hah,' said Dr Svensson. 'The citizens of Thebes expressing their views.'

'This was a personal interview,' Ulf went on. 'The Moderate Extremists were barely mentioned. They wanted to talk to Björn about his childhood and early years — his time at university.'

Dr Svensson was interested. 'Did he mention you?'

'In passing,' said Ulf. 'Which suited me: I have no desire to be under the public gaze. Who does?'

Dr Svensson smiled. 'Oh, many do, believe me. Many crave it. They read about these appalling, shallow celebrities and think how wonderful it would be to be one of them. To be famous for being famous — that sort of thing.'

'Not for me,' said Ulf.

'Of course not. You're not that type. But this programme . . . what about it?'

'It was that programme where people are asked for their six favourite pieces of music, and the conversation goes on around that. Then they start talking about what books they like to read, films they like, and so on.'

Dr Svensson said he had often heard it. 'It's very revealing,' he said, 'about what people would like people to think they are, rather than what they really are. And your brother? What did he say about you? What was this passing reference to you?'

'I may have mentioned my uncle to you — the one

in Stockholm; I think I have. Well, he was the one who did well with a chemical process he had invented. He was a bachelor — although there was always a woman friend in attendance. We used to go and stay with him when we were young. He had a very large garden and we were given the freedom to run around in it.'

Dr Svensson looked out of the window. 'The gardens of our childhood are always large,' he said.

Ulf thought about this. Every so often Dr Svensson came up with an aphorism that Ulf believed he coined then and there. The previous week he had said, 'We are all archaeologists of our individual pasts,' and had followed this with 'Each of us, in our own particular way, is Odysseus.' Now there was this observation on childhood gardens.

Ulf continued, 'It was an idyllic time, as you might imagine. An indulgent uncle, a sprawling garden with clumps of trees and paths for riding your bicycle on, and a treehouse at one stage — although it fell down one summer and Björn had to be taken to hospital. They were worried that he had broken his arm, but it was only a pulled muscle, or something like that.'

Ulf saw that Dr Svensson was making a note. It was a single word: *treehouse.*

'There was one drawback,' said Ulf. 'And that was the Bergman films. Our uncle had a private cinema in the house — an amazing thing in those days. Nowadays people have those large television screens and big armchairs—'

'And popcorn,' interjected Dr Svensson.

'Yes, and popcorn. But this was the real thing, with a projector and a pull-down screen. It would have been very exciting for us, if only a different sort of film were to be shown. But it was always Bergman.

148

Every day. Every single day.'

Dr Svensson made another note: *Bergman*.

'Our uncle was Bergman's biggest fan. He must have known every word of the scripts. He must have known every single moment of them. And he insisted that we sit there with him every day, for what seemed to us like interminable hours, and watch *Wild Straw-berries* or *The Seventh Seal*, or whatever it was that day. He had his own prints of the entire Bergman oeuvre, and at the end of each film he would sit there and tell us: 'We must think about this for a little while, boys.' And so we sat there, my brother and I, for quite some time, while we were meant to be thinking about Bergman. Then our uncle would stand up, rub his hands, and announce that his housekeeper would serve us a Coca-Cola and a piece of cake if we went to the kitchen. That was the moment of release, and I still think of it when I see a can of Coca-Cola. Freedom. Release.

'But the point of all this, is that my brother said on the radio the other day that he loved Bergman films. He said that he had been introduced to them as a child, together with his brother. I could hardly believe my ears. He said we looked forward to visiting an uncle who was a Bergman fan and who had a small private cinema. He said we loved watching them and would re-enact *The Seventh Seal* afterwards in the garden, pretending to be medieval knights. But we did not. We just did not. I have never re-enacted *The Seventh Seal* in my life — and neither has he.'

Dr Svensson remained silent when Ulf finished. After a few moments, he snapped his notebook shut. 'We shall need to talk about this at greater length,' he said. 'We don't have time now, and there is much

149

material there that needs to be considered.'

Ulf did not say anything. His therapy was being sponsored by his employers: was it a proper use of public money? He sighed.

Dr Svensson heard the sigh, and fixed Ulf with an intense gaze. 'You're still unhappy, Ulf,' he said quietly. 'There are sighs within you that have yet to emerge. But they will — they will. Give them time. All of us have sighs within us that will eventually come to the surface with time. Time. Time and patience.'

Ulf closed his eyes; he did not like Dr Svensson to look at him like that, as it gave him nowhere to go. Was he unhappy? He did not think so. So was he happy, then? He was not sure. Sometimes he was, and sometimes he was not. Was that normal? He suspected it was. He suspected he was perfectly normal, but he did not want to say as much. He wanted Dr Svensson, whom he liked, to be happy. And Dr Svensson, he suspected, would not be happy if he found out that Ulf was happy, because, in a curious way, he thrived upon the unhappiness of others — it was his justification, the reason he got out of bed in the morning. Björn, of course, was happy — there was no doubt about that — because he derived such pleasure from creating controversy. And rewriting the history of his childhood. That evidently made him happy. And he had his Greek chorus of supporters who echoed and endorsed everything he said. That would make anybody happy, presumably — to have people around one singing one's praises. And yet perhaps he was not really happy because an appetite for adoration could never be overcome — like the material appetites that the Buddhists said could, by their very nature, only be assuaged, not satisfied.

150

It was all very complicated, but it was now time to get back to the office.

★ ★ ★

Blomquist was waiting for him.

'The photograph you asked for,' he said, putting a piece of paper on Ulf's desk. 'I downloaded it from the internet. Lennart Solander.'

From the other side of the room, Erik, who had caught the name, called out, 'Solander? Lennart Solander? *The Heart's Reasons*?'

Ulf had not seen the film, but he had heard of it. And he had heard that Lennart Solander had been responsible for its massive success. 'Yes,' he said. 'That Lennart Solander.'

Anna joined in. 'And *To the End of the Earth*. He played the man with Tourette's. He was amazing.'

'He's a very fine actor,' said Carl. 'He steps right into a role. Some actors just play themselves — he doesn't. He becomes the person he's portraying.'

Ulf studied the photograph. A good-looking man in his late thirties was smiling into the camera. He was wearing a dinner jacket and bow-tie, and was holding some sort of award — a trophy in the form of a small golden palm frond. In the background was a large, highly coloured banner: *Television Awards — Recognising Excellence*.

Lennart Solander had perfectly regular teeth, exposed in a smile of satisfaction over his award. He had a head of luxuriant chestnut hair, smartly barbered, and eyebrows that looked equally carefully managed. He had a friendly, approachable look.

Blomquist waited for Ulf's reaction.

151

Ulf was pleased. 'Good,' he said. 'Now, The Divine Apollo.'

Carl looked up. 'You and Blomquist going off to a gay bar?' he asked.

'Yes,' said Ulf. 'Care to join us?'

Anna laughed. 'I'll come too.'

'You're not their sort,' said Carl. 'Sorry.'

Ulf said, 'You're being very juvenile.'

He and Blomquist left. The Divine Apollo was some distance away, on the other side of the city, and so they travelled in Ulf's Saab. Blomquist was silent at first, looking out of the car at the streets that were wet from a passing belt of rain. Then he tuned to Ulf and asked him whether he had heard anything about the anti-inflammatory properties of turmeric.

Ulf had read an advertisement to that effect, but had been uncertain as to whether to believe the claims that had been made for the spice.

'There's a lot of evidence now,' said Blomquist. 'People who take it swear by it.'

'I suppose that's the best evidence there is,' said Ulf. 'A good outcome should be pretty persuasive.'

Blomquist agreed. 'Of course, the drug companies don't want people to use things like turmeric. There's no profit in turmeric — or any other natural remedy — for them. They have a vested interest in questioning any evidence showing that natural remedies work.' He made a dismissive gesture. 'They don't care about anything but profits — making as much money as possible, as quickly as possible, out of human suffering.'

Ulf guided the Saab through traffic, thinking, I'm driving this beautiful silver-grey car on my way to a gay bar with a man who's going on about turmeric.

152

Would he ever have dreamed ten years ago, he asked himself, that he would be doing this — that the planets would align so that this exact concatenation of events would occur at this precise point?

'They have to make a profit,' Ulf said absent-mindedly. 'Nobody does anything for nothing.' Even as he said this, though, he realised that it was not entirely true. There were plenty of people who did things for nothing; some people devoted their entire lives to serving others for very little or no reward: doctors, nurses, teachers who went off to places where they were needed simply because they were needed.

'Oh, I know that,' said Blomquist. 'But they make immense profits, you know — immense. Some of these drugs can cost an arm and a leg. Some of them over one million dollars a year for each patient. One million dollars.'

'That's not good,' said Ulf.

'No, it isn't,' said Blomquist. 'The pharmaceutical companies sometimes target these very rare diseases — they call them orphan diseases — develop something to treat them, and then charge the earth for the drug. It's a deliberate strategy.'

'Very bad,' said Ulf.

Blomquist tapped the dashboard to emphasise his point. 'So there are people who know that their lives could be saved if only they could get the drug, but they can't afford it. The company says: if you don't have the money, you die.'

'Of course, the companies have to spend money on developing drugs,' Ulf pointed out. 'I read somewhere that one of these companies spent a billion dollars on a drug they developed, and then failed at the final hurdle. The thing didn't work. One billion dollars.

153

They have to get that back somehow, I suppose.'

Blomquist answered by pointing out that nobody had to develop turmeric — it was already there. 'And it's not expensive, you know — although you shouldn't go for the cheaper stuff. You should take at least a 1,000 milligram dose with 5 milligrams of black pepper. That aids absorption.' He paused. 'Or is it 5 milligrams per 500 milligram dose, which would make it 10 milligrams per 1,000 milligrams of turmeric?'

'I don't know, Blomquist. You raised the subject.'

'I wouldn't want to mislead you,' said Blomquist.

'I'll bear it in mind,' said Ulf.

They drove on in silence and on impulse, Ulf leaned forward to turn on the radio. If he did that, he thought, Blomquist might stop talking about supplements and drug companies. He found a station playing Bach, and he adjusted the volume so that although conversation might still be possible, it would not be easy.

'Bach,' said Ulf.

Blomquist listened for a few moments. Then, his voice raised, he asked, 'Which one?'

'Johann Sebastian Bach,' said Ulf. 'He's the default Bach.'

Blomquist grinned. 'Do you know how many Bachs there were? I mean, Bach musicians? I'll tell you. Over fifty.'

'That's a lot of Bachs,' said Ulf.

'Johann Sebastian Bach himself had twenty children, you know. Ten survived and became musicians. Music runs in families, obviously; ability to do mathematics, too, I think. I know somebody who . . .'

Ulf stopped listening — not out of discourtesy, but because his mind was drifting. He could drive and

154

think, but he could not drive, think and listen to Blomquist at the same time, and so he stopped following what Blomquist was saying about the inheritability of musical talent, and he thought, instead, of the investigation and their first exploratory steps.

The only information they had at present was that the putative owner of the painting had looked like a well-known actor, and that he might frequent The Divine Apollo bar. If you invite somebody to a bar — and he had invited Ivar — then there is a reasonable possibility that you know the bar in question. And so Ulf had decided that he would speak to the staff at The Divine Apollo, show them the photograph of Lennart Solander, and ask them whether there was any customer who looked like him. It was a long shot, but it was not unusual at the beginning of an investigation to start with unlikely lines of enquiry and then to find something that allowed one to progress to something more substantial.

They were now nearing the bar. This was in an affluent part of town, where fashionable coffee bars and hair salons jostled with upmarket delis and expensive restaurants. The Divine Apollo was on a corner, and was marked by a small rainbow flag hanging limply over the front door and a painted sign portraying Apollo with his lyre, backed by a benign and blazing yellow sun.

Blomquist gazed at the sign as Ulf parked the Saab.

'Was Apollo gay?' he asked. 'The original god, I mean — that fellow on the sign over there.'

'I think so,' said Ulf. He thought, and it came back to him. In his late teens he had been fascinated with Greek mythology and had spent long hours reading stories of endless heroic and impossible deeds. 'Things

155

were pretty fluid in those days. The gods were pretty even-handed in their affections — Zeus was keen on Ganymede, and Heracles was fond of his page. Apollo had Hyacinth until he killed him in a discus accident.'

'Unfortunate,' said Blomquist.

'Yes,' said Ulf, switching off the engine. 'I think a wind came up and diverted the discus. It could have happened to anyone.'

Ulf locked the car and together with Blomquist made his way through the front door of The Divine Apollo. It was unnaturally dark inside, blinds having been pulled down over the windows that looked out onto the street. Subdued lighting and muted colours gave the bar the feel of an expensive, impeccably tasteful nightclub. There was music in the background, but it was unobtrusive and, again, very tasteful. There were few customers, although one group, of five men and two women, seated in an alcove near the bar itself, was making its presence felt with raised voices and laughter.

They went up to the bar. From the other end, a barman, a man in his late twenties or early thirties, connecting a barrel of beer to a pipe, signalled that he would be with them when he'd finished his current chore.

The barman greeted them with a welcoming smile. 'Can I get you two gentlemen something to drink?'

Ulf declined, as did Blomquist. 'We're here on business,' Ulf said.

The barman smiled again. 'The manager's out at present,' he said. 'If you come back at five, he should be here then.'

Ulf shook his head. 'We're happy to talk to you.'

He reached into his pocket and brought out his

156

police identity card. The barman looked at it and frowned. 'The Department of Sensational Crimes?'

Blomquist corrected him. '*Sensitive* Crimes. The Department of *Sensitive* Crimes.'

'Sorry,' said the barman. 'The light's not very good in here.'

'We wanted to find out whether you could identify one of your regular customers,' said Ulf. 'Or rather, somebody who *might* be one of your regulars.'

The barman stiffened. 'I hope he's not in trouble — whoever he is.'

'No,' said Ulf. 'Not exactly. But we feel he may be able to help us in one of our current inquiries.'

The barman nodded. 'I'll do what I can,' he said. 'We like to co-operate with you people. We've not been in any trouble. We don't allow drugs.'

'Quite right,' said Blomquist. 'And, by the way, I think I know you. Or I know who you are.'

The barman looked confused.

'Your family name's Larsson. Am I right?'

'Yes,' said the barman. 'I'm Bobby Larsson.'

'You were a good ice hockey player,' said Blomquist. 'I've seen you play. A little while ago.'

'That was me,' said the barman. 'Then I had an injury. My knee.'

Blomquist's compliment was appreciated, Ulf noticed, and he could see that the barman was ready to co-operate. Extracting the printed photograph from his pocket, Ulf laid it on the bar. 'Do you have a customer who resembles this man? Anybody come to mind when you look at it? Not this actual man, of course — somebody who bears a resemblance to him.'

The barman studied the photograph. Then he

157

looked at Ulf, a smile playing about his lips. 'This is Lennart Solander,' he said.

'Yes,' said Ulf. 'We know that.'

'So, you want me to identify a customer who looks like Lennart,' said the barman.

Ulf confirmed this. 'Take your time,' he said. 'Somebody who resembles him. Maybe the same hairstyle, face, whatever. Who does this remind you of?'

'Lennart,' said the barman. 'This reminds me of Lennart. This is Lennart.'

Ulf was patient. 'I know that. It is Lennart Solander. We want to find somebody who looks like him.'

'Who comes in here?' asked the barman.

'Yes,' said Blomquist. 'You've got it.'

The barman's smile broadened. 'Lennart,' he said. 'You're looking for him.'

Ulf frowned. 'Somebody who looks just like him, not—'

'No,' said the barman, tapping the photograph. 'Lennart comes in here. Himself. Lennart Solander.'

Ulf and Blomquist exchanged glances.

'Oh,' said Ulf, after a few moments of silence. 'Oh, I see. So Lennart Solander comes in here. Does he live nearby?'

'Two streets away. We're his closest bar.'

Ulf folded up the picture and tucked it back in his pocket. 'Do you know his address?' he asked.

The barman's manner became guarded. 'I don't think I can give you that. Sorry. Working in a bar like this involves a certain amount of discretion, as you can imagine. There are still some people who make life hard for gay people.'

'We don't,' said Blomquist. 'And you can't complain about this city. It's gay-friendly through and

158

through. Everybody knows that.'

'Yes,' said the barman. 'But we've got those extreme right issues. Some people are still worried about them. So a bar still has to be a place where people can count on discretion — if they want it.'

'We're police,' said Ulf. 'And I can find out where Lennart lives by speaking to the local police office. It would just save a bit of time if you told us.'

The barman hesitated. Then, still a bit reluctantly, he reached for a piece of paper from under the counter and scribbled an address on it. He handed the paper to Ulf. 'Don't tell him I gave you his address.'

'Of course we won't,' said Blomquist.

'Lennart's a good man,' said the barman. 'He's kind. He doesn't boast about his success. He treats people well.'

'I'm sure he does,' said Ulf. 'And thank you for your help.'

The barman thought of something. 'Could I ask you a question?'

'Of course,' said Ulf.

'Could I join the police force? To be a detective, that is? Is it too late if you're thirty-two?'

Ulf laughed. 'Are you sure it's what you want?'

'Perhaps. Or yes, I suppose I am.'

'Then apply,' said Ulf.

'I'll sign your form for you,' said Blomquist. 'I'll write: *My mother knows this man's mother.*'

'That'll be a big help,' said Ulf.

The three of them laughed, and there was laughter, too, from the rowdy table in the alcove — as if in echo. Ulf glanced at those at the table, and one of the women glanced back at him, as if surprised that those standing some distance away should have heard their joke and joined in their laughter. Of course humour is infectious, he thought; we laugh when others laugh, even if we have not shared in what it was that made them laugh in the first place. Gloom's infectious too, he thought; not that he felt gloomy: this investigation was going remarkably well. They had found out that Lennart Solander was the owner of the painting. All they had to do now was to find out everything else.

12

Breathing Is Fairly Important

Ulf parked the silver Saab directly outside the expensive-looking apartment block. Looking at the building from the car, Ulf decided that this was exactly the right place for somebody like Lennart Solander to live. It was not ostentatious, and yet it was clearly well suited to somebody who might want security, quiet and protection from prying eyes.

'No surprises here,' he remarked.

Blomquist looked puzzled. He consulted the piece of paper on which the barman had written the address. 'It's the right place. This is what he wrote down.'

Ulf gazed up at the building. 'No, I meant this is exactly the right sort of place for somebody like Lennart Solander.'

'I suppose he's well off,' said Blomquist. 'Film people get well paid — if they get the work. It wouldn't be for me, though. Never.'

Ulf smiled. 'You might surprise yourself, Blomquist. I can see you doing well on the screen.'

Ulf was speaking playfully. He had a momentary vision of Blomquist in a film, suddenly going off-script to deliver a homily on vitamin D or turmeric, or the benefits of carotene. It would be unintentionally comic, which was often the most comic of all, and therefore possibly successful. Perhaps it was not as fanciful as all that.

And Blomquist, who had not detected the irony,

beamed with pleasure. 'Do you think so? I suppose I'd give it a try, if pushed.' He looked thoughtful. 'As it happens, I have a cousin — not a close cousin, you know, but a bit more remote — who's an actor. He's in television adverts. I'm sure you'll have seen him.'

Ulf looked doubtful.

Blomquist was undeterred. 'You probably have, but may have forgotten him.'

Ulf looked up at Lennart's building, wondering which windows were his.

'He's in one for lawnmowers that you ride on,' Blomquist went on. 'You know those things for people with very big lawns — or meadows, I suppose. They look like little tractors and some of them even have a reverse gear. Did you know that?'

'I did not, Blomquist. I didn't know that.'

'He got into it by accident, actually. He never went to acting school or anything like that. He married a woman who was a make-up artist in a television studio and he got his first job through her. She's a fantastic cook, by the way, and I think she should write a cookery book. Or a book about make-up. Both would be popular, I think. They met about eight years ago, and he started acting shortly after that. He's never looked back.'

'Ah. That's good. So many actors spend most of their time — what do they call it? — resting.'

Blomquist said that was undoubtedly true. 'It's an on-off profession. But not if you're in ads — there's always plenty of work for talented people. There'll always be lawnmowers to drive, cornflakes to eat and razors to use. My cousin was in an advertisement for safety razors once, but kept cutting himself. So they had to stop the filming and begin again because the blood got mixed up with the shaving foam and they couldn't have that. Imagine if the ad showed the actor bleeding all over the place. Imagine.'

'I don't think that would work.'

Ulf reflected on resting actors. Were there resting detectives? People waiting for a case to come along? Blomquist might rest a bit more, perhaps. He sighed.

Blomquist heard the sigh. 'Are you all right?' he asked.

Ulf wanted to say that he was not; that he wished Blomquist would talk just a little less; that he did not want to hear about Blomquist's remote relatives and their doings, on or off screen. He just did not want to hear about it. But kindness stopped him from saying any of this, because Blomquist was a good man at heart and Ulf had no desire to hurt him. So instead he replied, 'I'm fine, Blomquist. But I think we need to go in and see if we can find Lennart Solander.'

'Good idea,' said Blomquist. 'We shouldn't be sitting around here.'

Ulf looked at him. Sitting around? And whose fault was that? Who had been talking at interminable length about utterly irrelevant things, just like . . . Fidel Castro, thought Ulf. He could talk for hours, like Blomquist. He imagined Castro addressing a rally: a bearded Blomquist with that cap Castro wore with a red star in it, instead of which would be the symbol of the Malmö Police, and this Blomquist-Castro would be shaking his fist as he urged the cheering crowd to use turmeric.

He became aware that Blomquist was tugging at his sleeve.

'Over there, Ulf. Look.'

Lennart Solander had emerged from the front door

of the apartment and was beginning to walk purposefully down the street. He was dressed in casual clothes — a dark grey tracksuit — and was carrying a small sports bag.

'Going to the gym,' said Blomquist. 'Keeping trim for his next role. Perhaps something athletic — a sportsman, maybe, or a personal trainer. I think he'd make a convincing personal trainer because—'

Ulf opened the door. 'We'll talk to him.'

They hurried after the actor, whose stride suggested that his exercise period had already begun.

'Excuse me,' said Ulf, drawing abreast. 'Could we have a word?'

Lennart Solander turned to face his pursuers. There was a look of impatience on his face. But then he saw Blomquist's identity card being flashed before him, and his expression changed.

'Yes, of course.'

Ulf explained who they were. 'We'd like to talk to you about a painting.'

Lennart said nothing. Ulf noticed the side of his mouth twitching. He was stressed.

'A painting by Gaspard Dughet,' Ulf explained. 'You took it to an auction house.'

The blue eyes were fixed on Ulf. They shifted to Blomquist, then back again.

'Yes,' he said. 'I did. It's a painting I own with my brother and sister. What of it?'

'You didn't sell it?' asked Ulf.

Lennart hesitated. 'No. I didn't sell it.'

The eyes moved again. Now he was looking at neither of them. Then he turned to Ulf. 'I'm sorry, but I have an appointment with my personal trainer. I have to get to the gym. If I don't turn up on time, he'll

164

assume that I'm not coming.'

'You wouldn't want that,' said Blomquist.

Lennart's voice was cold. 'No, I wouldn't.'

'Could you possibly come to see us in the office?' asked Ulf.

Lennart took a few moments to reply. Then, when he did, his tone was warm and co-operative. 'Certainly. Where are you?'

Ulf explained the whereabouts of the Department of Sensitive Crimes.

'Sensitive Crimes?' asked Lennart. 'What does that mean?'

'What it says,' said Ulf.

'I've done nothing wrong,' muttered Lennart.

'I was not suggesting that,' Ulf reassured him. 'This is a routine enquiry.'

'I did not sell the painting,' Lennart said firmly. He looked at his watch. 'Look, I'm on set tomorrow and the day afterwards. The day after that?'

'Perfect,' said Ulf, and gave Lennart a card with the telephone number of the department. 'Call and make an appointment, if you don't mind.'

Lennart took the card, tucking it into a pocket. Then he started off again, leaving Ulf and Blomquist to return to the car.

'Guilty,' said Blomquist.

Ulf thought. 'Probably,' he said, and then added, 'Of original sin, at the very least. Like all of us — if you subscribe to that view of things, which I don't, I confess.'

'Is original sin a sin that nobody's thought of committing before?' asked Blomquist. And then laughed.

Blomquist thought his own joke very funny, and continued to laugh in the Saab. Ulf laughed in sympathy, although he thought the remark only mildly amusing. He turned on the radio. Bach was still there.

They listened together. The Suite No. 3 in D, with its solemn, dignified measures. Ulf thought: this is the opposite of chaos and confrontation. This is what I wish our city, our country, would be: calm, courteous, reflective, untroubled — all the things it used to be. But how could Sweden be all of that in a world that was so fretful and so riven by competition and dispute? He glanced at Blomquist.

'Do you believe the world is getting better, Blomquist?' he asked. It was a sudden question, unconnected with anything that had gone before, but Blomquist did not seem taken aback. 'Definitely,' he said. 'Look at life expectancy.'

'But what about life *expectations*?' asked Ulf.

'That's what I was thinking of,' said Blomquist.

It wasn't, thought Ulf, but no matter. Now he said, 'Thanks for all your help, Blomquist. I probably haven't said thank you before — not all that often. But thank you. I want you to know that I appreciate your assistance in these cases.'

Blomquist beamed. 'I'm proud to be able to help you, Ulf. And I think we make a great team.'

Ulf suppressed a smile. 'You're right,' he said. 'We get there in the end.'

'Even when we don't know what we're looking for,' said Blomquist. 'As in this case, where we don't know whether anybody did anything wrong; who they were; how they did it; or why. In fact, we know nothing at all, when it comes down to it.'

'There's nothing wrong with ignorance,' said Ulf. 'As a starting point, that is.'

166

* ★ ★

That afternoon, Ulf had to attend three senior management meetings, and had difficulty staying awake through two of them. These meetings were called every three months, and involved the discussion of administrative and logistical issues across all departments of the police force. Occasionally there was a subject of interest to Ulf, but for the most part the matters under discussion were exactly those with which he was least concerned. That afternoon, there was a lengthy discussion of photocopying facilities and of the way in which the cost of running photocopiers could be cut. A savings target had been set by the Commissioner, and in the course of implementing this, the Department of Commercial Crime had discovered that photocopying was the largest single item in the office budgets of most departments. The exception to this was the Department of Sensitive Crimes, where photocopying costs seemed to have been kept to a bare minimum. This had impressed the Commissioner, who had dryly observed that some of the other departments might do well to seek advice from Sensitive Crimes about how to keep costs in check.

This had not gone down well with the other departmental heads.

'The reason why their expenses are so low,' whispered the head of Traffic, 'is that they don't have anything to investigate. If you don't have anything to do, then your photocopying costs go right down.'

His neighbour at the table giggled. 'They have this fellow in their department — Erik — have you seen him? He's an actual filing clerk. Can you imagine? A filing clerk in this day and age! Anyway, I imagine

167

that he copies things out by hand like a medieval monk — a human photocopier.'

'Hah! I wonder if you can *adjust* him? Or whether he gets paper blockages from time to time.'

The Commissioner had thrown a discouraging look. He had heard the comments and did not approve. 'Perhaps you would tell the meeting, Ulf, how you keep your costs so low. Some of your colleagues, I think, might benefit from a bit of advice in that respect.'

Ulf had not been paying close attention, and was suddenly aware of narrowed eyes focused on him.

'In what respect?' he asked the Commissioner. 'We are very careful about costs across the board.'

'Photocopying,' prompted the Commissioner.

Ulf shrugged. 'That's simple. We read things.'

This brought a muted snigger from the head of the Department of Indecent Activities. He was always sniggering, thought Ulf.

'Now,' said the Commissioner. 'That's a very interesting point. Perhaps you might explain — for the benefit of those among us who have . . .' and here he looked at a sheet of figures in front of him ' . . . who have rather surprising photocopying expenses.'

Ulf thought quickly. Erik did not like the photocopier with which they had been issued as part of their inventory, and had put it in a cupboard. It still worked, Ulf believed, but its plug had been taken off by Carl to fit onto a kettle he had brought in to make tea. There was, Ulf believed, a ream or two of photocopying paper in the same cupboard, but that was now being used as notepaper by Anna.

'You read things,' said the Commissioner. 'Perhaps you might explain.'

168

Ulf smiled. There were certain Schadenfreude possibilities in any situation where the arrogant Department of Commercial Crime was put on the spot, but he was not one to provoke discord, and so he chose his words carefully.

'I'm not saying that one shouldn't use the photo-copier,' he began. 'I'm sure that those who do have a very good reason to do so. All I would say, though, is that many people, and I'm not suggesting that this applies to anybody in this room, have a tendency — just a slight tendency, of course, and I'm not blaming them in any way — to think that if you've photocop-ied something, you've internalised it.'

This was greeted with complete silence. Ulf real-ised that in spite of his cautious words, everyone in the room, with the exception of the Commissioner himself, believed his remark to be referring to him or her.

The silence was broken by the Commissioner. 'Very interesting indeed, Ulf. I must say that I've observed the same thing myself — without consciously observ-ing it, if you see what I mean.'

Ulf did not, but in general he felt that it was best not to ask the Commissioner to explain himself.

Now the Commissioner sat back in his chair and said, 'Tell us a bit more. I suspect that there are some here who might benefit from your insights.' The Com-missioner threw a quick glance in the direction of the head of Commercial Crime, who looked away sharply.

Ulf avoided the hostile gaze of the meeting. He studied his hands as he spoke. 'Photocopying is an excuse not to read something. You say to yourself, I'll photocopy this because it's worth reading, and you do so. But then you're not going to read the original,

169

are you? You think, I've dealt with it, but you haven't, have you? You put the photocopy in the in tray or you leave it on top of a filing cabinet, or whatever, *but you never read it.*' He paused. 'The carrying out of the external acts associated with a duty is not the same as the discharge of the duty itself.'

'Quite the psychologist,' whispered the head of Traffic to the head of Indecent Activities.

The Commissioner gave Ulf an encouraging look. 'Very interesting indeed. And you know something? As you were explaining, I was thinking of a similar example — not in the context of office activities, but similar nonetheless. Have you ever noticed when you see tourists traipsing around an old church or an interesting building, they photograph things all the time? Have you noticed that? Snap, snap, snap. But they don't look. Photography is a substitute for looking and for being there, in the presence of whatever it is that you're looking at. They take their photographs and then they go on to the next thing, but they've not seen anything — not in the real sense.'

Ulf agreed. The Commissioner was right; he had seen the same thing himself. 'That's what mindfulness is all about.'

The Commissioner leaned forward. He had become animated, and was being stared at suspiciously by the head of Traffic, the head of Commercial Crime, and the head of Indecent Activities.

'Mindfulness,' said the Commissioner. 'Exactly — mindfulness. We should all be more aware of where we are and what we are doing. We should all live more in the moment. I couldn't agree more.' He paused. 'You know, I've benefited greatly from going to a mindfulness workshop. We had a very good instructor. She said, right at the beginning, breathing is very important. Take a deep breath. *Now, think.* That's what she said. She said, 'Now, think; but first, breathe. Breathe, then think.'.'

'That's what they recommend,' said Ulf.

'I find breathing is fairly important to me,' whispered the head of Traffic. 'I'm all for it.'

The discussion of mindfulness continued for a further twenty minutes, and then it was time for a coffee break. During this break, Ulf was approached by the Commissioner, who discreetly took him aside.

'A word in your ear,' the Commissioner began. 'We have a vacant post coming up and I wondered if you had anybody in your department who might fit the bill.'

Ulf waited. Was the Commissioner about to offer him a new job?

'We need a schools liaison officer,' the Commissioner explained. 'It's not a very glamorous job, but somebody has to do it. I thought that you might have somebody you could suggest for the post.'

'Possibly,' said Ulf.

The Commissioner continued, 'We have a very bright young detective who's made his mark up in Stockholm but who wants to come back to Malmö. His wife's people are from here, apparently, and they want help with childcare. Anyway, he's had glowing reports from everybody and he might fit rather well with you in Sensitive Crimes. I think you'd be lucky to get him. But you'd have to lose somebody.'

Anybody but Anna, thought Ulf. And then he went on to think: Blomquist.

'Would you have a think about it?' asked the Commissioner. 'I could put this young man somewhere else — Commercial Crime would jump at him, I imagine — but I thought I'd give you the chance.'

Ulf thanked him and said that he would give the matter careful thought. Then the Commissioner looked at his watch and brought the coffee break to an end. 'We have a lot still to talk about,' he announced to the group. '*Tempus fugit*, as they say.'

'Quite the classicist now,' whispered the head of Traffic.

The head of Indecent Activities spluttered over his coffee. 'Naughty!' he whispered back.

13

Man Wishes to Meet Woman.
Anyone Will Do

Anders and Bengta Kindgren lived in Nya Bellevue, in an avenue of expensive houses that were either slightly older, or made to look so, than most in the surrounding neighbourhood. Their house, one of the largest on the street, was surrounded by trees so planted as to conceal from passers-by both the Japanese garden and the kidney-shaped swimming pool, each, in its way, a signature of wealth. The house itself, although spacious, was in none of its detail ostentatious, and if there was money behind it — which there must have been — that money, Ulf thought, was old, rather than new. He tried to remember what Anders had said to him at their first meeting about his situation. He had remarked that he had enough money — more than enough — to be able to pursue an independent scholarly career. He had added something about a family property company on his father's side, and his mother's desire that he should go into that. A place like this could not have been bought on an academic salary, or on the fees to be earned from attributing paintings; this was a matter of . . . of what? Thirty million kronor?

Ulf had travelled by taxi, even though it was a fairly long ride from his flat to this part of the city. He was not a heavy drinker, but he was a scrupulous observer of the strict Swedish laws on drinking and driving, and he would not get behind the wheel after so much as half a glass of wine or even a low-alcohol beer. He might have abstained altogether, as this dinner party was taking place on a weeknight, a time when people generally frowned upon drinking, but he decided that he might allow himself a glass or two of wine, or maybe even something slightly stronger.

As he approached the front door, he saw that the party was taking place outside, in the pool area, where a series of tables and chairs had been set up under strings of small LED lights. The effect was just right; had the lights been coloured, they would have been too much, but they were discreet and white, avoiding any hint of showiness. Ulf did not ring the doorbell, but walked round the side of the house to find his hosts among the throng of guests beside the pool.

Anders saw Ulf approaching and detached himself from the small knot of people with whom he had been engaged. He welcomed Ulf warmly, shaking his hand and leading him towards a table covered with a white linen cloth that was serving as a bar. Behind this stood a young man in a smart white shirt and dark blue bow-tie; a student, Ulf thought, earning a bit of money acting as a barman.

'As you'll see,' said Anders, gesturing towards one of the bottles on the table, 'we have just about everything. There's a very good single malt if you like Scotch — which I do, as it happens.' He passed his own empty glass to the student for refilling.

Ulf looked at the bottle indicated by Anders. The whisky inside, it proclaimed, was twenty-five years old. Or so Anders hoped, thought Ulf: a few years previously Ulf had been involved in an investigation into fake whiskies, and had encountered a bottle that

174

looked exactly like that. It, too, had claimed twenty-five years in the cask, but the expert opinion the department had obtained had suggested that the whisky in question was barely five years old, had nothing to do with the distillery it claimed to be from, and had been bottled in Italy rather than Scotland.

He accepted the whisky, which was served over ice by the young barman.

'I believe they particularly appreciate this in Scotland,' said Anders.

Ulf smiled. This was a subtle statement of wealth. There was no other justification, he thought, for a twenty-five-year-old single malt: it was intended to say only one thing. Fifteen years would have been more than enough; twenty-five said, *I can afford this*. Ulf sipped at the drink, complimenting Anders on the choice.

'The Scots like a drink, of course.'

Anders laughed. 'It's a northern weakness, isn't it? The Scots, ourselves, the Finns, the Russians . . . Is it something to do with the weather, do you think? Do northern latitudes somehow incline us to the consolations of alcohol?'

'Or perhaps our genes do that,' said Ulf.

'Ah,' said Anders. 'So alcohol warms the genes as well as the blood.'

Ulf smiled. 'Whatever the reason, whisky like this is always welcome.' He knew that this was what was expected of him. This was not an encounter between social equals: this was an independently wealthy man, a connoisseur with an international reputation in the fine arts, receiving a minor government functionary in his house and treating him to something he would never be able to afford himself. They were in an egalitarian society, but not that egalitarian. Yet Ulf did not mind: he was completely at ease with himself. He knew where he had come from and where he belonged. And he knew, too, that ultimately he had *power*: he had the authority of the state behind him. He could, in theory, arrest even the Prime Minister if he were to transgress the state's laws. That was the difference between Sweden and places that were not Sweden. There were so many countries where ordinary people were oppressed and put upon by their rulers, where they toiled and suffered without a glimpse of the freedom that was taken for granted in Sweden. How lucky he was to have been born where he was, and at this particular time of history, when it was possible to shine light into the darkest corners, when obfuscation and superstition had been driven into retreat — not vanquished, perhaps, but dealt a mortal blow.

Anders led him back to join the other guests. 'I must introduce you,' he said. 'There are people here I'd like you to meet.'

There was something in his tone that roused Ulf's suspicions that this was not to be a simple social occasion. That did not matter, of course: he could slip in and out of his detective's role at will, and a social occasion, he believed, was as good a time as any to acquire the background information that might prove the key to an investigation.

'My wife has gone off to check on something in the kitchen,' Anders explained. 'She'll be back in a moment. In the meantime, come and meet Marlene and Oscar Johansson. And Vera Lagerstrom. Old friends — all of them.'

There was something odd in the way in which

Anders used the word *friends*, as if in inverted commas. Was that affected cynicism, or irony perhaps, or was Ulf imagining it? Some people had a slightly arch way of speaking, which was of no real significance — perhaps it was that. He remembered the name Marlene Johansson: she was the art historian whom Christina Berks had described as completely ruthless. A viper in the bosom of the party? It was unlikely. Christina was jealous, perhaps.

The introductions made, Ulf was aware of the eyes of the guests upon him. He discreetly reciprocated their glances. Marlene, he observed, was a tall, elegant woman in her early fifties, perhaps. There was evidence of cosmetic surgery, Ulf thought — a small tightening around the eyes, slight tension in the skin across the brow — but that might just have been the light. The eyes themselves disclosed intelligence, he decided, and a lot of it. And the ruthlessness to which Christina alluded? Yes, thought Ulf — that was easy enough to imagine.

Oscar, her husband, was a well-built man, running slightly to fat. There was nothing about him, though, that would single him out in a crowd. He could be any middle-aged man with a receding hairline and the comfortable clothes and self-confidence of the haut-bourgeois. He would be confirmed in all his views, untroubled by envy because he had everything he would ever need, and tolerant of others. He was middle-Sweden in his outlook: sensible, unemotional, and a bemused observer of the excesses of the rest of the world.

The third guest, introduced as Vera Lagerstrom, was younger than the others. She was a woman somewhere in her late thirties or early forties, dressed in what Ulf thought was a rather ill-fitting silk shift. Her arms were almost pudgy, he noticed — a feature exacerbated by the tightness of two large brass bangles she was wearing above her right wrist.

Oscar was looking at Ulf with interest. 'Varg?'

Ulf nodded. 'Ulf.'

Oscar took a sip of his drink. 'You aren't anything to do with Björn Varg, are you?'

Ulf sighed inwardly. He was used to this, though, and indeed had come to expect it. 'My brother,' he said. And then added, with a smile, 'Sorry about that.'

Marlene and Oscar laughed, as did Anders. Vera looked away, as if pained by the revelation.

'It must be strange to have a famous name,' said Oscar. 'I don't have that trouble with Johansson.'

If there had been any tension, this remark dispelled it.

'My brother and I don't agree,' Ulf went on. 'But there's a good side to him — believe it or not.'

'Oh, I'm sure there is,' said Oscar. 'And he's not a *real* extremist, is he? He's not a fascist, by any means. A lot of what he says could even be seen as leaning to the left. He's . . . I suppose he's an iconoclast, which is not an entirely bad thing to be.'

'He likes challenging entrenched positions,' said Marlene. 'There's something to be said for that. We shouldn't expect everybody to think the same way.'

Now Vera made her contribution to the conversation. 'There has to be social consensus,' she muttered.

It was a very Swedish comment — one that should surprise nobody at all, and yet Anders gazed at her in a strange way when she said this. Ulf noticed that his look had an aspect of pity to it. Why should he pity this woman? Had she been invited as an act of charity of some sort? We all had heart-sink friends, after all, whom we felt we had to entertain from time to time. Perhaps Vera fell into that category.

Anders had been looking over his shoulder, and now he said that he needed to see if his wife needed help in the kitchen. He excused himself, while Vera struck up a conversation with Marlene, who, Ulf noticed, looked bored. She did not want to talk to Vera. Oscar moved slightly, so that he was standing between his wife and Ulf. It was a gesture that cut out the other two.

'Anders said you were a detective,' he said.

'Yes,' replied Ulf. 'I work in a department of the CID.'

'Homicide?' asked Anders. 'Something like that?'

Ulf smiled. 'No, I'm happy to say it's not homicide. I have colleagues who have to do that sort of thing. Fortunately, I don't.'

'And so what exactly do you do?' pressed Oscar.

'I'm in the Department of Sensitive Crimes,' said Ulf. 'We deal with . . . well, I suppose, unusual offences. Often rather minor things — but they can be troublesome in their way, for the people on the receiving end.' He wanted to steer the conversation away from the department. 'And you — you're an engineer, I believe.'

Oscar looked surprised. 'I assume Anders told you,' he said.

Ulf did not correct him. 'Mechanical?'

Oscar nodded. 'We have a light engineering works in the family. My father set it up. We made grinding and cutting equipment — still do. We have works here in Malmö and a branch in Germany — in Stuttgart. And a much smaller one in Slovenia. I'm not hands-on

179

with the other branches — we have very good local management.'

'That must help.'

'It does,' said Oscar. 'It allows me to get on with things I like to do. I have a small line in miniature cars. Scaled-down battery-driven models. People buy them for their children. They have a regulator that stops them from going more than ten kilometres per hour. Children love them.' He smiled. 'It's an innocent occupation. Some of my fellow engineers make weapons systems, after all.'

'And your wife?' Ulf asked.

'She's an art historian,' said Oscar. 'She teaches a bit — now and then, not very much. She writes too. There's a book she's been working on which takes her off to various places from time to time. Berlin, Milan. I lose track.'

Ulf waited for a few moments. He wanted the next question to sound innocent. 'And does she do any work for dealers?' he asked. 'The sort of thing Anders does for the auction houses?'

Oscar shook his head. 'Now and then. She'd like to, of course.'

'But there's not much of that work about?'

Oscar nodded. 'So I believe. And it tends to be dominated by relatively few people.'

Ulf had his next question ready. 'Have you heard about what happened to Anders? That business over the fake?'

Ulf had not expected what followed. Oscar laughed. 'Serves him right,' he said. 'Over-confidence. He thinks he knows everything.'

'Pride comes before a fall?' asked Ulf.

'You could say that.' Oscar paused. 'I don't, but

180

others might.'

Ulf waited for a few moments. 'What did your wife think about it?'

Oscar took a sip of his drink. He lowered his voice. 'Actually, she was pleased.' He hesitated. 'Our host, I'm afraid, has not always been entirely kind to his fellow art historians. He reviewed Marlene's last book very badly. He was polite, of course, but if you read between the lines, you got the message. She was very upset. She said that it effectively halted her career.'

'In what way?' asked Ulf.

'If she were to apply for a chair at one of the universities, it would count against her. There would be bound to be somebody on the committee who'd remember the review and say 'Not very sound scholarship', or something like that.' He shook his head. 'Academics! They live in such a narrow, petty little world. They think it's the be-all and end-all, but it isn't really.'

'Has she forgiven him?' asked Ulf, conscious of the fact that the woman they were discussing was standing only a short distance away. But she was now engrossed in a conversation with Vera, her earlier boredom apparently having evaporated. 'After all,' Ulf added, 'you're here this evening, aren't you?'

Oscar raised an eyebrow. 'Yes, odd, isn't it? We hadn't expected an invitation, but he got in touch. He said there was somebody we might like to meet. That was you, I suppose — we know the others.'

'And you came,' said Ulf, 'in spite of the past.'

'We did,' said Oscar. 'And I'm glad we did. I don't believe in leaving hatchets unburied.'

Ulf would have liked to ask, 'And your wife?' but he did not. He imagined what the answer to that might

181

be, anyway, and if you already knew the answer to a question, then why ask it?

A few minutes later, Anders returned from the kitchen, accompanied by his wife, Bengta. Anders introduced her to Ulf, and then went off to speak to a couple of guests whom Ulf had yet to meet.

'I'm glad you were able to come at relatively short notice,' Bengta said. 'These days it seems that you have to book most people weeks in advance.'

'People lead busy lives,' said Ulf. 'In my case, I suppose I don't get that many invitations.'

Bengta looked surprised. 'Am I expected to believe that? An attractive man like you?'

'I just don't,' said Ulf. 'And it's probably my fault. I don't bother much with a social life.'

'You live by yourself?' asked Bengta.

Ulf nodded. 'I get by. I have a dog.'

'And you've always been single?'

He shook his head. 'Not always. I am now, but I wasn't always.'

Bengta lowered her voice. 'Anders said you were very helpful. He had been worried that the police wouldn't take him seriously. He said that you did.'

'It was a serious complaint,' said Ulf.

'I'm glad you look at it that way. He's really suffered, you know. It means a lot to him that there's somebody who sees it from his point of view.'

Ulf looked at her. He liked her, and yet he remembered what Anders had told him about her having an affair. How did that square with her concern for her husband? Of course, people had affairs and still loved their spouse or their partner. There were plenty of people who seemed capable of having room for more than one lover in their life. He did not see himself doing that, but then he was not everybody.

Now he asked her who she thought might be behind the campaign.

His question amused her. 'But that's something we're counting on you to find out.'

'I need assistance,' said Ulf. 'I'm not psychic.'

Bengta looked about her. 'I'd say the person is present here tonight. That's why we've invited this particular group of people. One of them is the person you're looking for.'

Ulf had assumed that this was the rationale behind the guest list. Now he repeated his question. 'But who do you think is responsible? You don't have to give any reason. Just tell me who you think it might be.'

Bengta hesitated. 'Marlene,' she said at last. 'That woman is seething . . . and I mean *seething* with envy. She'd love to *be* Anders, but she isn't. So I think she's doing the only thing she can think of — which is to get him out of the way, to destroy his reputation. Discredit him. She'd be the winner if that happened.'

Ulf looked across the patio. Vera was now talking to another couple altogether whom Ulf had yet to meet.

'What about that woman over there?' he said to Bengta. 'Vera . . . '

'Lagerstrom. Vera Lagerstrom. Oh, poor Vera — she's an editor, you know. She's fairly close to the bottom of the academic food chain. She has a soft spot for Anders — she'd never do anything to harm him. She worships the ground he walks on. It embarrasses him.'

'And how do you get on with her?' asked Ulf.

The question took Bengta unawares, and she had to collect her thoughts before she replied. 'I feel sorry for her. She's one of those people who live on the margins of other people's lives.' She gave Ulf an almost conspiratorial look. 'You know the type. You must have met people like that. Rather weak characters, I'm afraid.'

Ulf hesitated before he asked his next question. He had slipped into his detective's role rather more quickly and more completely than he had imagined. This now had the tone of an interrogation rather than a social conversation with his hostess. But he did not want to miss the opportunity.

'You mention your husband's embarrassment over Vera's attachment to him . . .'

Bengta was looking at him quizzically, and he decided that no offence was being taken. He went ahead. 'You don't feel that he has reciprocated her interest at any point?'

It was too direct, he thought, and he blushed. Anybody asked such a question might feel, with justification, that a marriage was being pried into. But Bengta simply laughed. 'Oh certainly,' she said. 'Anders had a fling. What man wouldn't? If a woman throws herself at a man, there are very few men who aren't at least tempted. And most, I suspect, would do something about it — out of curiosity, if nothing else.'

'You have a low opinion of us,' said Ulf.

'I'm a realist,' Bengta retorted. 'And anyway . . .' She looked sideways at Ulf, as if assessing whether he could be trusted with a sensitive disclosure. 'And anyway, Anders and I have an understanding. Our marriage is a tolerant one. We may have particular friends and the other party will not go off in a huff. It's an adult arrangement.'

Ulf remembered what Anders had said about his

184

wife's lover, Linus — the philosopher, the author of the book on Kierkegaard.

'I might as well tell you that I have had one or two close male friends,' Bengta continued. 'Anders has never minded. We're very fond of one another, you see, and these things are not all that important, when it comes down to it. What happens is being there for one another in the long run. That's important.'

'I see.' Ulf took a sip of his whisky, which was now almost finished. It really was twenty-five years old, he decided. And it was Scottish, not Italian. It was not a fake: the whisky was genuine; the marriage was not. Or was it? There were different visions of marriage, and this one had presumably lasted.

'So, there you have it,' said Bengta. 'If you were inclined to think that I had anything to do with what's been going on, you are very, very wrong, I'm afraid.'

Ulf decided to be direct. 'But if you were to have a male friend, and he were to feel jealous of Anders, you don't think he — that male friend, I mean — might be inclined to show his hostility in some way?'

Bengta stared at Ulf in frank disbelief. Then she said, 'Linus? You mean Linus?' And then she burst out laughing again, loudly. From a short distance away, one of the other guests looked at her with amusement. Ulf wondered if she had had too much to drink. Her glass was full, he noticed, but she had not touched it while she had been talking to him.

'I take it you know about Linus,' she said. 'He's no secret. In fact, he was going to be joining us this evening, but he had something else on.'

'Your husband doesn't mind?'

'Of course not. I told you — we're tolerant of that sort of thing. And anyway, Linus doesn't mean a great

185

deal to me. I feel sorry for him, I suppose. He's lonely and a bit of a lost soul. It's not going to last forever — I know that.'

'But what does he think? Linus, I mean. Might he not resent your husband?'

She rolled her eyes. 'Resent? Poor Linus is hardly aware of him. He lives in a world of his own, you see. I don't think Anders is real to him — his head is completely in the clouds. He's a philosopher, you see.'

'So I'd heard.'

Her eyes narrowed. 'Who told you?'

Ulf almost replied 'Your husband', but did not do so. That might be a mistake, he thought. He decided to return to the subject of Vera.

'You don't think Vera might have had anything to do with that business with the journal article?'

'Well,' said Bengta, 'she would be well placed to do it — she works for the publishers of that journal. But frankly I don't see Vera doing anything that requires the slightest degree of courage. She's awfully mousy. She lives with an aunt. She doesn't have much of a life, I'm afraid.'

Ulf gazed across the pool to where Vera was standing. Her bangles caught the light and flashed back at him. 'You'd be surprised what mousy people can do,' he said. 'Some of the worst crimes in the country are committed by people who wouldn't say boo to a goose. Or that's what everybody thinks until suddenly one of these people snaps and does something awful. That's what happens, you know.'

Bengta affected dismay. 'You mean Vera might be capable of something serious?'

'No, not necessarily. But I wouldn't rule it out. Anybody can do something dramatic. But fortunately,

186

that's not what we're talking about here. We're talking about a minor act of revenge, I suspect.'

'A minor act with potentially major consequences,' said Bengta. 'Anders feels that his career is jeopardised by this.'

'I wasn't playing anything down,' said Ulf.

'Good,' said Bengta. 'Because it's serious, and I, for one, would really like you to find out who's doing this to Anders. And then deal with him. Prosecute him, or whatever.'

'Him?' asked Ulf.

She stared back at him. She held his gaze. And then she smiled. 'I know what you're thinking. I think you're making a sexist assumption. You're thinking: this is spiteful reasoning — typical of a woman. That's what you're thinking, Ulf Varg.' She wagged a finger playfully. 'Oh yes you are.'

'I'm not. You think I'm thinking along those lines, but how do you know what I'm thinking?'

'Because I know that's the way men think. They think they're dispassionate. They think they don't experience any of the emotions that women fall victim to — jealousy, the desire for revenge, that sort of thing. Well, men do. Men are just as capable as women are of that sort of thing. Men can be really petty once they set their minds to it.'

She gave Ulf a challenging look, but it was not unfriendly. And now she said, 'Forgive me for being so direct. I didn't mean to be rude — I'm not entirely serious.'

Ulf's smile defused the situation further. 'I didn't think you were.'

She put her glass down on a nearby table. The wine was untouched. 'Let's get everybody to table,' she said. 'As you see, we have several smaller tables set out, rather than one big one. We can move around between courses. It's the thing to do these days, as I'm sure you're aware.'

Ulf was not, and he suddenly felt socially disadvantaged. So people were having dinner parties where they moved about between courses: that made sense, as it saved one from being stuck. But he had not experienced it himself because he had so few invitations. And that, he told himself, is my fault. I sit in my flat and do nothing while people are enjoying themselves. I must get out more — that classic reproach, but pertinent in my case. I must get out more. I must stop thinking about Anna, because I shall never have a life with her and I might as well admit that. I shall go online, to one of those dating services for the thirties to fifties. I shall type in *Police officer, single, with dog* . . . No, I shall not. People will think: dog? What sort of dog? And then they'll think: that dog's a problem — obviously. Of course, I could say, *Man with silver Saab* . . . No, I shall not say that either. Perhaps *Man wishes to meet woman. Anyone will do.* That would be a mistake, of course, but it would be a kind thing to write . . .

14

Quod Erat Demonstrandum

The following morning, as Ulf stood under the shower, he thought about how he might handle the Commissioner's offer. By the time he had dried himself, combed his hair and dressed for work, he knew exactly what he would say to the Commissioner when he phoned him later that day. He would accept the offer of the promising new trainee from Stockholm and, assuming that he had already spoken to Blomquist, he would go on to confirm the availability of a member of his staff for the swap. He would not dodge that part of it, he thought: he could, of course, leave it to personnel to inform Blomquist of his fate, but that, Ulf felt, would be the easy way out. He would tell Blomquist about it personally, over a cup of coffee that very morning, just before going into work. He would not put it off. It would not be easy, but he had to do it.

Ulf telephoned Blomquist to set up a meeting over coffee. It was a short conversation, and Ulf felt a momentary pang at Blomquist's friendly tone and his eager acceptance of the invitation. The other man had something he wanted to tell Ulf, he said — but did not want to speak about it over the phone. No details were given, but Ulf suspected it would be something to do with diet or vitamins, or possibly enzymes — it was a moving field in which the focus could shift at any moment. The reason why Blomquist would not want to speak about it over the phone would be simple enough: the new advice would touch on some intimate medical problem — a 'male issue', as Blomquist would put it. It would be something to do with zinc deficiency and men's health, Ulf imagined.

Ulf sighed inwardly — both at the thought of a discussion of zinc and also the thought of what he had to say to Blomquist about his transfer. He steeled himself. 'I look forward to seeing you,' he said.

And Blomquist replied, 'And I you.'

Ulf rang off. He looked out of the window at a blue, untroubled sky. Human affairs were so messy. You could do your best to lead a quiet life, to keep out of unnecessary conflict, to put in your forty years or whatever it was of working to the best of your ability without creating too many ripples, but there were always difficult decisions needing to be made. And however hard you tried, there would be times when you could not avoid causing pain to others, because pain and disappointment seemed an inevitable concomitant of human life. The moment you accepted any promotion, any slight advantage over those below you in the pecking order, you had to accept that you might have to do things that others would prefer you not to do — make rulings that would dash the hopes of others, give one person advantage over another, make people do things they would rather not do. All this came with seniority; all this came with working in a hierarchical organisation; all this came with simply being human.

He tried to put these thoughts out of his mind as he delivered Martin to Mrs Högfors. The widow appeared to have forgotten the confiscated air rifle. Ulf knew he would have to speak to her about it in due course, and arrange for its return to her nephew, but that could wait a day or two. There was also the problem of that business with the cucumber man. She had made no formal complaint, and Ulf would prefer it to remain that way, as any official inquiry would reveal that she had fired the rifle at her would-be assailant. That could be awkward. The neatest solution, Ulf decided, would be to allow the whole thing to blow over. The man would have learned a lesson, Ulf thought, and Mrs Högfors had emerged unscathed. Vigilantism was not something that the police should encourage, even if there was sometimes a rather appealing justice to it. If you confront people with cucumbers by night, and they discharge an air rifle at you — well, what could you expect? The squirrel, of course, was another matter altogether. He would have to speak to her about that. You could not have elderly widows persecuting squirrels in the park in an ordered society — you simply could not.

Martin had made good progress. The wounds on his snout had now healed, and in a day or two he could be taken back to Dr Håkansson to have his stitches removed. The sutures on his nose could be dealt with at the same time, Ulf thought, even though the nose was now beyond all doubt upside down. Both Ulf and Mrs Högfors had got used to its new alignment, and Ulf even thought that the reversal somehow improved Martin's appearance.

'Nobody will notice,' he said to Mrs Högfors. 'They might think there's something a bit odd, but I doubt if people will think much of it.'

Mrs Högfors scratched Martin's back, a courtesy that he always greatly appreciated. 'Poor Martin,' she said. 'It's not easy being a dog, is it?'

Ulf was not sure whether the question was directed at him or at Martin. He replied, though, on Martin's behalf. 'I get by,' he said. 'As long as you people remember to feed me. And, of course, give me plenty of exercise.'

Mrs Högfors smiled. 'But that's in the contract, Martin. That's in the contract between dogs and man.'

* * *

Blomquist was already in the coffee bar when Ulf arrived. Joining him at the table in the window, Ulf signalled for his coffee to the young man behind the bar before turning his attention to his colleague.

Blomquist had been reading a newspaper. He folded this now and tucked it into his jacket pocket.

'Anything in the paper?' Ulf asked.

'The usual,' said Blomquist. 'Something about your brother, though.'

Ulf sighed. 'What's he been saying now?'

'He's suggesting that people could be chipped — you know, like those chips that vets put under the skin of cats and dogs. Name and address of owner — that sort of thing. Not in this case, of course: this would be a sort of subcutaneous ID card.'

Ulf's sigh became a groan.

'Actually,' Blomquist continued, 'he has a point. You could use it in all sorts of ways. Paying for things, for example. If the chip had your credit card detail all you'd have to do is wave a hand over the machine. Going through airports there'd be no need for passports — the machine would recognise you and open the gates.'

'And the civil liberties angle?' asked Ulf.

Blomquist said that he was not sure about that, but the advantages to the police were clear enough. 'It's a question of balance,' said Blomquist. 'One has to weigh the right of privacy against the social interest.'

Ulf's coffee arrived. 'Of course,' he said, wiping a fleck of stray foam off the rim of the cup, 'everything's a compromise. That's what life is like — not that I think my brother and his Moderate Extremists are great ones for compromise.'

Blomquist was looking at him intently. 'Don't be too hard on your brother,' he said. 'You don't have another one, do you?'

Ulf was taken aback. He was used to distancing himself from his brother and his opinions — he had to do this all the time. And yet Blomquist was right: Björn was his brother, after all, and a brother was irreplaceable.

'He means well,' Ulf muttered. 'It's just that—'

'I know,' said Blomquist. 'He embarrasses you, doesn't he?'

Ulf nodded.

'I'm embarrassed by my own brother,' said Blomquist. 'He's in a rock band. They're dreadful. They're all well over forty and yet they behave as if they're eighteen. He hasn't grown up.'

Ulf smiled. 'That can't be easy.'

'No,' said Blomquist. 'It isn't. And he has a really unhealthy diet, you know — really unhealthy. He eats hardly any vegetables or salads.'

Ulf shook his head. 'He'll be vitamin D deficient, I imagine.'

He was not sure why he'd said that; he had not really intended to, but the remark had somehow slipped out. It was the Blomquist effect, he decided.

193

Blomquist nodded sadly. 'He's beginning to have prostate issues,' he said. 'I told him about pumpkin seed extract, but do you think he listened to me? He did not. He laughed. He thinks it's a joke.'

'He'll learn,' said Ulf.

'I'm afraid so,' agreed Blomquist. He took a sip of his coffee. 'But let's not talk about brothers, Ulf. I have some interesting news for you.'

Ulf cleared his throat. 'Blomquist, there's something I need to talk to you about too,' he began.

'Sure,' said Blomquist. 'I'm in no hurry. But I need to tell you something about the Kindgren case. I've done a bit of asking around.'

Ulf frowned. He was running the Kindgren investigation and he did not expect Blomquist to go off and make enquiries without first telling him about them. Blomquist sensed Ulf's reservation, for he now explained. 'I'm not going off in a direction of my own,' he said. 'Don't worry about that.'

'I'm pleased to hear that,' said Ulf. 'But what's this about 'asking around'?'

'Talking to my mother,' said Blomquist, with a smile.

'Your mother?'

'Yes,' explained Blomquist. 'My mother knows Lennart Solander's mother, as it happens. They're in the same book group.'

Ulf smiled. Talking to Blomquist, nothing would surprise him.

Blomquist leaned forward. 'Well, I was visiting my mother last night. She lives in one of those semi-sheltered apartments; you know the deal — there's somebody onsite who can deal with any problems, but the residents are all independent. They have their own kitchens and so on, but they can take meals in a central dining room if they want to. They serve pretty nourishing food there, actually — very little red meat, lots of fish. Fresh vegetables. Lots of roughage for the old folks — you know how it is. It's important they keep regular — really important.'

Ulf pursed his lips.

'My mother swears by senna,' Blomquist continued. 'If she finds that she's getting a bit bunged up, she takes some senna. Have you tried it, Ulf?'

Ulf took a deep breath. This is Blomquist on steroids, he thought. Or Blomquist on senna . . .

'I have not,' Ulf said, through gritted teeth. 'I don't need to.'

Blomquist looked at him quizzically. 'Never? You never have periods when you could be more regular? Never?'

'Listen, Blomquist,' said Ulf, struggling to keep his voice even, 'I don't really want to discuss my stomach with you, if you don't mind.'

'Stomach?' said Blomquist. 'I'm not talking about your stomach, you know. I'm talking about your—'

Ulf raised a hand to stop him. 'You were talking about your mother.'

'Of course,' Blomquist said. 'My mother. Well, I was round there checking up on her and I happened to mention Lennart Solander. I didn't give her any confidential information, in case you're worried about that, but I can tell you that she already knew about the painting.'

Ulf was intrigued. This was typical of Blomquist — there would be any amount of irrelevant detail, and then suddenly there would be a gem of insight or information.

'And?' Ulf prompted.

'And she said that Lennart's mother had already spoken to her about it. His mother said that Lennart had taken the painting to the auction house with absolutely no intention of selling it. He wanted a valuation without disclosing to his siblings — who are joint owners, remember — that he was having it valued. So he pretended to be interested in selling it, but really was not at all minded to do that.'

Ulf digested this information. Then he asked, 'So he didn't take it back?'

'No,' said Blomquist. 'Not only did he not take it back to the auction people — he took it to his mother's house and suggested she should hang it on her wall for a while.'

'Why would he have done that?'

'Because Lennart couldn't afford to insure it in his own place. Apparently, he's in debt. He's really pushed for cash.'

'So who's insuring it?' asked Ulf.

'It's covered by his mother's household policy, I gather.'

Ulf wondered why Lennart would not have wanted to sell it if he was financially pressed.

'Because his two siblings who are joint owners won't agree to that,' said Blomquist. 'One of them takes the view that Lennart should get an ordinary job rather than waiting for acting jobs that might not materialise. The other likes the painting too much and doesn't need the money. She point-blank refuses to sell.'

'Why doesn't she buy him out then?'

'That's what I asked. And my mother said that the sister would never do that because she's too mean. Apparently, she won't spend a cent on anything. She

196

wears cast-offs from charity stores and survives on cheap soup. She's not going to pay however many thousands to her brother when she can stop the painting from being sold just by refusing her consent.'

Ulf looked up at the ceiling. This was interesting information, but did it take them any further? One thing was apparent: it identified a motive on Lennart's part. If he was so hard up, then he might well have succumbed to the temptation to have a copy made and try to sell that. But if that had been his intention, then why should he have taken the painting to his mother's apartment? Was that, perhaps, to provide it with an alibi?

Ulf drained his coffee cup and signalled for a refill.

'That's very interesting, Blomquist,' he said. 'But I still think we need to speak to Lennart at some point.'

'We can,' agreed Blomquist. 'But I don't think he's our man.'

'Why do you say that?'

'Because according to my mother, Lennart's mother said that he was planning an insurance fraud.'

Ulf's eyes widened. 'His mother said that to . . . to your mother?'

'Yes,' Blomquist confirmed. 'Lennart planned to have the painting stolen from his mother's place. He thought he could bring her in on the plan, because she's never said no to him on anything — she's always backed him up regardless. So he thought he could get her involved in his fraudulent little scheme. The painting would be stolen by some friends of his from The Divine Apollo, who would then destroy it. Lennart would claim the insurance — which he'd share, of course, with his siblings. But there would be enough for him to pay off his debts.'

'Very cunning,' said Ulf.

'Yes, except for one thing: his mother drew the line at insurance fraud. She refused to play ball. And she told my mother — because she tells her everything, apparently.'

Ulf was silent as he worked out the implications. Lennart was not involved in any scheme to discredit Anders — that, at least, was clear. He had planned a quite separate fraud and they could follow that up if they so wished. It would be difficult to prove, though, and they had enough on their hands as it was.

He looked at Blomquist. 'So we don't need to speak to Lennart again. Agree?'

Blomquist nodded. 'Somebody else made a copy of the painting — from a photograph, I assume.' He paused. 'What about those people you met last night? Did you suspect any of them?'

'Yes,' said Ulf.

'Who in particular?' asked Blomquist.

Ulf thought about this. 'We'll need to talk about that some other time,' he said. 'It's a bit complicated. And there's something I need to talk to you about, Blomquist.'

Blomquist looked at him expectantly. 'Fire away,' he said. And then he added, 'I really like talking to you, Ulf — I really do. A lot of people . . . ' He hesitated. Ulf watched him. 'A lot of people, you see, don't seem to be interested in talking to me. I'm under no illusions — I'm not the most exciting person in town. They think I'm boring, I suppose. But you never give any sign of thinking that. You're too kind. You listen to me.'

Ulf caught his breath. 'Oh, I don't know—'

Blomquist cut him short. 'No, it's really good of

198

you, Ulf. You listen. I feel I can speak my mind to you.'

Ulf swallowed. Blomquist was not making this easy.

'And I want you to know, Ulf,' Blomquist continued, 'that I really appreciate everything you've done
for me. In particular, I can't tell you how grateful I
am that you've taken me on in Sensitive Crimes. That
has made all the difference to me — all the difference.
I was stuck where I was before. I was going nowhere.
Now . . . Well, now I find myself impatient to get into
work every day — now that you've involved me in this
case, and others like it. I feel my career has turned a
corner.'

Ulf looked at Blomquist in dismay. How could he
now say what he had planned to say? It was impossible — he could not bring himself to end something
that clearly meant so much to this man.

And so, rather than break the news of Blomquist's
impending transfer, which now, of course, was not
going to take place, he said, 'I'm glad you're happy in
your work, Blomquist. So many people aren't.'

'But I am,' said Blomquist. 'Thanks to you.'

Ulf mentally rehearsed what he would say to the
Commissioner. He might tell him that there simply
was not enough work in the department to justify
their taking on of this highly regarded rising star from
Stockholm. Or he could say that Blomquist was proving invaluable to him and should be left where he was.
Or he could simply forget about the whole thing. It was
well known that the Commissioner tended to move
on from issue to issue and often never followed up on
suggestions he made. This might be just such a case,
and Blomquist would stay where he was — by default,
in a manner of speaking. Moreover, it occurred to Ulf
that if it were let slip to Commercial Crime that there

was a very promising young officer coming down from Stockholm and that if they moved quickly they might get him, then they would be only too happy to poach him from under the nose of the Department of Sensitive Crime. Either that, or they might let Indecent Activities apply for him on the grounds that they needed somebody young and unshockable to strengthen their team.

He looked at Blomquist. 'We need to make a plan,' he said. 'We need to work out where our time is best spent. We need to work out who might wish to harm Anders — and why.'

'It sounds as if it's a long list,' said Blomquist.

Ulf admitted it was. 'This is the way I see it,' he said. 'We have his wife, and her lover Linus, the philosopher. That's just to start with.'

'You can strike her off the list,' said Blomquist. 'Wives don't do that sort of thing.'

Ulf raised an eyebrow. 'Really?'

'Well, it's unlikely. What about her lover?'

'He sounds very unworldly,' replied Ulf. 'From what I heard the other night, he doesn't really know what's going on. He's a philosopher, you see.'

'Ah. All right, let's not bother with him. What about others?'

'I met a woman called Vera Lagerstrom,' said Ulf. 'She's some sort of editor. She would have been in a position to sabotage his article.'

'But why would she?' asked Blomquist.

'She was his lover,' said Ulf. 'But no longer.'

Blomquist raised a finger. 'Ah! Hell has no fury . . . et cetera, et cetera.'

'Perhaps. But she's very mild. Not the sort to do much, I wouldn't have thought.'

'Just the sort then,' Blomquist said. 'Powerlessness spurs people on. I once had to arrest a nun, you know, who poisoned the abbess of a convent. She was the most junior nun in the place and she felt put upon. She put large quantities of strychnine in the abbess's tea. She survived, of course — some of those people have the constitution of an ox. Did you know, by the way, that strychnine used to be used as a medicine? It causes convulsions, you see, and they believed that—'

Ulf cut Blomquist short. 'How interesting. All right, we can keep her in mind.' He thought of the other suspects. 'There are some professional rivals. A woman called Marlene Johansson, for starters. I was told that Anders once wrote a bad review of one of her books.'

'We should look closely at her then,' said Blomquist. 'Authors are terrible people, for the most part. They are slow to forgive a slight and they have very long memories. Remember that critic in Copenhagen who was shot in the leg with a crossbow? It was an author who did that. The critic had written a bad review of his book and he went out and bought a crossbow to retaliate. The critic was lucky to survive.'

'Poor man — an occupational hazard, I suppose.'

'Yes,' said Blomquist. 'I gather he wrote nothing but enthusiastic reviews after that.'

'I don't blame him,' said Ulf. 'If somebody was going to shoot me with a crossbow I would be *very* complimentary.'

'Any others?' asked Blomquist.

'There's a Professor Hans-Dieter Kaufmann. He's German and teaches at Lund. He's married to a Finn. He stands to gain if Anders misses out on work. He was at the dinner party, but I didn't meet him. We

201

were sitting too far apart to talk.'

'Perhaps we should go and see him,' said Blomquist.

Ulf agreed.

'Who's the most unlikely of all those?' asked Blomquist. 'In your opinion, that is.'

'I don't think any of them seem very likely,' Ulf replied.

'But if you had to choose?'

'I think that perhaps Vera Lagerstrom is,' said Ulf. 'I just can't see her doing something like this.'

'Then she's probably the one,' said Blomquist. 'It's almost always the least likely suspect who proves to be responsible.'

Ulf could not agree. 'You have to be more scientific than that, Blomquist,' he said good-naturedly.

'That is perfectly scientific,' retorted Blomquist. 'It's the theory of least likely likelihood. Shall I explain it to you?'

Ulf looked at his watch. 'Not right now,' he said. 'Some other time, perhaps.'

He relented. It was tempting to fob Blomquist off with that sort of promise, but it was wrong to do so, Ulf decided. If Blomquist was a full member of his team, which he was, and would now continue to be, then he was owed a hearing.

'Actually,' Ulf said, 'I'd very much like to hear your theory, Blomquist. Please tell me about it.'

Blomquist looked pleased. But at the same time, he was concerned. 'I don't want to waste your time, Ulf. I'd never want to do that.'

That, Ulf thought, might be inscribed above the door: *Blomquist has promised not to waste Ulf Varg's time*. This would mean fewer discussions of things

202

that had nothing to do with the matter in hand: no turmeric; no vitamin D; no Q10 enzymes; nothing, really, except departmental business. No, thought Ulf, that would be draconian — and impossible. Ordinary life depended upon the exchange of inconsequential snippets. We liked to talk about small things — about things that people had said; about the little, unimportant transactions of life; about the fleeting, often rather silly, thoughts that went through our heads. Of course we did.

And so he listened politely to Blomquist, who told him about his theory. At the end of the explanation, Ulf said, 'So, Blomquist, this is what it amounts to: you say that people will only do things that they think they can get away with. Is that correct?'

'It is,' said Blomquist.

'And so, in deciding what to do — if it's something that may get them into trouble of some sort — they put themselves in the shoes of an external observer looking at the situation.'

'That's what they'll do,' Blomquist confirmed.

'And then they work out what an external observer would think of who might do what?'

'That's it.'

'And then they proceed to do what they planned to do, provided it isn't what an external observer might think is likely to be done? Have I understood it correctly?'

Blomquist nodded enthusiastically. 'That's exactly right.'

Ulf scratched his head. 'I see.'

'So there you have it,' said Blomquist.

'And in this case,' Ulf suggested tentatively, 'what does this theory imply?'

Blomquist looked away. 'I don't know,' he said at last.

Ulf looked at his watch again. 'Most interesting,' he mused.

And then, quite suddenly, Ulf had an idea. It was, he thought, a lightbulb moment. He looked at Blomquist, who, noticing Ulf's expression of intense concentration, realised that something important was about to be said.

'Blomquist . . .'

'Yes?'

'Let's think about what Anders does for a living.'

Blomquist frowned. 'Good question. A pretty easy existence, if you ask me. Looking at paintings; going on about paintings; turning up at conferences and talking about paintings. Not exactly strenuous work.'

'Authenticating,' said Ulf. 'Giving a painting its papers, so to speak. And that involves money.'

Blomquist shrugged. 'So, he gets paid. No surprise there.'

'That's not the money I'm thinking of. The money I'm wondering about is the money involved with the painting — the value of the painting. What it's sold for. That's what counts.'

Blomquist said nothing.

'The point is this,' Ulf continued, convincing himself as he went on. 'The point is this, Blomquist. If Anders says that a painting is an important painting by some artist for whom people will pay large sums, then the person who has asked his opinion becomes much richer than he otherwise would be.'

'All right,' said Blomquist. 'And so . . . ' He started to smile. 'I see where this is going. If he says a painting is not what the owner wants it to be, then you may

204

have a very angry owner.'

Ulf felt as if he were a mathematician explaining a proposition. They were now approaching the quod erat *demonstrandum* moment. 'What we need to look for,' he said, with a flourish, 'is a recent occasion where he has declined to authenticate a painting — in particular, we need to find out whether he has ever refuted a painting's previously accepted attribution.'

Blomquist asked for a further explanation of this, which Ulf now gave him.

'If I have a painting, Blomquist,' he said, 'that everybody has accepted as being the work of, let's say, Brueghel — the original Brueghel, that is . . .'

'There were more than one?' asked Blomquist.

'Yes. They were a family of painters. But the one that everybody thinks of—'

He did not get the chance to finish. 'Like the Bachs?' asked Blomquist.

'Yes, a bit like the Bachs.'

Blomquist became animated. 'There were something like fifty of them,' he said. 'Fifty! If anything proves that things run in families, then that, surely, is proof enough for anyone.' He paused. 'Fifty musicians in one family.'

'You told me that,' said Ulf. 'We talked about them.'

'Mind you,' Blomquist continued, 'I've always believed that you get most of your abilities from your genes. Do you know about those twin studies? Where they look at twins who've been separated at birth and then discover that they behave almost exactly the same way, in spite of having been brought up separately. Have you seen those, Ulf?'

Ulf knew that he had to guide the conversation back to Brueghel if they were to avoid a long discussion on

205

nature versus nurture. There might be time for that later — in the Saab one day, perhaps, on a long trip on some case — but not now.

'Brueghel,' he said firmly. 'If you think you've got a Brueghel and I come along and say, 'Oh, that's not *the* Brueghel, not Pieter Brueghel, that's Jan Brueghel the Younger,' then you might be pretty cross, don't you think? Suddenly thirty million kronor has become two hundred thousand kronor, or something like that.'

'I'd be cross,' Blomquist agreed.

'And you'd be cross with whom?' Ulf prompted.

'With you.'

'Exactly. And would I not want to say, 'That man doesn't know what he's talking about. He doesn't really know one Brueghel from another.' Wouldn't I want to say that?'

'That depends,' said Blomquist, after a few moments' thought. 'That depends on how important the thirty million kronor is to you.'

Ulf felt a momentary irritation. 'Of course thirty million kronor is important. Who wouldn't be interested in that sort of money?'

'It would count more to some than to others,' Blomquist said. 'That's all I meant.'

Ulf was about to dismiss this, when he realised that Blomquist had a point.

'Are you suggesting that we look for somebody who really needed an attribution — to save himself from bankruptcy, for instance — and then was denied it by Anders? And then . . .'

'And then wants to get even,' Blomquist supplied. 'Or wants to get the attribution back by destroying Anders' reputation — by making his attribution hardly worth the paper it's written on.'

206

'There you have it,' said Ulf. 'That's where we should be looking.'

They were both silent for a while, each thinking his own thoughts, but each deciding that this was the explanation for which they had been searching — but, up until now, not finding.

Then Ulf broke the silence. 'So what I'd like you to do, Blomquist, is to go and see Anders. Get from him a list of all the attributions he's been asked to give over the last, say, three years. He should have a record of these, I imagine. We won't be interested in all of them — find out if there were any cases where he took something away — where he said a painting was not what its owner hoped it would be. And, in particular, where the owner really needed the attribution.'

Blomquist smiled broadly. This is what he had hoped he would be doing when he joined the Department of Sensitive Crimes. This was real detective work — the sort that required thought and skill and knowledge.

'That'll be our man,' he said. 'That'll be somebody with a real grudge.'

'Possibly,' said Ulf, adding, 'Or woman.' And he realised that he made this proviso not just out of non-sexist sensitivity, but because there was something about this whole matter that made him feel a woman was involved. He could not say 'This is a woman's crime', because you were discouraged from saying such things, but you could still *think* them. Your nose could tell you things that reason might miss. And you had to trust your nose.

That made him think of Martin. He would be taking Martin to Dr Håkansson shortly to have the stitches taken out of his nose. Poor Martin — and yet he had only himself to blame. At the end of the day, that applied to most of us: we had only ourselves to blame. Except sometimes, of course.

15

Knowing Where to Look

Martin had always liked Dr Håkansson, a fact that the vet was proud of and made a point of mentioning to Ulf at their consultations.

'I'm used to being disliked by animals,' Dr Håkansson said as he gently picked the dog up and placed him on his examination table. 'Martin is an exception, I'm happy to say.'

'I suppose they associate you with a painful or confusing situation,' said Ulf.

He stroked Martin's flank. In spite of his apparent calmness, he felt a shiver beneath the dog's coat. Martin was being brave.

'Yes,' agreed Dr Håkansson. 'There's that, but there's also the smell. I think smell might be the main thing — particularly for dogs. They smell the antiseptic we use on the surfaces in here. We splash it about a bit, I suppose. They don't like it.'

The two men were standing round the table. Ulf held Martin's collar lightly, to keep him in place, while Dr Håkansson undid the protective cone around his neck.

'You'll be pleased to get rid of this lampshade, old fellow,' the vet said as he removed the ungainly apparatus.

Martin gave his head a shake, surprised, it seemed, by the sudden return of freedom. Dr Håkansson leaned forward and touched the dog's snout. Then,

209

with a movement so deft that Ulf almost failed to notice it, he snipped the stitches one each side before doing the same to Martin's nose. '*Voilà*,' he said as he completed the procedure.

Ulf smiled. He was pleased that he had a vet who said *voilà*. It was not necessarily what one expected from somebody whose profession was so physical, so matter of fact. Chefs might say voilà as they extracted some elaborate creation from the oven; an artist might say voilà as he put the final touch of paint to the canvas; a couturier might utter the word as he revealed a new outfit — but not a vet; nor, for that matter, a dentist, nor, a *fortiori*, a fireman, as he played the final jet of water over the dying embers of a fire.

Dr Håkansson peered closely at Martin's nose. As he did so, the dog turned towards him and sniffed appreciatively.

'Not at all bad,' mused Dr Håkansson. 'I see what you mean about the angle, but I don't think it makes much difference to a dog.'

Ulf bit his tongue. He had been expecting Dr Håkansson to offer some apology, but none seemed forthcoming; quite the opposite, in fact: it seemed to him that Dr Håkansson was proud of his handiwork rather than being ashamed.

'How did it happen?' Ulf asked, trying not to sound accusing.

Dr Håkansson was casual. 'What? This nose business? Oh, a dog's nose is a very odd thing, you know. It's like a bit of sponge. Pretty formless. You can't really tell which way is up and which is down.'

Ulf frowned. 'Is that really so?'

Dr Håkansson glanced at him. His tone became defensive. 'Yes, it is. Otherwise I wouldn't say it.'

210

'I suppose you know best,' said Ulf.

Dr Håkansson nodded. 'Yes, I do.'

Ulf looked away. He liked Dr Håkansson, and had known him for some years. At Christmas they exchanged greetings, Dr Håkansson sending him the same Christmas card every year, addressed to 'Ulf and Martin Varg', and featuring a picture of a wolf standing in the freshly fallen snow, looking up at Santa Claus and his reindeer-drawn sleigh. The wolf looked confused — as well he might, thought Ulf. It was a peculiar image, and Ulf wondered whether it was chosen for him because of his name, but Mrs Högfors had told him that her friend, who was also a client of Dr Håkansson, received an identical card.

But Dr Håkansson had more to say on the subject. 'Of course, you could opt to have plastic surgery. I wouldn't recommend it, but the option's there.'

Ulf waited for him to explain.

'There's a new cosmetic surgery service,' Dr Håkansson continued. 'It's a partnership that opened up six months ago. They're in Copenhagen, but they obviously take Swedish patients.'

'Are you talking about me?' Ulf asked. 'Or Martin?'

Dr Håkansson laughed. 'Martin, of course.' He gave Ulf a sideways glance. 'I don't think you need cosmetic surgery, Ulf. Not you. You're very fortunate, you know, looks-wise. My wife says you could easily get a job in the films.' He paused. 'I could do with a bit of help, I suppose. My wife says my ears are a bit odd.' He paused again. 'Do you think they are, Ulf?'

Ulf looked at Dr Håkansson. 'Not really,' he said. 'I've never looked at your ears, I must admit. Ears are ears, as far as I'm concerned.'

'That's because you're a man,' said Dr Håkansson.

'Men don't look at each other's ears — not critically, I suppose.'

'Possibly not,' said Ulf.

'But I suppose if I'm being honest with myself, I must admit mine do stick out a bit.'

Ulf looked at the vet again. 'I don't think so,' he said. 'Not to the extent of being a hazard to passers-by.'

Dr Håkansson laughed. 'Well, that's a relief.' He touched his right ear, as if to reassure himself. 'I don't really care what I look like, do you?'

Ulf shrugged. 'I don't think about it much.'

'That's because you don't have any issues,' said Dr Håkansson. 'If your ears were like mine, you might think differently.'

'There's nothing wrong with your ears,' said Ulf.

Dr Håkansson looked distracted. 'I know somebody who had his ears pinned back. He was in my class at vet school. He was Norwegian. He came from Bergen, I think. Anyway, he met this Swedish girl when he was at university here and she was quite a looker. She was a model, actually, and you used to see her on the cover of magazines. They married just after he graduated. And the next thing I heard was that he had had his ears pinned back. It looked odd.'

'Odd?'

'Yes. Most ears stick out a bit — his now were flattened back against his head. It made him look windswept.'

'I suppose there are worse things than looking windswept,' said Ulf. And he thought: such as having your nose upside down. But he did not say that.

Dr Håkansson became business-like. 'I'm going to give you some worming pills for Martin, and I'm just

212

going to check his blood. Then, I think, we can let you go home. Unless you want to discuss the cosmetic surgery issue further. I don't recommend it. I don't really like the idea of people taking their dogs to have a facelift — you know, tightening the skin around the eyes — that sort of thing.'

'I quite agree,' said Ulf. 'It's . . . it's ridiculous.'

'Unethical, in my view,' said Dr Håkansson.

The vet took a blood sample. Martin either did not feel the needle or was simply unconcerned. Then, after giving a small packet of worming pills to Ulf, Dr Håkansson opened the consultation-room door and ushered them out.

'I'll take a look at him in a year or so,' said the vet. 'If the bloods come up with anything, I'll let you know. But I suspect all will be normal.'

Ulf thanked him and made his way to the reception desk. He stopped. Hilma, the usual receptionist, had been replaced during the time he and Martin had been in the consultation room. Now there was a different woman sitting where he expected to see Hilma.

'Hilma?' asked Ulf.

The new receptionist smiled. 'Hilma's gone home. She's going to be on holiday for three weeks. I'm the replacement.'

Ulf looked at her. 'I'm Ulf. And this . . .' He gestured to Martin at his feet. 'This is my dog, Martin.'

The receptionist's manner was warm and friendly. 'I know. I was looking at the records.'

'Of course,' said Ulf. 'The bill.'

'I've printed it out. Here.' She handed him a piece of paper, and Ulf reached for his wallet and the credit card it contained.

'I'm Juni,' she said.

He reached out to shake her hand across the desk — and gave her a discreetly appraising look. She was about his age — perhaps a little younger. He looked again. The second look counted; he had learned that in his encounters with suspects. The first look told you very little; the second was very different. She was undoubtedly attractive, with the high cheekbones and colouring of the Nordic beauty. She might have emerged, he thought, from a Scandinavian vitalist picture, one of those paintings where flaxen-haired women stood with the wind in their hair, the picture of glowing beauty and health. They had not thought of it in those terms, those artists of the time, but they were only a short inch away from the glorification of the physical in fascist art. One had to be so careful. One step further and the blonde became frightening, even distasteful: the cold, the unfinished, the too pallid, and the concomitantly cruel. But not here.

His gaze wandered to Juni's left hand — the hand with which she had given him the bill. There was no ring. He was a detective, after all, and it was his job to notice such things. Or so he told himself, and then admitted that that was not the reason he had looked.

He said, as he handed her the card, 'Are you from Malmö?'

She shook her head. 'Not originally. I came here when my husband took a job.'

He felt unexpected disappointment. A husband — of course. So often there was a husband, or a boyfriend, or somebody.

'But then he went back to Gothenburg. We separated. I stayed here in Malmö. Gothenburg's fine, but we'd have kept bumping into one another if I'd gone back there. You know how it is.'

Ulf felt his heart give a leap. 'I see.' He smiled at her. 'You obviously like it here.'

'Malmö's great. I like the people. I like the atmosphere.'

Ulf smiled again. 'Yes, you hear people saying Malmö's cool. You hear that all the time.'

'Well, it is,' said Juni.

She processed the payment and then handed the card back to him.

'Martin here is deaf,' Ulf said.

He was not sure why he mentioned this, but he wanted to prolong the conversation, and that was at least something that might spin things out.

It did. 'Poor Martin,' Juni said. 'I saw that in the notes, actually.' She pointed to her computer screen. 'Dr Håkansson has written about it.'

'I've taught him to lip-read,' said Ulf. 'People find that hard to believe, but he can do it. Just a few words, of course, but I think he's the only dog in Sweden who can lip-read.'

'But that's wonderful!' exclaimed Juni. 'You must be so proud of him.'

'I am,' admitted Ulf.

'Will you show me?'

'Of course.'

Ulf turned to face Martin. 'Martin!' he commanded. 'Sit, Martin!'

He articulated the words carefully, making sure that his lips were fully visible to the dog. Martin stared up at him. There was adoration in his eyes. Ulf was God. Ulf was the principle that drove the world about him, that moved the greater spheres above that dogs rarely saw, but could smell. Ulf was everything to Martin. And of course Martin would sit. If God said sit, we sat.

Martin sat, and Juni clapped her hands in delight. 'Bravo!' she said. 'That's amazing.'

Ulf thanked her, in a self-effacing way. He looked at her left hand again. She noticed, but said nothing. He looked out of the window.

'You wouldn't be — ' He broke off. He was aware that she was looking down at her hands, folded on her lap, demurely. He was emboldened. She had not frowned. She had not busied herself with some task to avoid him. She simply looked at her hands. It was so easy; so easy; but it had been so long since he had done it that he had almost forgotten how simple it was. You asked somebody and they said yes or no. You said 'Coffee?' or 'A drink?' And you usually received your answer there and then, which in this case was yes. 'Yes,' Juni said, 'I am free after work, as it happens. Yes, let's meet for a drink. Why not?'

He suggested they meet in a bar — the first bar that came to mind. It was a place that a young, well-heeled set liked — rowdy, but only at the weekends. On weeknights there was a different, less boisterous clientele. It was a place, they said, that was popular with blind dates as there was a fire exit you could use if you needed to get away discreetly. She said, 'I used to go there with my ex.'

'Ah. Perhaps not.'

'No.'

Ulf took a deep breath. 'Look, let's skip bars altogether. Would you let me cook you dinner? At my place?' As he issued the invitation he wondered what he would give her. There was no food in the flat, a visit to the supermarket being long overdue.

'I'm not sure . . .'

'I'm perfectly respectable,' said Ulf. 'Ask Dr Håkansson.'

'That won't be necessary,' said Juni. 'I can tell that you are.'

Ulf was pleased, but then he thought: was it a good thing to look so obviously respectable? Was that what he wanted? Was it not better to look ever so slightly dangerous — not actually be dangerous, of course. Women liked men who had a slight air of danger about them. That added spice to a relationship — if one wanted spice. But did he? He was not sure. And as he thought about it, it came to him that he knew perfectly well what he wanted. It was Anna.

But he had to go on. There was no point in hankering after what could never be.

He said, 'Just dinner. I'll drive you home.'

She glanced out of the window. 'Is that your car there? That lovely Saab?'

'It is.'

'What time?' she asked.

* * *

Ulf left Martin with Mrs Högfors.

'I'm entertaining somebody this evening,' he explained. 'If you wouldn't mind having Martin for a while . . .'

Mrs Högfors was immediately curious. 'What's her name?' she asked. And then laughed at her own question, adding, 'Not that I'm the nosy neighbour, Ulf.'

'There's nothing wrong with nosy neighbours,' he responded. 'We get a lot of information from them in the CID. People phone up with all sorts of snippets about their neighbours — mostly false, of course, but

217

there's the occasional nugget.'

Mrs Högfors looked furtive.

'Is there anything you'd like to tell me?' asked Ulf, half in jest, but half in the belief that Mrs Högfors' expression meant that there was something she wanted to say.

'I don't like to burden you,' she said. 'You have enough on your plate, I imagine.'

Ulf assured her that he always had time to hear her concerns.

'I heard something,' she said. 'It was the other day, when I was taking Martin out for his morning walk. You had gone into work early — remember?'

Ulf nodded. 'Please go on,' he said.

'Well, when we reached the park, I noticed that there were two men on the bench near the gate. You know the one? It's just behind that notice about not cycling on the grass.'

'I know it,' said Ulf.

Mrs Högfors lowered her voice. 'They looked suspicious. I'd never seen them there before and they looked as if they were up to something.'

Ulf waited.

'They were talking to each other, and one gave the other something. I couldn't see what it was, as it was wrapped up in brown paper. He put it in his pocket and shortly after that he stood up — the one who had been given the parcel — and walked off. The other one stayed on the bench. When he saw me, he pulled his hat down over his eyes. It was very deliberate.'

Ulf raised an eyebrow. 'It certainly sounds like suspicious behaviour to me,' he said.

'Doesn't it?' Mrs Högfors agreed. 'But there's something else. They were speaking Russian — I'm sure of it.'

For a few moments, Ulf said nothing. Mrs Högfors had many good points, and he often told himself how lucky he was to have her as a neighbour. But like all of us, she had her faults, and her antipathy towards the Russians was the most obvious of these. So after a while, Ulf said, 'It could have been innocent, you know. There are plenty of perfectly law-abiding Russians who may need to use the park from time to time.'

Mrs Högfors was clearly not convinced. 'But what was in the parcel?' she asked. 'That's what I'd like to know.'

Ulf shrugged. 'People give one another parcels,' he said. 'Innocent parcels — in the majority of cases. It happens all the time.'

Mrs Högfors looked away. 'I know that you're very trusting when it comes to Russians, Ulf. I know that. But the Russians probably know it too, and get away with all sorts of things.' She paused. 'Swedish values are under pressure, you know.'

Ulf struggled. There *was* a problem of foreign crime in Sweden, but it was not as simple as some people would have it. The official line, of course, was that there was no real problem. People always blamed others for crime — and those of a foreign background were an easy target. That could quickly lead to the demonisation of entire communities, most of whose members would be as innocent as anybody else. And yet what if it were true that organised bands of people from elsewhere were coming to Sweden to prey on a liberal and trusting society? If you were a petty thief from a place of grinding poverty, where the pickings were small and the criminal courts harsh, would it not make every sort of sense for you to move to Malmö

219

or Stockholm, where there was so much more to be stolen and where punishments were mild? There was a big difference between an Albanian prison and its Swedish equivalent.

And if this criminal tourism were to be noticed by people like Mrs Högfors, should they be prevented from complaining? Were they to be dissuaded from remarking on the evidence of their own eyes? Perhaps they had to learn to accept imported crime as an inevitable concomitant of the fact that the world's borders were now more porous, and that the walls of distance that protected people from others had been irretrievably breached. We were inhabitants now of a single rock in a sea of suffering and need. That, perhaps, was the uncomfortable truth to which people needed to adjust. Yet they would still hanker, he suspected, for lost days when the intimacy of a homogeneous society, and the personal ties that bound one to another in such smaller worlds, meant that crime was, on the whole, rather rare. In a society of strangers, by contrast, crime was as hard to control as it was easy to commit. It was not hard to rob a victim you had never met, and with whom you shared no common past, no language, no nursery rhymes or fairy tales; it was not hard to shoot or stab one whose name you did not know, with whom you had never been ice-skating, with whom there was no shared everyday cosmology. He sighed. 'Don't make matters worse,' the Commissioner had once said when addressing a meeting of senior officers. 'Feel your way through situations. Love, not hate, is the balm that a divided society needs.' Ulf had written this down, verbatim, as surprised as every other member of the audience that the Commissioner should sound this note. And yet, he reflected, he was absolutely right. It was hard to remain tolerant; it was hard to do the right thing; but we simply had no alternative. Oppression and violence brought sorrow — and more violence. And that would make things worse — the Commissioner was right about that. We cannot go back to a Sweden that no longer exists, Ulf thought. We had to make a new Sweden that would not jar too much with the Sweden we had lost.

Mrs Högfors was satisfied that she had now done her duty, and returned to the subject of Ulf's guest. 'I'm pleased you're entertaining,' she said. 'I worry about you, Ulf. There's no reason for you to be on your own. You'd make such a good partner for somebody. You don't need to be lonely, you know.'

He thanked her, but added, 'I'm not sure whether anybody would have me, you know.'

'Nonsense,' said Mrs Högfors. 'You're a very good-looking man. You don't drink too much — unlike some men. You don't go on and on about football — a serious male weakness. You have good taste when it comes to . . . well, to everything, really. So why not share your life with somebody?'

Ulf looked away. 'I'd like to,' he said. 'I've wanted to for some time.'

'But why the reluctance, then? What's holding you back.'

He brought his gaze back to her. Suddenly, he wanted to confide. She knew just about everything about him anyway — why hold back on the one thing that really mattered in his life? His therapist, Dr Svensson, had once said, 'Mrs Högfors, you know, is your mother,' and he had laughed. But the insight behind that analysis was profound. She was. She was

221

his mother, and to Martin she was, he imagined, Gaia — if dogs believed in the old gods.

He made the decision. 'I've been in love, you see. All this time. Years.'

She stared at him. 'With somebody who hasn't loved you back?'

He hesitated. He was not sure whether Anna loved him. She liked him — that was plain enough. But that was different from love. So he said, 'I'm not sure about that. It may be that she loves me in the way in which I love her — I don't know. But what I do know is that we could never be together.'

'Because she's married?'

Mrs Högfors had gone straight to the kernel of the matter, and Ulf realised that this was because she was a woman. Women had a far finer feeling for these things than men did. Women understood intuitively the currents and courses of the heart.

He bit his lip. *Because she was married.* It was that simple. And that final.

'Yes. Because she's married to somebody else.'

Mrs Högfors reached out to take Ulf's hand. She had never done that before, but the gesture seemed entirely right in the circumstances. 'Dear Ulf,' she said.

He found himself fighting back tears. He loved Anna so much. That was where the tears came from; from his feeling for her. Love makes you cry as reliably as any onion. He loved her as he had never loved anybody before. She was his all, his everything, the totality, the essence, the person who made sense of everything for him, and yet he could not be with her as *himself*, as the man who loved her. It seemed so hard, although he knew that there were cases of greater hopelessness.

222

There were men who loved other men who could only love women; or women who loved other women who could only be with a man. That was hopelessness of a different order — like yearning to be a swan when you were demonstrably a bird of a different feather; or wanting to be able to sing when you had no voice; or wanting to be anything you could never be. Oh, it was so hard, so bitter, for so many people on the outside looking in, and although you wanted to tell them that it was fine for them to be what they were, you knew that would never assuage the desire they nurtured for the unattainable state of grace.

He thought: don't be self-pitying. You can't have everything you want in this life. Everybody had to compromise; everybody had to make do with the hand they'd been dealt. Self-pity was a railing against fate, really, and that was completely pointless; and, for others who witnessed it, merely tedious.

'I'm sorry,' he said. 'I shouldn't have involved you in this.'

'But you should have. You should have.' She shook her head as she went on, 'You men — you're all the same. You spend so much time trying to be strong when what you should do is have a good cry.'

He smiled weakly. They had said, at a training course, detectives *could* cry; and that had been a comfort to a number of them, even if not to those supercilious, urbane types in Commercial Crime. They did not feel the need to cry because they saw so few of the things that everybody else saw: the horrible things that people did to one another; the distress, the sorrow, the pain of victims. They had none of the chores that Traffic had: the dreaded calls to break the news to relatives of a fatal pile-up; or Homicide's sad

223

trips to identify the deceased at the morgue; or the Drug Squad's wading through the degrading squalor of addiction. There was so much to cry about, so much; although he had to admit that in Sensitive Crimes they were rarely called to see anything really disturbing — laughable, yes, because the crimes they investigated were so unusual, and revealing of the oddest corners of human nature, but not disturbing.

He said to Mrs Högfors, 'Thank you. You're probably right.'

'Yes, I am right — about this, at least. And now, this person you're seeing this evening — is she the one you've been in love with?' There was a note of disapproval in Mrs Högfors' voice. She did not want Ulf to be an adulterer.

'No,' Ulf reassured her. 'This is not that other person.'

'This is a new friend? Somebody you've just met?'

He nodded his confirmation. He wondered whether he should say that she had been introduced by Martin — which was true, in a way: if it weren't for Martin, they would never have met.

'That's very good,' said Mrs Högfors. 'And you feel this might be the beginning of something?'

'Yes,' said Ulf. 'Or possibly. Or maybe not. I don't really know.'

Mrs Högfors looked thoughtful. 'Falling in love with somebody requires preparation, you know.'

'Oh yes?'

'Yes. You have to open yourself up to the process. You have to be *ready*. If you have the defences up, then it won't happen.'

He looked at her — and smiled. He found himself wondering about the part that love had played in her life. There had been the husband, whom Ulf had never met — the man she referred to simply as 'Högfors'. She spoke of him as if he had been the fount of all wisdom, the paragon of all virtue. She would have loved him deeply and with complete loyalty, Ulf imagined. She would have dedicated her life to him with unquestioning willingness. And Ulf hoped that he had done the same for her; he thought that this was probably the case. How fortunate to find in this world an anchor, a fixed point in one's life, that dispels all doubt and loneliness. How lucky were such people as Mrs Högfors and the late Högfors — fortunate that their luck had held even after the demise of one of them; for the memory of love, it seems, is almost as strong a consolation as love itself.

Ulf decided that he would not try to forget Anna. He would remember that he once loved her, and would draw from that the strength to start loving somebody else. As long as . . . as long as one could *choose* to fall in love. What Mrs Högfors had said implied that one could; that love was preceded by a state of readiness that was indeed chosen. It was like preparing a field, perhaps, for the planting of a crop. You cleared away the stones; you broke the ground; you drove away the raiding birds. All of that you did deliberately and in pursuit of a goal that you had chosen. Love was choice. We could *choose* to love after all.

He looked down at Martin, who stared back up at him with a love that, although rarely celebrated in the human arts, was as strong as that of Pyramus for Thisbe, Rodolfo for Mimi, Dante for Beatrice. And everywhere, Ulf thought, this adoration is on show in our lives, in the simple, everyday sight of a human and a dog, walking together, bound by a love that seems so ordinary that we take it entirely for granted. Dogs, of course, did not choose to love. Their love was deep in their DNA, deep in their instincts. But so was ours, thought Ulf; so was ours . . .

Mrs Högfors was staring at him. 'Are you feeling all right, Ulf?' she asked.

He assured her that he was.

'Martin can have a sleepover,' she said.

'He'll love that,' said Ulf, adding, 'He's very fond of you, you know.'

Mrs Högfors took the compliment in her stride. 'There is nothing larger than a dog's heart,' she said. 'Beside their hearts, ours are small and narrow, selfish and jealous — I'm sorry to say.'

One word in this observation stood out: *jealous*. And Ulf thought: that is the key to this whole unpleasant business that Blomquist and I must try to sort out. The more they looked into it, the more complex it became, and yet jealousy was never complicated: it was simple and could rarely disguise itself with any skill. The important thing was to look in the right direction — then the motivating jealousy would be laid bare, exposed in all its malevolence and its ability to disturb the surface of our lives.

He sighed. That particular insight was not all that helpful. Knowing where to look was the problem, even if the looking itself was not.

16

Women Who Love Men

'You're looking pleased with the world,' said Blomquist when he met Ulf in the coffee bar the following morning.

Ulf looked up from his newspaper and then set the paper aside. It would be hard to be pleased with the wider world this morning, in view of what was happening. Disaster might not yet have struck, but the paper implied it might not be far off. Italian banks, he had been reading, were in dire straits — a time bomb primed to go off at any moment, the newspaper's financial editor had warned. *When, not if, the Italian banking system collapses* . . . Of course they had been saying that for years, and yet the Italian economy, Byzantine in its ways, half concealed from the prying eyes of auditors and the taxman, continued with its feats of legerdemain. Ulf had not quite finished the article by the time Blomquist arrived, but he had had sufficient time to ponder the existential question mark that hovered over Italian banks. Swedish banks were safe and solid, as were their German equivalents. What was it about *latitude* that made all the difference in banking? Of course, latitude was not actually the problem — the real issue was what lay behind latitude; what mattered was Protestantism, and its historical shadow. He sighed. These were thoughts that would have to wait — unless, of course, he asked Blomquist for his view. What, he wondered, did Blomquist think about Italian banks? Would his views be as strong as were his opinions on salt in one's diet, vitamins, enzymes and the rest?

'Pleased with the world?' he said, in response to Blomquist's observation. 'Well, perhaps I am.'

'Been on a date?' asked Blomquist, signalling to the barista to bring him his coffee.

Ulf gave a start. 'How did you know?'

Blomquist tapped the side of his nose. It was a very irritating gesture, Ulf thought. He did not like people to tap the side of their noses like that.

'I can tell these things,' said Blomquist.

Ulf decided to tell him. Blomquist was right — he was happy, and the reason for that was that his dinner with Juni had been a conspicuous success. He had cooked a cheese soufflé that had been preceded by smoked halibut that he had found in his local deli. Juni had said, 'I love halibut — it's my favourite fish,' and then had said, of the soufflé, 'There is nothing I like more than a cheese soufflé — nothing.' And of the dessert he had prepared — pears in wine with cardamom, she had said, 'I've always loved pears in wine with cardamom — always.'

They had talked until midnight, and the hours had fled. Then Ulf had driven her back to her flat in his silver Saab and she had said, 'I just love old Saabs.' They had parted with an embrace that lasted slightly longer — just a few seconds — than the embrace with which ordinary friends might leave one another, but that was enough for Ulf to know that there was a future to this relationship. And that instinct was confirmed when she had accepted his invitation to meet the following evening, although she had insisted that on this occasion she would cook for him. 'Do you like

228

pasta?' she had asked. 'Do you like crab linguine?' And he had replied that he loved it and that he had been thinking of eating more crab linguine in the future. And they had both laughed, and he had kissed her goodnight and driven away in his silver Saab.

He suddenly felt the need to share all that with Blomquist, but instead he said, 'Blomquist, why do you think Italian banks are so shaky?'

Blomquist did not seem to be surprised by this question, and responded as if it was entirely normal to be asked this, first thing, by one's superior officer, over coffee. It was as if he had his answer at the ready, like a well-prepared interview candidate.

'Italian banks?' he said. 'Oh well, the reason for that is the Italians themselves. Look behind any Italian bank and what do you see? Italians.'

Ulf laughed. 'One wouldn't expect anything else. But do you think Italians can't run banks? They're highly intelligent people, in general. Extremely competent. They're creative. They're charming. Musical. Great engineers. They make wonderful things. They're the best forgers on the planet. The list goes on and on.'

'Yes, I agree with all that,' said Blomquist. 'But they're too exuberant. That's the problem. And too sympathetic. They invented the word *simpatico*, remember? Bankers should not be sympathetic. Bankers need to be retentive personalities. They need to hoard. The Italians are better at spending than hoarding. Simple.'

Blomquist now gave Ulf a look that suggested that the topic had been adequately dealt with. There was nothing more to be said about the Italian banking crisis: it would doubtless continue as long as Italian

229

banks existed. There was not much point in exploring it further. But then Blomquist said, 'Of course, there's their diet. Diet has a lot to do with how people are, you know, and if you look at what the Italians eat—'

Ulf stopped him. 'We need to talk about our case,' he said.

Blomquist reluctantly left the Italian diet unexplored. Ulf thought: I'm having crab linguine tonight.

'Yes,' said Blomquist. 'I have the information you asked for.'

He handed Ulf a sheet of paper. 'I went to see Anders. I'm pleased to say that he keeps very good records. He was able to identify three paintings that he has had his doubts about in the last few years. He said we could go back further if required, but I thought four years would do.'

Ulf agreed. Revenge, as everybody knew, was a dish best served cold, but not that cold. Grudges nursed for too long tended to have the edges removed and might not inspire a programme of calculated reprisal.

He saw that Blomquist had written down three names, each followed by a couple of sentences. One of the names had been underlined in red ink. Ulf noticed that, and looked up sharply. So it was Blomquist who did that — who took a red pen to the newspapers and magazines the coffee bar provided for its customers.

'I see you've underlined this name,' Ulf said, pointing to the top of the list. 'Viggo Blix.'

'Yes,' said Blomquist. 'Viggo Blix. Have you heard of him?'

Ulf searched his memory. The name was vaguely familiar, but he could not think why. It was an arresting name: Viggo was suggestive of strength and determination, and Blix was one of those odd, short names that were such a welcome contrast to the patronymics that everybody used to have. Viggo Blix would be a man of achievement, thought Ulf — if nominative determinism had anything to it. And then he remembered the item in the newspaper. There had been a picture of a man handing over a cheque to a smiling recipient. There had been something about a grateful hospital.

'Dotcoms,' said Ulf. 'Isn't he one of these dotcom people who made a lot of money . . . ' He waved a hand in the air. That was the domain of these people — the ether, out of which they conjured implausible fortunes.

'In California,' supplied Blomquist. 'Yes. He went to San Diego twenty years ago, or thereabouts. He set up some sort of design site. If you wanted a part made for something, you could use his software to design it and then that would be automatically sent to just the right people in China who could make it for you. It took off.'

'Lucky man,' said Ulf.

'He made a real packet,' Blomquist continued. 'He sold the company to a firm in Indiana, and pretty much retired at the age of forty-eight. That was five years ago. He was from this part of the country and he came back. He has a house just round the corner from the Villa Lindhaga Montessori School. You know the place?'

Ulf knew the school. Mrs Högfors' niece worked there and at Halloween she passed on to her aunt the flesh of the pumpkins that the children hollowed out for lanterns. Mrs Högfors made pumpkin pies for her freezer and gave some to Ulf. He did not like pumpkin pie but was too embarrassed to reject the gifts.

He passed them on to Carl in the office, who received them gratefully.

'I'm not sure about Montessori education,' Blomquist said. 'There's a lot of freedom in it, you know, and you learn when you want to learn. But what if you don't feel in the mood — what then?'

Ulf cleared his throat. This was not the time to discuss the Montessori method. And he would be firm about that. 'I think we should—'

But Blomquist was determined. 'I went to a conventional school,' he said. 'We sat in rows and we had lessons according to a timetable. We did what we had to do, when we had to do it.'

Ulf looked up at the ceiling. 'But that can kill a child's interest in learning,' he said. 'I had a dreadful history teacher. He frightened us. He made us read out loud from a very dull book. Page after page. Can you imagine? But look, Blomquist, we must get on with the matter in hand.'

Blomquist glanced at the piece of paper. 'Viggo Blix is in Malmö. The other two aren't — one is in Stockholm and the other now lives in Milan. The client in Stockholm is a Catholic priest, a Monsignor, who was left some paintings by his grandfather. He's a member of a well-off family. The paintings weren't anything very special, but some might have been by an artist called Carl Larsson. Apparently that would have been a good thing. But they weren't — they were by somebody who wanted to paint like Larsson. But I don't think a Catholic priest would try to get back at Anders, do you?'

'No,' said Ulf. 'Highly unlikely.' And yet . . . He had arrested two ministers of religion in his career — one for fraud, and another for —

232

Blomquist interrupted his thoughts. 'And Anders says that the one in Milan isn't at all well. He's got one of those nasty neurological diseases, poor man.'

'He's not likely to be doing anything criminal then,' said Ulf. 'If you have something like that, I think you tend not to be interested in pursuing vendettas. You forgive, I imagine. You try to tie up loose ends.'

'I would,' said Blomquist.

Ulf remembered something. 'Mind you, I remember reading about a Spanish conquistador on his deathbed. The priest said to him, 'And have you forgiven your enemies, my son?' And the conquistador replied, 'Enemies? I have no enemies. I have killed them all.'.'

Blomquist frowned. 'And had he?'

Ulf stared at him. 'Who knows? Probably.' He cleared his throat again. 'Anyway, let's not worry about conquistadors. This Viggo Blix — I seem to recall that he was in the papers after he had given something to somebody.'

Blomquist was prepared. 'I looked him up. He gave five million kronor to one of the hospitals. They needed to buy a fancy scanner from Canada. Viggo Blix came up with the cash.'

Ulf approved of that.

'He's a big collector, apparently,' Blomquist went on. 'Anders says that he has some pretty impressive paintings. Early stuff — as well as some nineteenth-century and contemporary Scandinavian art. He was asked to give an insurance report on the collection and that's when the trouble began.'

Blomquist's coffee arrived, and he blew across the top of the cup to cool it down. A few small flecks of milky foam landed on Ulf's jacket. Ulf looked down, but did not brush them off. It was best to ignore these things — as when somebody inadvertently spits on you while speaking. The mortification of the other is attenuated by our not noticing such things, or at least pretending not to notice them; only the most ill-mannered will remove a flake of dandruff from the shoulders of a visitor.

Blomquist revealed what Anders had told him about the painting evaluation he had carried out for an insurance company. 'The sums involved were very large. If you look at what I've written there you'll see I noted some of the artists involved. You'll probably know their names — they don't mean anything to me.'

Ulf examined the sheet of paper. 'Matisse?' he said. 'Well, well. And Domenico Ghirlandaio. And Hockney. You've heard of Hockney, Blomquist? Swimming pools in California — that sort of thing.'

'Perhaps,' said Blomquist.

'Anyway, this is very impressive. These are museum pieces.'

'Yes, that's what Anders said. And everything was genuine, Anders said, except for one painting that simply wasn't what Viggo claimed. You'll see the name written down there. See?'

Ulf read. 'Alessandro Bonvicino, known as Il Moretto.'

'That means a.k.a., as we say it,' said Blomquist. 'Il Moretto was a sort of nickname. But he didn't paint the painting that Viggo has in his collection. Anders said that it was just from his studio — painted by an apprentice or somebody — not by the man himself. It so happens that this is an artist Anders has particular knowledge about. He wrote some articles about Il Moretto, he said, and that if he says something isn't

234

by him, then a lot of people are going to believe him.'

'I see,' said Ulf. 'And Viggo was none too pleased?'

'That's putting it mildly,' said Blomquist. 'Apparently he went through the roof. Ballistic. He was furious. Anders said that his reaction was out of all proportion to the issue. There he was with this fantastic collection and only one comparatively unimportant painting had had a question mark put over it. Why should he be so furious?'

Ulf shrugged. 'Collectors can be obsessive. They can be sensitive.'

'So it would seem. He yelled at Anders. He threatened to sue him. He turned purple with rage, Anders said. He could have had a stroke.'

'Yes,' said Ulf. 'A bit of an over-reaction.'

Blomquist looked thoughtful. 'He probably has blood pressure issues. A lot of people do, you know. They have blood pressure issues that they don't know about. That's why they call hypertension the silent killer.'

Blomquist fixed Ulf with a concerned stare. 'Do you have your blood pressure checked regularly, Ulf?'

Ulf had to admit that his visits to the doctor were infrequent. 'I see a psychotherapist, as I think you know. But he doesn't take my blood pressure.'

'Is he a qualified doctor?' asked Blomquist.

'Yes,' said Ulf. 'He's a fully trained psychiatrist. He will have had a proper medical training.'

'He'll know all about blood pressure then,' said Blomquist. 'I don't see why he can't take your blood pressure. It's not difficult.' He paused. 'Do you like salty things?'

'I do. They're a bit addictive, aren't they? You eat one salted cashew nut and then you end up eating the whole packet.'

Blomquist shook his head. 'Very dangerous. Salt is not a good idea if you have high blood pressure.'

'But I don't think I do,' said Ulf. 'And anyway, Blomquist, let's concentrate on—'

'Yes, all right,' said Blomquist, 'but I don't think you can say that you don't have high blood pressure. How do you know that?'

Ulf bit his lip. Working with Blomquist would lead, he feared, to constantly punctured lips. People would wonder why his lips were swollen, and he would have to explain.

Blomquist returned to the point. 'Anders said that he thought it had all died down. He heard no more from Viggo Blix and he said he thought that he had moved on to other things. Apparently he had a bit of a reputation for having rows, and people like that get hot under the collar for a little while and then move on. He thought it very unlikely that Viggo would be behind this campaign against him. He has far bigger fish to fry, Anders said.'

Ulf thought that this was not for Anders to judge. 'We're the ones to decide that, Blomquist,' he said. 'I think we should go and see this Viggo Blix and have a word with him.'

'I agree,' said Blomquist. 'In fact, I've already arranged an appointment for us at eleven-thirty this morning — at his place.'

Ulf's surprise showed. 'That's very efficient, Blomquist,' he said.

Blomquist beamed with pleasure. 'Thank you,' he said. He blew over his coffee once more, and once again small flecks of foam landed on Ulf. Ulf picked up his own cup of coffee and blew over it too, hoping

236

that flecks of his foam might reach Blomquist and thus make him more careful next time. But they simply landed on the sleeve of his own jacket. I deserved that, he thought; it was a very childish thing to do, and he felt ashamed.

'Careful,' said Blomquist, reaching out to brush the foam off Ulf's clothing. 'Milk stains, you know. And I'll tell you something, Ulf, if you spill a bottle of milk in your car, watch out. Milk turns rancid and it'll take months to get rid of the smell. It's awful. I know somebody who had to sell his car because he couldn't get the smell of sour milk out of the carpets in the footwell. He just couldn't. He tried everything. Bleach was no good. Some of those special enzyme cleaners — you know, the ones they use if somebody is sick over something — but they were no good either. It hung around like a . . . bad smell.'

★ ★ ★

You would know, thought Ulf, that the imposing, stone-faced house, painted eggshell blue, was the home of somebody substantial, although you would not necessarily guess that it contained a Matisse and a whole collection of similar paintings. You might notice, though, the watching cameras and the blinking alarms; you might comment on the height of the surrounding wall and the sharpness of the ornate, pointed fleur-de-lys that spiked its top; you might also observe the well-tended garden with its ornamental fountain and its marble benches. Whatever your focus, the conclusion would be the same — that you were in the presence of significant funds.

237

Blomquist drew in his breath. 'Money,' he said simply.

Ulf smiled. 'Lots of it, Blomquist. So much for our egalitarian society.'

'I suppose he pays his taxes,' said Blomquist.

'Lots of them,' remarked Ulf. 'If he does.'

They made their way to the front door and pressed a discreet brass buzzer. Above their heads a camera light blinked red, blinked again, and then turned green. The door opened.

A major-domo would have completed the picture, but it was Viggo who greeted them in the doorway.

'Inspector Varg?' he said. And then politely, 'And Officer Blomquist?'

They shook hands. Then Viggo ushered them into a large drawing room immediately off the hall. 'Coffee is being fetched,' he said. 'But let's not wait. Please tell me what I can do for you.'

Ulf glanced at the walls as he sat down. It seemed as if the jewels of the collection were on display here — that was the Matisse over the mantelpiece; that was a Léger by the window; and that, he thought, was unquestionably a Renoir. Viggo noticed. 'You're interested in art?' he asked.

Ulf said that he was. 'I take an interest above all in Scandinavian art,' he said. 'But I very much enjoy the rest.'

'I don't know much about it,' said Blomquist, awkwardly.

Viggo was relaxed. 'The French are here,' he said. 'Swedish and Danish art is in the dining room. Earlier paintings — the Dutch and Italians — are upstairs. I can show them to you, if you'd like to see them.'

'I would,' said Ulf. 'I mean *we* would.' He glanced

238

at Blomquist, who nodded his agreement.

Viggo sat back in his chair. He looked at Ulf expectantly.

'We're investigating an incident connected with the Berks auction house,' Ulf began. 'A short time ago there was an issue there over a painting that was withdrawn when it was discovered it was not what it claimed to be.'

He watched Viggo's reaction. If he was behind what had happened, he might be expected to be cool and impassive, but there could be giveaway signs of guilt in his body language. Ulf treated body language with caution, but there were times when it could be helpful.

He did not expect what happened next. Viggo clapped his hands together and burst out laughing. 'Hah! Wonderful! The funniest thing that's happened in years!'

Ulf could not conceal his surprise. 'You mean . . . You mean you know about it?'

'Of course I know about it. Everybody does. It was the talk of the artistic community. I would have put it up on my billboard — if I had one. That poseur shown up for what he is: a chancer. A complete, eighty-four horsepower, twin-carburettor chancer.'

Ulf sat open-mouthed. Blomquist blinked.

'I can't tell you how pleased I was,' Viggo continued. 'I had a problem with that man, and how! I have a Moretto upstairs, a lovely painting — I'll show it to you. It's beautiful.' He enumerated the points of his argument on outraged fingers. 'It's classic Bonvicino — a delicate Madonna and wise-beyond-his-years infant. With that silvery look that Brescia school paintings have. It's all there. I have a provenance from a very

239

reliable dealer in Venice. I have literature on it from reputable Italian art journals. And then along comes this . . . this backwoodsman and pours cold water on its attribution. I was due to lend it to an exhibition in Copenhagen, but after they heard about what this character, Kindgren, said, they backed out and said they didn't want it. That was the kiss of death. It didn't matter what the scholars in Italy said, a big public gallery was saying no to it. The press got hold of that story and of course the whole thing then came out in the open. My painting, my Moretto, was now the work of some wretched apprentice.'

'You were upset by that?' asked Ulf.

'Upset? I was livid. I freely admit, I have a bit of a temper, and on this occasion I'm afraid I let rip a bit. But I was in the right, you know. I had every excuse.'

Blomquist spoke now. 'You don't particularly like him?'

Viggo looked as if he was struggling to understand the question. Then he said, 'Don't particularly like him? I loathe him. More than that, I despise him.' He paused. 'If he was on fire, gentlemen, I'm afraid I would not be the one to call the fire brigade.'

Silence descended on the room. Ulf was appalled by the display of vitriol. This man, who had so much, was bitter because somebody had questioned a single painting in his collection: bitter and unforgiving. Narcissistic personality disorder? He would ask Dr Svensson the next time he saw him.

From the hall outside came the sound of clinking cups.

'Our coffee is arriving,' said Viggo. 'And by the way, why do you want to talk to me about that Dughet business? Has somebody stolen it?'

Ulf shook his head. 'I just wanted to ask you whether you knew anything about it — whether you could help us in any way.'

'I'd help you if there was any chance of convicting Kindgren of something,' said Viggo. 'I'd do anything — perjure myself, if you like. Concoct evidence. Anything.' He laughed. 'Well, maybe not, but you get the gist of my feelings about him.'

Ulf smiled. 'You certainly make yourself clear.'

Their coffee arrived. Ulf said that there was nothing more that he wanted to ask Viggo about, and the conversation moved to Swedish art in the nineteenth century. 'I love those landscapes,' Viggo said.

'Me too,' said Ulf. 'Those magnificent skies.'

'It's interesting that there are no vapour trails in the sky in those paintings,' said Blomquist. 'Has either of you noticed that?'

★ ★ ★

They climbed into the Saab and drove away, in silence at first, both of them shocked by what they had heard.

'I hate that sort of thing,' said Blomquist at last. 'It leaves you feeling somehow sullied.'

'It does,' agreed Ulf. 'Hate is never edifying.'

'But it tells us something,' said Blomquist. 'It tells us something loud and clear.'

'It's not him? Is that what you think?'

'Yes,' said Blomquist. 'That's exactly what I think.'

'And I'm sure of that too,' said Ulf. 'If he were responsible for the campaign against Anders he would have been much more circumspect. But he had no hesitation in disclosing a glaring motive — sheer detestation. And I think that takes him off the hook.'

Blomquist nodded. 'Unless, of course, he knew that's what we'd think.'

Ulf considered this, but decided eventually to discount it. 'It was heartfelt,' he said. 'That man's no actor.'

'I agree,' said Blomquist. 'So where does that leave us?'

'Not much further forward,' said Ulf, his tone one of regret. He paused, lost in thought as he drove the silver Saab back across the city. Then he said, 'I still think there's a woman involved in this. I think we should look at female suspects.'

Blomquist agreed. 'You know something, Ulf?' he ventured. 'The women who set out to harm men are often the ones who love them. I've noticed that in quite a few cases I've been involved in.'

Ulf frowned. Blomquist's theories had to be taken with a large pinch of salt, and yet . . . and yet. Love and hate were neighbours in the territory of human emotions. So who were the women who might harbour feelings of animosity towards Anders? He had spoken of his mother, and of her disappointment at his choice of career. Then he had mentioned his wife and had disclosed her affair with the philosopher, Linus Wallin. Finally, there was Vera Lagerstrom, who was apparently harbouring a longing for Anders and who might be annoyed at being ignored. Anders' wife could probably be excluded: it simply did not seem likely that she would resort to an elaborate plot to tarnish his reputation. So, if they were to concentrate for the moment on female suspects, that left the mousy Vera and the unknown quantity that was Anders' mother.

He suggested this to Blomquist, who said, 'Yes, I

think so too — on the basis of what you've told me. And . . . ' He stopped. Then, 'Both of them?'

Ulf looked at him.

'Just a suggestion,' said Blomquist. 'But if we imagine for a moment that they are both involved, then that gives us the opportunity to play the oldest trick in the book on them.'

He explained to Ulf what he had in mind. Ulf laughed. 'Come on, Blomquist! That works on screen. It would never . . . ' He stopped. Perhaps he was wrong. 'I suppose we could try,' he concluded.

'Good,' said Blomquist. 'Who first?'

'Let's visit mother,' said Ulf.

'When?' asked Blomquist.

'Tomorrow. Can you get her address without letting Anders know we're going to see her?'

'Easy,' said Blomquist, tapping the side of his nose.

'I see,' said Ulf. Then he added, 'The oldest trick in the book may have been played any number of times, but for the person on whom it's played, it's usually the first.'

'True,' said Blomquist. 'It's a bit like jokes, isn't it? An old joke is new to the person who's never heard it. Of course, I always seem to hear jokes well after they've been heard by everybody else.'

'Here's one,' Ulf offered. 'Did you know that when the Commissioner went to a police conference in Italy recently, he went to a bar and ordered a glass of prosciutto?'

Blomquist looked puzzled. 'And?' he asked. 'Did he get it?'

'No,' said Ulf.

243

17
Crab Linguine and Happiness

The following morning, Ulf was first to arrive in the office. Blomquist had texted him to say that he had obtained an address for Anders' mother, and had contacted her to arrange a meeting at eleven a.m. that day. 'The address will surprise you,' he said — a remark that Ulf found hard to interpret, but then everything about this investigation was surprising as far as he was concerned. He was enjoying it, of course, as he was interested in anything to do with art, but he had always held that cases had an 'atmosphere' about them, and there was something here that smacked of irresolution. He could not quite put his finger on it, but this case, he thought, was not going to end with a clear determination. Some cases came to a very clear and satisfactory resolution: you found out who had done what, why it had been done, and you handed the case over to the prosecution authorities, all set out in a neat file. That, he felt, was not going to happen here, although he could not say exactly why he thought that.

Arriving in the office before anybody else had its advantages. There were several reports that he had to write, including — and these were the trickiest of all — the annual review statements of each of his colleagues. This was a task that Ulf was required to do as head of the Department of Sensitive Crimes, and it was not a duty that he enjoyed. Ulf believed in consensual leadership; he felt uncomfortable with hierarchical structures, and believed that in general one got the best out of everybody through collegiate arrangements. He did not like to give orders, and as a result he never told anybody to do anything. Indeed, he did not even describe himself as head of the department, preferring the terms *co-ordinator* or even *conductor*. The latter had occasioned a certain amount of derision from other departmental heads, in particular from the head of the Department of Indecent Activities, who had said at one meeting, quite openly, 'Are you an orchestra over in Sensitive Crimes, Ulf? What instrument do you play yourself?'

This had brought sniggers from the head of Traffic, who was a close friend of the head of Indecent Activities. The two of them had been at school together and were members of the same badminton club. Anna had also discovered that the wives of these two were cousins who taught in the same high school. There was nothing objectionable about their closeness, of course, although Carl, who was not particularly given to humorous observations, once wittily dubbed them Stanley and Oliver, after Laurel and Hardy — a sobriquet that had stuck and had become widely used throughout the force. Unfortunately, the victims of this nickname had heard of the implied insult, and had retaliated by coining a nickname for Carl. This was the Boy Wonder — Carl was youthful in appearance — but it had completely failed to register. They had then tried to get people to refer to him as Elvis Presley, again for no particular reason — Carl bore no resemblance to the late singer — and once again the name withered on the vine. Finding a nickname was an art, Ulf decided, which requires a delicate and perceptive sense of the essence of others — and those two did not seem to have it.

But as conductor of a department it was his inescapable duty to write at least two paragraphs about each member of staff, to be considered in the annual appraisal; even the Commissioner himself, to whom everyone was required to submit their reports, had to do the same. Ulf had wondered who wrote the Commissioner's appraisal, but had never found out the answer. Erik had suggested that it was probably the Deputy Commissioner, but Anna took the view that the Commissioner wrote it himself. 'When you're that senior,' she said, 'you can self-assess. You're assumed to have the necessary judgement to do it fairly.'

Ulf doubted that and had eventually plucked up the courage to ask the Commissioner about his experience of appraisal. He had done this when the Commissioner had addressed departmental heads when reviewing the whole annual review process — the 'review review', as it was called. (There had subsequently been a review of the review review.) Ulf had been tactful, and had raised the issue incidentally, saying, 'I find the annual review process a very good way of helping people to fulfil their potential. The appraisal part is particularly useful — as I'm sure you'd agree, Commissioner. I take it that even you have to go through that . . . and who does yours, by the way?'

The Commissioner had listened attentively, but when Ulf finally posed his question, he had simply raised a finger to his lips in a hushing gesture and smiled enigmatically. He often did that, Ulf had noticed, and it was intensely irritating. It was, he thought, something that should be mentioned in the Commissioner's own appraisal — *has a tendency to*

246

say hush when anybody raises any awkward issue — but of course that would never happen.

Now Ulf sat at his desk with the appraisal forms before him. He had an hour or so before any of the others arrived, and he hoped to complete at least two of the reports by then. He would start with Anna, because that would in one sense be the easiest, even if in another it was the most difficult. It was straightforward because of the impossibility of finding any fault in Anna's performance of her duties. She was never late, she was always ready to work extra hours if the need arose; she never argued with colleagues or was in any way obstructive; and she was, most importantly, effective in the performance of her duties.

It was a litany of praise, and, as he read over what he had written, an element of doubt began to creep in. An appraisal was not a hagiography: shortcomings should be mentioned because it was expected that everybody, even the most appreciated employee, would have at least some weaknesses. It also occurred to Ulf that if he sounded no notes of caution about Anna — even very modest ones — the Deputy Commissioner, who read every report and was known to be a hard-nosed cynic, might conclude that there was something not quite right. Romantic attachments between members of staff working loosely together were discouraged where one was senior to the other. It was not a hard-and-fast rule, as the authorities recognised that people could fall in love with, and even marry, those with whom they worked every day, but there was sensitivity to the possibility of abuse of power. A forty-year-old head of department who became involved with a twenty-year-old member of section could expect to find himself or herself watched very closely — and with good reason, thought Ulf.

Of course there was no age disparity in the case of the relationship between him and Anna — but then there was no relationship of that nature anyway. He might have strong feelings for Anna, but that's all they were — strong feelings. He had never declared himself to her; he had never done anything that could reveal what was really going through his mind when he was with her. He may have longed to tell her how he felt; he may have longed to shower her with tokens of his affection; he may have longed simply to take her hand in his, but he had done none of this. He had denied such urges time and time again — not that he awarded himself any marks for moral merit: he did this because it was the right thing to do. He had decided that he would do nothing to threaten Anna's marriage, and he had stuck to that decision. So if the Deputy Commissioner thought that his positive appraisal had anything to do with an inappropriate relationship between the two of them, Ulf could look him in the eye and issue a denial with complete conviction.

And yet, why run the risk of that sort of thing? Mud sticks, thought Ulf, and the thinking of mud, even without any justification, stuck as much as real, cloying mud. And it was not just to protect himself that he should avoid such suspicions — it was also for Anna's sake. It would be equally distressing to her — more so, perhaps — if their names were to be linked in idle gossip. That could reach her husband — it might even reach her children, because Ulf knew that her two girls socialised with the children of other police colleagues at swimming events. Children picked things up; children heard their parents talking about adult

248

affairs and passed on snippets of gossip — taken out of context, as often as not, and distorted, but quite capable of causing real harm. So it would be better, Ulf thought, to say something in the appraisal that would forfend any suspicious thoughts on the part of the Deputy Commissioner.

But what could this be? Ulf sat at his desk and pondered how he could say something that suggested mild reservations and yet was not of such a nature that it might be held against her. He also had to bear in mind that the rules allowed Anna to read her appraisal and discuss it with him, and so anything he wrote would have to be able to survive such scrutiny. He tried to remember any recent cases in which Anna had been involved where there had been any issues, but he could think of nothing. Had there been any complaints against her? He did not think there had been. Had she been involved in any disputes with colleagues? Again, he did not think so: Anna had an equable disposition and avoided unnecessary conflict. She was liked by everybody with whom she worked, Ulf thought.

And then it occurred to him. During a recent investigation, Anna had forgotten to inform Carl that she had decided to send the inquiry off in a different direction. Carl had then spent an entire day conducting pointless interviews. He had been annoyed by this waste of his time and had told Anna that she should be more careful to keep everybody informed. She had accepted responsibility for this and had apologised. Carl was placated, and nothing more was said, but Ulf had been aware of his colleague's irritation.

He now looked for just the right words to register the incident without being too censorious. And so he wrote, 'This colleague is usually punctilious in the discharge of her duties, but could perhaps make greater efforts to ensure that all those involved in an investigation are kept fully informed of decisions made and matters prioritised.' He liked the phrase 'matters prioritised', because it was the right language to use in a form of this nature. Ulf had discovered that the best way of dealing with bureaucracy was to use the form of words it wanted you to use. If you did that, then very little attention would be paid to the content of what you wrote, and your documents would sail through. It was a form of box-ticking that was pervasive and powerful, an act of obeisance to whatever policy fad was current at the time — a shibboleth.

He completed Anna's appraisal with relief. The Deputy Commissioner could hardly imagine that somebody who was watching another's prioritisation of matters would have the inclination to become romantically involved with that person — far from it. Satisfied, he now turned to Erik's form. Erik did his job conscientiously and efficiently — the only problem was that there was just not enough for him to do. He had his eyes on retirement, which he planned to spend fishing, as far as Ulf could make out. That was a perfectly understandable goal, and Erik would deserve his leisure when the time came. So Ulf wrote a glowing report on Erik's fastidious filing and his willingness to retrieve information quickly and effectively. He wrote about the fact that his desk was always tidy — an inspiration to those whose desks were normally cluttered. The reason for that, of course, was that Erik kept his fishing magazines tucked away in a drawer — but Ulf did not mention that.

He looked at Blomquist's form but decided to

leave it to a later date. And that would require much more thought. It would be a positive appraisal, but he would have to battle with the temptation to spell out some of his impatience over Blomquist's long-winded expositions of the merits of various vitamins and food supplements. Perhaps he could make the point obliquely and write something like 'This officer takes great pains to maintain his vitamin D levels.' Or 'Nobody would accuse this officer of being uninformed on health and safety matters.' Or 'This officer leaves no stone unturned when it comes to any matter at all.'

He sighed and put the remaining forms back in their file. He looked at his watch. Having started work early, he decided he could pay a quick visit to the coffee bar where he might read the papers and order his thoughts for the day ahead. He did not want to spend too much time on the Anders Kindgren inquiry and today, he hoped, there might be a breakthrough. They were getting close, he thought, even if he was not sure why he thought that. That did not matter, though; for all the talk about method in investigations, Ulf was convinced that the one thing that mattered above all others was intuition. If your intuition told you something, then it was a good idea to trust it. Intuition, in his view, was really just another name for a judgement based on experience, and another name for judgement based on experience was wisdom. That's what Ulf believed, although coffee — and beyond coffee, duty — now called, and thoughts of this nature could be put off until an altogether more leisurely moment.

★ ★ ★

251

Blomquist had said that the address he was going to furnish would be a surprise, and it was.

'This is next door to Anders,' Ulf exclaimed as they reached their destination. 'I thought the road sounded vaguely familiar.'

'Well, there you are,' said Blomquist. 'Anders and his mother are neighbours.'

Ulf parked the silver Saab on the street. 'I don't know what we can conclude from that,' he said as he switched off the ignition.

'There are all sorts of possibilities,' Blomquist replied. 'One is that the parents owned two houses — one next to the other — and then gave one to their son. The other is that one of them lived here first and the other then bought the next-door house when it came on the market.'

'Either suggests closeness,' said Ulf. He shook his head. His doubts were surfacing once more. 'I'm not sure whether we should — '

Blomquist did not let him finish. 'Let's try,' he urged. 'You never know. What do they say? Cast bread upon the waters and see what it brings in.'

'Yes, but—'

'We have nothing to lose,' said Blomquist.

'She may be grossly offended,' Ulf pointed out. 'She may complain that we were harassing her. And then we'll end up in Lund's office.'

Blomquist seemed unfazed by the prospect of a disciplinary referral. 'Don't worry about that. His bark is worse than his bite — as I gather you discovered recently.'

'It's all very well for you,' said Ulf. 'I'm the senior officer. I'll be the one on the carpet — not you.'

'It won't happen,' said Blomquist.

The house was larger and even more expensive than those around it. In the driveway, under the shade of a spreading oak tree, two slick cars had been parked — instances each of the higher reaches of German engineering. They were of the same marque, and there was a distinct his and hers feel to them. This was a display.

They rang the doorbell. A minute or so later, the door was opened by an elderly woman, wearing a plain grey trouser suit. She had a commanding presence. Her hair was swept back and held in position with a discreet black Alice band, while around her neck was a string of large pearls. Ulf quickly decided that this woman, presumably Anders' mother, was not a person on whose wrong side one might care to be. But then he thought: there is no reason for me to be intimidated. I am the head of the Department of Sensitive Crimes and if anybody should feel intimidated it should be her.

She introduced herself as Margareta Kindgren and said she had been expecting them. Then she led them into a formal sitting room where they were both invited to sit on a sofa while she took a Louis XV armchair. As they sat down, she fixed them with a gaze that was disapproving but also tempered by something else. Ulf could not decide what that was at first, but after a few moments he understood its nature. She was afraid. This wealthy, elegantly dressed woman was afraid.

'I'll come straight to the point,' he said. 'We are investigating an incident involving your son, Anders. More than one incident, in fact.'

She looked down at the floor. 'What has my son done?'

It was, Ulf decided, an inept attempt to deflect him,

253

and its effect was to make him all the more certain.

'Your son has been the victim of a hostile campaign,' he said, keeping his voice steady as he spoke. 'He has been harassed and intimidated, and, more seriously, his reputation has been damaged.'

She looked up. She did not say anything — and her silence, Ulf realised, was further confirmation of what he now suspected.

'I feel I should tell you straight out,' he said. 'The others have confessed to us.'

'A full confession,' Blomquist interjected. 'Everything.'

'So I suggest you make a clean breast of it,' Ulf went on. 'If you do, it will be easier for you in the long run.'

This was, as Blomquist had described it, the oldest trick in the book. It was also the most unsubtle, but now, as Margareta looked from Ulf to Blomquist and then back to Ulf, it became clear that it was working.

Ulf explained further. 'If you make a confession too, then the prosecutor might be lenient. We would certainly make a recommendation of that nature.'

'It's your best chance,' said Blomquist. 'Otherwise . . . well, this is the sort of offence that could easily attract a prison sentence.'

Margareta stared at Blomquist with wide eyes. 'Prison?' Her voice faltered. And then she added, 'Me?'

'You,' said Blomquist. 'Sorry.'

She lowered her head into her hands and sat wordless and immobile for some time. Ulf did not disturb her silence; the deception needed time, and interruption might impede it. Then she looked up, and Ulf saw that she was weeping.

Ulf waited tactfully. At last he said, 'Why did you

254

do it? To your own son . . .'

She stared at him imploringly. 'It was for his own good.'

With those words, Blomquist's scheme was vindicated. Now Ulf spoke calmly. 'I don't see how it could possibly be for his own good, but we can come back to that. What I suggest you do now is tell us, from the beginning, why you did it.'

'But you said they've already told you,' Margareta sniffed.

'They have,' Ulf said. 'But I want to hear it from you. In particular I want to know why you did it.'

She wiped at her eyes with a small white handkerchief. 'Why? Why? Why do we do anything? Or, more to the point, why does a mother do anything? To protect her son, that's why.'

'Protect him from what?'

'From everything. From making the wrong choices — disastrous choices. We never wanted him to spend his time gazing at dusty old paintings. We never wanted him to try to make ends meet from a few scrappy fees here and there. We never wanted — '

'We?' asked Ulf.

'My husband and I. We felt the same about this — always. But he was not involved in any of this, by the way. He doesn't know anything about it.'

'I'm prepared to accept that,' said Ulf.

'Anders had such promise,' she said. 'There would have been a place for him in the family firm — and there still is. And then he went and married that dreadful woman who has affairs, you know. She's currently carrying on with a perfectly ghastly philosopher, of all things. A dreadful man. And you should see him. His shoes.' She shuddered. 'I can't forgive her for that,

255

you know. She's blatant. She says Anders accepts it, but I know his heart is broken. And so I thought I'd get him out of the whole mess. I'd somehow persuade him to come back to the firm . . .'

'By destroying his reputation as an art historian?' prompted Ulf.

'I wouldn't put it that way. I'd say that I was simply helping a career change.'

Ulf took a risk. 'So you and Vera worked out how to achieve that?'

It paid off. 'Yes, Vera put me in touch with that young man who works for Christina Berks. It transpired that he's very disaffected because Christina is having an affair with his father, and his mother isn't taking it well. I assume that he told you how we did it?'

Ulf was impassive and Margareta continued before he had the chance to reply.

'He arranged for the copy to be made and delivered to the auction house. And Vera arranged to interfere with the article. It was all very easy.'

'And the fish?' asked Blomquist. 'What about the fish?'

Margareta looked confused. 'Fish?'

'Fish were dumped on his car.'

Margareta shrugged. 'Nothing to do with me,' she said. 'And why would anybody do that?'

'No matter,' said Ulf. 'But tell me this: why did Vera become involved?'

Margareta hesitated, but evidently decided to continue. 'Because she's always loved Anders. Because she wants to get him away from that wife of his. I think she felt that this might move a log jam in his life and he would be prepared to consider her again.

I wasn't so sure, but I could see why she thought the way she did.'

Blomquist asked Margareta whether she would have welcomed a switch in Anders' affections. 'Of course I would,' she replied. 'Anyone would be better than that wife of his. Anything — even modest little Vera. I rather like her, if the truth be told.'

They left Margareta's house. Ulf had administered a formal caution, and had told her that she would be visited again over the next few days. 'We shall see how things develop,' he said. 'Your co-operation will certainly stand you in good stead.' She seemed reassured by that, but when they took their leave she had started to cry again. 'I feel very ashamed of myself,' she said, fingering the string of pearls in her agitation.

Outside, on the street, Ulf hesitated. It would be simplest to go straight to Anders, as they were directly outside his house. They would call in and reveal to him what Ulf was sure would be utterly unexpected news. He swallowed hard. He felt shocked and uncomfortable and he could tell that Blomquist felt the same way.

'Blomquist,' Ulf asked, 'have you ever encountered anything — and I mean *anything* — remotely like this? A mother — a mother! — who does something like that to her son?'

Blomquist shook his head. 'Never. Although . . .' He hesitated. 'Although, we have to bear in mind that she thought she was acting in his best interests. That's maternal enough.'

Ulf conceded that was true. 'I suppose every mother thinks that.'

'Parents can make it difficult for their children,' Blomquist said. 'Fathers, mothers . . . but I suspect that fathers do more harm than mothers, although

257

it depends on whether you're a boy or a girl, doesn't it? Mothers and sons . . . that can be complicated, as we've just seen, wouldn't you say?' He looked thoughtful. 'I don't know, though. I'm not a psychologist.' He looked away, as if remembering something. 'The most difficult thing about being a parent is knowing when to let go. That's the single hardest thing, you know.'

Ulf thought about this. Blomquist was right, he suspected. You had to let go — not just in the parent–child relationship, but in so many other areas. You had to know when to step away from an argument; you had to know when to stop advising a friend when the friend was about to do something foolish; you had to know when to retire and to let those younger than you take over.

Ulf thought of Dr Svensson. He would have to talk to him about this case — anonymised, of course. And he could ask him about something that had just occurred to him: what was Freud's relationship with his mother? We heard very little about Frau Freud, he thought, but her influence must have been considerable. Without Freud's mother, would we have had Freudianism? It was an interesting question, but not one to be discussed outside Anders Kindgren's house, in departmental time, with an awkward task to be performed.

'It's not going to be easy,' Ulf said to Blomquist. 'But I suppose we'd better do it. He is, after all, the complainant.'

Anders was in, and greeted them courteously.

'I've been expecting you,' he said. 'I saw your nice Saab parked outside and I wondered if it was you.'

'We were visiting your mother,' Ulf said. 'And then we thought we'd drop in to see you.'

Anders raised an eyebrow. 'Mummy?' He laughed. 'What's Mummy been up to now?'

Then his face clouded over. 'Is everything all right?'

'She's fine,' said Ulf. 'But I have to tell you: there's a rather tricky issue we need to discuss.'

Anders listened in silence as they told him of his mother's confession. Ulf was not sure what his reaction would be. He half expected Anders to stop him, to protest that this was all fantasy, but nothing was said, and the information was received impassively, in silence.

At the end of Ulf's account, Anders simply sighed. He seemed neither surprised nor angry. 'Silly Mummy,' he said. 'She never gives up, you know. Silly, silly, interfering Mummy!'

Then he laughed.

Ulf looked grave. 'There will be a prosecution, of course.'

Anders gasped. 'Not Mummy? Oh no, please don't even think of that.'

'You don't want it?' asked Blomquist.

'Certainly not.'

Ulf felt deflated, although he had anticipated this, few men being keen on prosecuting their mothers. Without a complainant, there was no point in proceeding in a case such as this. In a curious way, he was relieved — nothing would be served by delving further into this strange skein of family issues. Jealousy, ambition, spite, unrequited love: all of these things were present here, but they had reared their heads within the context of a family, and families — and lovers — were best left to sort out their own pathology. Vera and Ivar, the intern at the auction house, were the outsiders involved in all this, and they could be pursued if it was thought necessary to do so. But was it? A warning would probably suffice in their case. Was that weak? Should he do more? No, this was the Department of Sensitive Crimes and sensitive solutions were sometimes just what was needed. And anyway, taking the case further would be difficult: this would be classed as a family matter, and if Anders declined to co-operate, the prosecutor would be very unwilling to proceed.

Ulf addressed Anders. 'You need to talk to your mother.'

Anders nodded. 'I shall.'

There was a silence.

Blomquist had something to add. 'We haven't worked out who dumped the fish on your car.'

'Do we need to know that?' asked Anders. 'Can't we treat that as just being some sort of . . . what do you people call it — some sort of red herring?'

Blomquist looked interested. 'Were they herring?' he asked.

Ulf looked out of the window. A small sprig of creeper, of ivy perhaps, tapped at the pane. There was a clear sky beyond — pale blue, untroubled. It was the sky of the landscapes he so loved, those nineteenth-century paintings that placed you under just such a sky, where north, and cold, and the purity of nature were presences on the palette alongside the dabs of pigment. He wanted to go home.

* * *

Ulf completed the appraisal forms the following morning, working on them in the privacy of his flat before going into the office. Under the rules of the

260

annual review procedure, he was obliged to show each member of staff what he had written. This was not a task that he relished, although in his case, where few critical remarks needed to be made, that process was not too painful. On this occasion, though, when he showed Anna what was on the form, her reaction was one of shock — and hurt.

'Why did you write that?' she said, pointing to the offending sentence. 'Why?'

Ulf had not expected her to be offended. The tone of what he had written about the need to keep colleagues informed was hardly objectionable.

He defended himself. 'It's not really a criticism, you know. It's meant to be helpful.'

'Helpful?' snapped Anna. 'Do you really think it's going to help me if the Deputy Commissioner, not to mention Lund and all those people, decide that I'm a bad communicator?'

Anna had never raised her voice to Ulf — not once in all the years they had worked together. Now she did, and he was stunned into silence. On the other side of the office, Carl looked up from his desk and glanced over towards where Ulf was standing beside Anna.

'Please don't make a fuss here,' Ulf whispered.

'If you don't want me to make a fuss,' Anna hissed, 'you should have thought twice before you put your pen to paper.'

She had lowered her voice, but only slightly. Now Erik looked up, and exchanged glances with Carl.

'Look,' said Ulf, drawing her aside, 'let's go over to the coffee bar. We can talk there.'

Anna closed her eyes. It was clear to Ulf that she was very angry. When she opened them, she did not meet his gaze, but looked away evasively. 'You go,' she muttered. 'I'll see you there in five minutes.'

Flustered, Ulf left the office, aware that his departure was being followed discreetly by Carl and Erik, both of whom were pretending to be immersed in their work. He did not look back at Anna; suddenly, oddly, he thought of Orpheus, who looked back and lost Eurydice. *I have lost her without looking back . . .*

* * *

He sat in the coffee bar, staring into an untouched cappuccino. This was a disaster. He had offended Anna — the very last person he would ever wish to hurt. Her anger had left him shaken and raw. And although he had not intended his words to have this effect, he now realised that he had miscalculated their impact. He had been naïve, even foolish, and now she felt that he had somehow betrayed her. It was too late to do anything about it: even if he changed his appraisal, as he would have to do, the damage was done. Trust and friendship had been shattered.

She came in and sat down opposite him at his table without ceremony. He looked across at her, but once again she did not meet his eyes.

Ulf could not put it off. Now he said, 'I want you to know this: the reason I wrote what I did was to . . .' He faltered. He was not ready to confess to her how he felt about her. Yet, if he did not do that, his entire story made no sense.

She looked at him. 'You've no idea how you've hurt me,' she said.

'I think I have, actually. I can tell I've hurt you, but I wrote that so that they wouldn't suspect something.'

She frowned as she tried to make sense of what he had said. 'Suspect what?'

He looked down at his coffee. 'Suspect that I was having an affair with you.'

Anna's eyes widened. 'Why would they think that?'

'They might think that if I didn't write anything critical.'

Anna stared at him. 'But why?' And then, after a moment, she added, 'Are people talking? Is that what's happening?'

He was quick to reassure her that he had not heard anybody talking about them in that way, but that he thought they might. 'And the last thing I would want would be for that to happen — because, you see, I'm very fond of you, Anna.'

It was the first time he had said anything like that, and he regretted it the moment he uttered the words. This was not what he had intended. But the effect of the words on Anna immediately allayed his fears. From looking at him with distrust, her face broke into a warm smile. It was as if the argument had never taken place.

'I'm fond of you too, Ulf,' she said. 'Very fond.'

And then she added. 'But not in that way, of course.'

Time stopped for Ulf Varg.

He shook his head. 'Of course not. Of course not.'

'So I think we just forget about it.'

He said that he would take out the offending comment, but she said that she did not want him to do that. 'It might be for the best, you know. Now that you've explained things.'

Ulf took a sip of his coffee. The rift had been healed, but her words hung in the air between them. *Not in that way, of course* — those unintentionally cutting words that no would-be lover would ever wish to hear. The coffee was lukewarm now, and so he drank the rest quickly. They would get back to work — he and his colleague, for that was all Anna now was. Colleague and friend, but no more than that.

They walked back to the office.

'I'm sorry,' said Anna, as they started to climb the stairs.

'There's nothing to be sorry about,' said Ulf.

She seemed to weigh this. Then she said, 'What I meant was that I'm sorry if I've made you unhappy.'

He pretended to be surprised. 'Why should I be unhappy?' But then, almost immediately he switched to the truth, and said, 'I think I'm going to be happy anyway. I've met somebody.'

Anna stopped. She was a stair above Ulf and she turned to look down on him. He was not sure he could read her expression, and he decided not to try. But she leaned forward and kissed him lightly on the cheek — a kiss that meant nothing and everything, at one and the same time.

* * *

Ulf telephoned Juni at her work. In the background, he heard a dog barking and the sound of Dr Håkansson's voice rising above the din.

'Change of plans,' he said. 'Let's go to a restaurant.'

'You don't want crab linguine? I thought you liked crab linguine.'

'I love it,' said Ulf. 'But I haven't been to a restaurant — a good one — for I don't know how long. There's a place just outside town that I've been reading about. It's had pretty good reviews. There have been rumours there's a Michelin star in the offing.'

Juni required no persuading, and Ulf picked her up at her flat at seven that evening. He had Martin with him, sitting in the back of the Saab. It was unusual to take your dog on a date, but if you were dating a veterinary receptionist, then that was perhaps not entirely out of order. And when Martin greeted her with enthusiasm, and she reciprocated with delight, Ulf knew that he had done the right thing. Martin did not accompany them into the restaurant, of course, but was happy to sleep on the back seat of the Saab. He had a lot of sleeping to do in life, and whether this was done in the Saab or at home, on his blanket, made very little difference.

Inside the restaurant, Ulf and Juni scanned the menu.

'There's crab linguine,' said Juni, pointing at an item.

'So there is,' said Ulf.

He looked across the table at her. She looked back at him. He noticed her eyes. He said, 'I'm glad I met you.' Then he said, 'I love your eyes.'

It was a kind thing to say, but true. And there is a certain nobility in statements that are both kind and true.

We do hope that you have enjoyed
reading this large print book.

Did you know that all of our titles
are available for purchase?

We publish a wide range of high
quality large print books including:
Romances, Mysteries, Classics
General Fiction
Non Fiction and Westerns

Special interest titles available in
large print are:
The Little Oxford Dictionary
Music Book, Song Book
Hymn Book, Service Book

Also available from us courtesy of
Oxford University Press:
Young Readers' Dictionary
(large print edition)
Young Readers' Thesaurus
(large print edition)

For further information or a free
brochure, please contact us at:
Ulverscroft Large Print Books Ltd.,
The Green, Bradgate Road, Anstey,
Leicester, LE7 7FU, England.
Tel: (00 44) 0116 236 4325
Fax: (00 44) 0116 234 0205

Other titles published by Ulverscroft:

THE TALENTED MR. VARG

Alexander McCall Smith

Spring is coming slowly to Sweden — though not quite as slowly as Detective Ulf Varg's promised promotion at the Department of Sensitive Crimes. For Varg, referred by his psychoanalyst to group therapy at Malmö's Wholeness Centre, life now seems mostly a circle of self-examination: something which may or may not be useful when it comes to the nature of his profession, and the particularly sensitive cases that have recently come to light.

One of his new investigations involves fellow detective Anna Bengsdotter; it will require every ounce of self-discipline he has in order to remain professional. The other, more curious case is centred around internationally successful novelist Nils Personn-Cederstrom. According to his girlfriend, Cederstrom is being blackmailed — but by whom, and for what reason?